MIRACLE IN MARCH

JULIET MADISON

Re-published in 2024 by Bloodhound Books.

www.bloodhoundbooks.com

Print ISBN: 978-1-916978-62-1

To Jay, my first miracle.

CHAPTER ONE

Emma Brighton had been waiting for this day for what seemed like forever. At thirty-seven years old, she'd never been overseas, and while friends had gone off on grand adventures, she'd worked, saved, and dealt with life's unexpected challenges. But now — now was the time. *Her* time.

'Just book the thing already.' Jen placed a cup of steaming tea on the table next to Emma's laptop as she browsed travel websites.

'Are you trying to get rid of me?' Emma slid a glance towards her dearest friend and roommate.

'Well, yes. The sooner you go have an adventure, the sooner you'll bring back souvenirs and tell me the juicy details about gorgeous foreign men you had passionate affairs with.'

Emma removed her hands from the keyboard and tilted her head at Jen. 'Yes to the souvenirs, no to the passionate affairs. This is *my* trip. I'm not looking for love, I'm looking for...'

'What exactly *are* you looking for?'

Emma returned her attention to the screen and scrolled down the webpage that showed pictures of Tuscan villas framed with green spreading vines and bright red flowers. 'Nothing. I don't have any expectations; I just want to see more of the world than my little part of Sydney. And feel... free, for a change.'

Jen sat next to Emma and sipped her green tea, while Emma sipped her chai. 'So, Italy first? France? What's the plan?' She draped her arm around her friend.

Emma clicked on the other tab she had opened for Paris. 'The City of Lights,' she said with a smile and a flutter of excitement in her belly.

'And the city of *luurve*.' Jen wriggled seductively and Emma laughed.

'I figure I'll put my French language skills to good use first, give me some confidence before I lose it completely in Italy.'

'So, teaching French to your first-graders has made you an expert, huh?'

'Not really, but at least I know the basics.'

Jen smiled. 'All I know is something about *voulez-vous coucher avec moi...*'

Emma nudged Jen. 'That's enough, missy! And when I get back, I expect to hear all about *your* juicy gossip and passionate affairs with... Australian citizens.'

'I'll tell you about mine if you tell me about yours.'

Emma smiled. 'Deal.' They shook hands. 'Now, this is where I'm thinking of staying in Paris, you like?' Emma pointed to the screen and her phone rang its chirpy ringtone. 'Oh, Mum's calling. Guess I should take the opportunity to tell her the good news, finally.' She pressed answer. 'Hi, Mum.'

'Em. Oh, Em!' Panic shook her voice.

'What's wrong?' Needles of fear pricked Emma's nerves. There was only one other time she remembered her mother sounding this way.

'You need to come to Welston hospital, *now*. It's your father.' She sucked in a loud breath. 'He's had a stroke.'

In an instant Emma was on the road, heading south along the coast towards Welston, the country person's city; small compared to others, but a major township for south coast dwellers with all the necessary amenities. And also the place where Emma had grown up, until she'd swapped the small city for a big one while her parents moved further south to Tarrin's Bay.

Lights flanking the highway blurred and elongated as she drove, both from her speed and the tears spreading across her eyes and preparing to spill.

Please stay alive, please stay alive...

All she knew was that her dad was having some sort of procedure or tests to deal with a clot in the brain. It didn't sound good, but she knew how resilient the human body could be.

In just over an hour she was there, finding a parking spot, finding the hospital entrance, then finding out her father's fate.

'Emma!'

'Mum!'

Barbara and Emma Brighton rushed to each other and embraced.

'They're still working on him. He's not out of the woods yet, but they think he's got a good chance of surviving.'

'Oh, thank God.' Emma sunk into her mother's arms. 'Has there been any significant damage?'

'They won't know for a while, but he had numbness down his left side when the ambulance took him. His speech was...' She gulped then sobbed a little. 'Oh, Em, it was so scary! One minute we were talking and the next, he got his words jumbled and his face looked all strange.' Barbara covered her mouth with a shaky hand.

Dread sank to the pit of Emma's stomach, but she couldn't

let it show. Her mum needed her. 'Let's sit here and wait for an update, Mum.' She led her to a cold, empty row of chairs.

'Oh no! I have to call Amelia and get her to handle things at the cabins. How will I, how can we...' Her eyes darted side to side searching for answers. That was the problem with having your own business — never being able to call in sick.

'She's working tomorrow anyway, isn't she? Why don't we send her a text to let her know the situation and that we'll call when we know more?'

Barbara nodded. 'Okay. I just don't think I can talk to anyone else right now.'

'I know. Here, I'll do it.' Emma took her phone from her handbag and found Amelia in the 'contacts', then sent her a message. She was an efficient and reliable employee, she'd be happy to help out as much as possible, though as a busy single mother with teenagers she wouldn't want to take over the place completely. Tarrin's Bay Beachside Cabins and Caravan Park would need an extra set of hands. Now.

'Oh, Em, you have to go to work tomorrow! Do you think you could take the day off, or the week even?'

Emma managed a feeble smile. She still hadn't told her mum the good news that she was officially on holidays and had enough money to live on for the next year. 'Well, Dad sure picked a convenient time to cause problems, because I don't have to go to work tomorrow. I'm officially on leave. I have a year.' She'd miss her students, but she'd promised to send a postcard to the school for their replacement teacher to show them. Whether or not they'd get one now she didn't know. Unless she sent one from Tarrin's Bay.

'A year!' Emma's mother exclaimed. 'How in heaven's name did you manage that? What aren't you telling me? Is everything alright?' She put her hand on her daughter's arm.

'Yes, I'm fine. I've been saving up. I was going to tell you this

4

week actually, but...' No, she couldn't tell her about the overseas trip. For now, all her mum needed to know was that her daughter was here and ready to help, here to be with Dad and support him in his recovery. She didn't want her mother to feel guilty for Emma having to change her travel plans.

'Do you think... could you possibly...'

'Yes, Mum. Don't worry. I'll take over the running of the cabins in the meantime, and then we can reassess once we know how Dad is.'

'Oh, darling.' She rested her head on Emma's shoulder. 'What would we do without you?'

Emma didn't answer. She took that moment to take a long awaited deep breath, silently wishing that everything would be okay. How bizarre, that a couple of hours ago she was getting ready to put her travel plans in motion. But now those plans would have to be put on hold. A shame, but she couldn't allow herself to dwell on disappointment. Family was more important, and like they'd been there for her when she'd needed them, she'd be there for them.

They sat together in silence for a while, until squelchy footsteps approached on the shiny but scuffed hospital floor. Emma looked up into the tired eyes of the doctor as he greeted them.

CHAPTER TWO

ONE MONTH LATER

James Gallagher stepped up onto the porch of cabin number one, his son Jackson already at the door, banging on it with his palm.

'Hang on, mate, gotta unlock it first.' James put his bags on the porch then stuck the key into the lock, Jackson running on the spot on tiptoes. At least the four-year-old seemed keen to be here; James was never sure how he'd react to different environments.

'Okey dokes, let's go inside and check out our makeshift home for the next week.' James went to push the door open but Jackson beat him to it, barging through like a one-kid stampede, a high-pitched squeal accompanying him. James opened his mouth to say, 'Not so loud', but shut it again. It never did any good anyway, and right now he couldn't care less if anyone had a problem with his child's behaviour. He wanted to get unpacked, find something to occupy Jackson for at least half an hour, and sit on the porch to admire the beachfront view. At least they'd been able to secure the cabin at the far end of the holiday park, with his sister and brother-in-law in the cabin next to his, and his parents in number three. As for the caravans behind, they weren't that close. Luckily the cabins had been booked a year ago, or they wouldn't have had any chance of getting this perfect location at the front.

Jackson inspected every corner of the open-plan living room and kitchen, picking up object after object, familiarising himself with his surroundings. He noticed the television and bounced on tiptoes, flapping his hands with excitement and nervous energy, then dashed into one of the bedrooms. James followed him, making sure the place was reasonably Jackson-proof, if such a place existed. He leaned against the doorframe and smiled at his son's excitement. This was a good sign. Once, when they'd travelled and stayed in a motel, Jackson had screamed and cried almost the whole time. Something about the place just hadn't gelled with him. But now, he seemed enlivened by the cabin, which was good, because he was here with his family to do something very important and there was no going home until it was done.

'C'mon, let's check out your room, buddy.' James gestured for Jackson, and he ran past his father and into the adjacent room. There was a single bed and a bunk bed. Jackson immediately leapt onto the single bed, and James laughed. Most kids would go for the top bunk. Not Jackson.

Loud applause filled the room. Jackson had pressed a button on his Sound Machine, the handheld gadget he stored in his pocket that featured sixteen different sound effects, and formed the soundtrack to his young life. Applause was good. That meant he was satisfied with his temporary bedroom. Had he pressed the screaming or crashing glass sound, then all hell would break loose.

James left his son to inspect the premises and went back to the porch to bring in the bags, plonking them on the queen-size bed that would be his, and only his, for the next few days.

The clang of the screen door sounded and James dashed to

the living room. 'Jackson, hang on!' But the boy was out the door, rushing up onto the porch of cabin number two. James followed.

'You want to see our place too?' asked Lizzie, holding the door open for her nephew. Jackson burst inside and James stood on the path in front, waiting for him to do his thing. Lizzie smiled. 'It's nice when he's happy,' she said. 'I think he'll like it here, and it'll be good for you guys to have a change of scenery for a while.'

James nodded. 'And good for you to put your feet up while soaking up the ocean view. Speaking of which, shouldn't you be doing that now and letting André get things unpacked?'

Lizzie stepped onto the porch and held her large belly. 'Guess you're right. Damn that doctor, doesn't she know how hard bed rest and "taking it easy" is for a woman like me?'

James understood. He didn't know how to take it easy either; he and Lizzie had been genetically programmed with their father's workaholic genes. But he also understood what life was like with a new baby. 'I wouldn't worry, another month or so and you certainly won't be taking it easy. Enjoy it while you can, I reckon.'

James' sister eased into the white, wicker chair and it crackled as it stretched under her weight. 'God, hope I don't break this thing,' she said with a chuckle. 'Five minutes into our stay and I'll have to pay for repairs!'

An overexcited squeal came from inside.

'Is the place to your satisfaction, *garçon?*' Lizzie's French husband, André, asked, though everyone knew he would not get a reply. James liked that his family talked to Jackson as though he was any other boy. Apart from his father. Martin Gallagher still tried to get words out of his grandson and got frustrated easily, so after a while he'd stopped trying.

Applause sounded again and Jackson pulled open the door.

For a moment his eyes connected with James', but just as quickly they diverted elsewhere. 'Let me guess, Nan and Pop's cabin next?' James followed Jackson to his parents' cabin. 'Just doing the rounds, Mum,' he said with a brief smile when they arrived at the door.

'No problem at all, my little one.' Marie Gallagher leaned down and tried to kiss her grandson on the head, but only managed to brush lightly against his overgrown mop of brown hair as he whizzed past. The boy didn't stop for anyone or anything. Get in his way and he could easily knock you down like a prize bull. He slammed against his pop's leg, almost dislodging the precious item in his hands.

James gasped. 'Careful, Jackson.'

'Hey, fella, take it easy!' Martin Gallagher said. 'This is *very* important.' He placed the glossy wooden urn on top of one of the kitchen cupboards. Now, Nonna Bella would have a bird's-eye view of her favourite room — the kitchen. Figuratively speaking.

James' Irish/Italian grandmother was supposed to be here with them. Instead, they'd be saying goodbye to her, spreading her ashes in her favourite location in Tarrin's Bay, on the day that would have been her ninetieth birthday.

If she'd only lasted two more weeks.

James shook his head at the injustice. Bad timing seemed to run in his family. Knowing his luck, when he was old and grey, he'd probably cark it during the countdown to New Year's Day... *5, 4, 3, 2, 1... Happy New—Croak.*

He shook his head again, this time trying to shake out the morbid thoughts that sometimes popped into his head. They'd started appearing after Jackson was born; intrusive thoughts springing out of nowhere that made him question his sanity. Sleep deprivation, he was told. And stress. It was as though his mind tried to prepare him for the worst at every available opportunity, so that if something untoward happened, it wouldn't be as much of a shock. The mind was a crazy thing, even for the non-insane.

When Jackson was satisfied with the three cabins, he ran outside and then...

Oh no.

'Jackson, not another one. That's not ours.' James scooped up his child just as he'd landed on the porch of cabin number four. Jackson thrashed in his dad's arms and screamed. 'This one belongs to someone else, mate. C'mon.' James carried his heavy, crying son off the porch, eyeing an apology to the couple who'd approached the doorway. They didn't seem perturbed, but neither did they seem impressed. Oh well, what could he do, short of handing out information brochures on autism to every person he came across?

As usual, James' mother was ready with her help, dashing into cabin number one and back out to the porch with Jackson's favourite toy, a stuffed fabric owl. A pink one, at that. 'Here we go,' she said, handing the toy to Jackson. He grabbed it, holding it tight to his chest.

James wished his son would do that to him. He was affectionate sometimes, in his own way, but never the way he was with Owly.

'You go settle in and I'll watch him out here if you like,' Marie said. Jackson wriggled out of James' hold and placed Owly on the grass beside the path, rocking him side to side and pressing the bouncy spring sound on his machine.

'Thanks.' He took the two steps to the porch with one stride, turning around briefly to double-check his son, then entered the cabin. With military precision he arranged things in Jackson's room the way he'd like them, unpacked their belongings, and freshened up in the bathroom with a splash of water on his face. He glanced at his reflection in the mirror. Subtle speckles of grey were becoming visible in the dark hair on his temples. He was only thirty-eight, but time seemed to be slipping away faster and faster these days. He rubbed his jaw between his thumb and fingers, easing the tension from the clenching he often forgot he was doing, but that his dentist said he needed to deal with. He ran his hands through his thick wavy hair, and a random memory crept into his mind...

She's here already? James spread the remaining hair mousse through his waves to tidy them, then washed his hands quickly. He checked his teeth and adjusted his shirt to show the right amount of chest, not too much, not too little, and headed for the front door.

He could see her silhouette through the glass, her long hair merging with the curve of her shoulders, a few strands lifting to the side by way of the breeze. He opened the door and smiled, her heart-shaped face a vision of feminine beauty. 'Good evening.'

'Good evening to you too.' Her white teeth gleamed under the outdoor lamp and he wanted to take hold of her then and there and pull her close, wrap his arms around her body and tell her all he wanted to say with one kiss. But it was only a first date, and that wouldn't be appropriate.

'I'll grab my keys,' he said instead, then led her to the car and opened the door for her.

'It's a beautiful night,' she said.

'Beautiful indeed,' he replied.

James took a deep breath and tried to erase yet another memory from his mind. Why couldn't the brain have a delete key like a computer?

Voices chattered outside and he went back to check on Jackson. His son made soft, lyrical sounds, clearly having some kind of private conversation with Owly. He had his own language, and it was only through his tone that James was privy to at least some idea of what his child might be trying to say.

His mum was talking to another woman. A younger woman, with her back to him. The woman took a punnet of strawberries from her shopping bag and handed them to his mother, then took one out and offered it to Jackson. He eyed her hand cautiously at first, then plucked the fruit from her grasp. Strawberries were his favourite. James was about to say that out loud, to thank the woman for her generosity, but as she turned to the side her heart-shaped face and her smile sent his heart plummeting to his stomach. He froze.

The woman turned around completely and caught his gaze, her carefree smile giving way.

Emma.

CHAPTER THREE

Emma never thought she'd see those dark brown eyes again. But there they were, right in front of her, staring, unblinking.

'James?' She phrased it as a question though she knew the answer.

He crossed his arms, his biceps tight aside his chest. 'What are you doing here?'

Emma glanced sideways at the woman she'd been talking to, who looked a tad confused, then back at him, her heart pounding. 'I um, I work here. I'm running the place temporarily for my parents.'

'Your parents own the place?'

Emma nodded, shifted on the spot, an uncomfortable twinge tightening her muscles. 'I'd, ah, better go and leave you to it.' She smiled at the woman and the boy, though he didn't look at her, then turned away.

'Wait.' James stepped off the porch. 'We don't see each other for over five years and that's all you've got to say?'

She'd been dreading the possibility of this moment catching up with her. Emma scratched her head and squinted as the afternoon sun caught her eye. 'I really should go, I have to get these inside.' She held up the bag of fruit and fresh bread, but it was her that needed to get inside. The air was thick with untold secrets and she could hardly breathe.

The older woman knelt down to the boy and spoke to him, making an effort to join in his play, obviously trying to shield him from any argument and give James a chance to talk to Emma.

Emma walked but James rushed up beside her, then turned back briefly. 'Mum, can you watch him?' She must have nodded because James walked alongside Emma's fast steps. Her skin buzzed with the closeness of his presence. 'Emma, wait. Don't you think I deserve an explanation?'

She kept her focus ahead. 'I'm sorry, I can't talk right now. I have to go.' She picked up her pace until they reached the garden beside the playground.

'Stop! Emma, just stop.' He grasped her arm and she glanced at it then looked him in the eye. His gaze bore into hers and she trembled.

'Not here, please, James.'

'Then over here.' Still holding her arm he led her through the small garden and behind a thick tree. 'I'm not leaving till you talk to me.'

'Look, James, I'm busy. It's my day off, and I need to get some things done before work tomorrow.' She removed her arm from his grasp, though his touch lingered hot on her skin.

'I think explaining why you left the man you supposedly loved without an explanation should factor in your To Do list, don't you?' He crossed his arms again.

Emma sighed and looked at the ground where tree roots bulged beneath, as though they too were trying to unearth secrets from times gone by. 'I told you, I took a job interstate and couldn't handle the idea of a long distance relationship. It was easier that we had a clean break.' Big. Fat. Lie. Although Emma had hated to do it, the alternative was worse, and she hadn't been prepared for the consequences, not then, not now.

'I don't understand why you had to lie. I know you didn't go to Melbourne. I heard you were living and working in Sydney. I wouldn't call Welston to Sydney a long distance relationship.'

He'd looked her up? But she'd done her best to become invisible.

'Look, not now. I have to go.'

'So you keep saying. I guess you're used to walking away.'

Emma sucked in a sharp breath. It hurt her to think of the past, and she knew it hurt him, but it had been for the best. She opened her mouth to speak but closed it again. She expected him to probe further but he just stood there, arms crossed, eyebrows raised, awaiting a response. His eyes were darker than she remembered, and fine lines crinkled at the corners.

'Go then. Just go.' He flicked a hand towards the pathway. 'I'll be here for a week. That's plenty of time for you to get your act together and do what you should have done five years ago.' He turned and stormed off.

Each beat of her heart pumped guilt, dread, and pain throughout her body. She was about to walk off the way she'd been desperate to go, back to the cottage, but couldn't bring herself to look away. She watched him, his back to her, as he marched back to his cabin, and it was only then that it hit her. *He has a son? Did that mean he also had a wife?* Oh, what did it matter? She'd left him, he deserved someone better. Someone who could be the person he needed.

Emma tightened the grip on her shopping bag and walked to the one bedroom cottage behind the reception office, her home for however long she was needed here. She plonked the bag on the kitchen countertop and sighed. *Crap.* She forgot to take the fresh bread to her parents' place behind the walking track. Her dad was expecting his favourite sourdough and olive bread, and she didn't want to keep a sick man waiting. Especially the way he was with the brain damage after his stroke. He would snap at her for the slightest thing. It hadn't affected his intelligence, mainly his mobility and inhibitions, meaning he had none of either. Yesterday he'd told her that the colour of her skirt looked like puke. At first she'd laughed, but when he mentioned how she had put on a couple of kilograms it had hurt. People weren't supposed to say things like that out loud, especially not your own father. She was still slim but had rounded out somewhat over the past few months. Her mum had said it was good to see some healthy meat on her, trying to make her feel better about her father's remark, but that night she'd cried.

Just like she was going to do now.

CHAPTER FOUR

E mma dabbed her face with a cold cloth to reduce the redness, then sculled a glass of water. Seeing James again was overwhelming, and combined with her father's delicate state, her emotions were bubbling up beneath the surface into a rolling boil. When the day was over she'd call Jen and have a good chat; the last thing she wanted was to keep anything else bottled up inside.

Emma slid her sunglasses on, grabbed the bag of bread and her keys and stepped outside, the afternoon sun low on the horizon giving the beach a warm glow. She followed the path around the cottage and glanced to her right. Her mother was walking in her direction.

'Em, oh good. I saw you earlier and thought you were maybe ducking inside to the bathroom before bringing the bread over, but when you didn't come out I thought I'd come check.'

'It's okay, you didn't have to come. I was just on my way over.' Emma handed her mother the shopping bag. The homely scent of fresh bread gave her some comfort, but so did the fact that it wasn't necessary to visit her father right now. Though that brought guilt along with it. 'Do you need me to come over and help with anything?'

'No, all is good. Your father's sleeping right now so I thought I'd get some fresh air while I can. The home nurse will be visiting tomorrow, and now that his INR levels and medication dosages are all sorted he should be a bit more stable from now on. Hopefully.'

Emma nodded in relief. 'Good. Don't forget to take up Penny's offer for some respite, she'll look after him for a day or so here and there.'

'I know, but he's not overly keen on having my sister nurse him. It doesn't bother her one bit, I know that, but he's got his pride. Easier to have someone not in the family do the sensitive jobs.' She glanced in the direction of her house.

'Yeah, I guess. But Penny is such a good nurse, if he gets too much, just call her. She'll be happy to help.'

'I will.'

Emma sniffed and adjusted her sunglasses.

'Are you okay?' her mother asked, stepping closer.

'Yeah, I'm fine.' Emma rubbed her nose with her knuckle.

'No you're not.' Barbara lifted her daughter's sunglasses. 'Your eyes are a bit red, have you been crying?' The soft skin of her mother's hand connected with her forearm.

'Oh, don't worry, it's nothing, I'll be fine.' Emma looked away.

Barbara tightened the grasp on her arm, turning her daughter's gaze back to her. She eyed her with a look that said: I'm your mum and you can't fool me. 'I don't mean to pry, but I saw you talking to someone near the park. None of the guests are being inappropriate, are they?'

'Not at all, no, he was just...' *the love of my life I tried so hard to forget.* 'Do you remember that guy I was seeing, back in Welston? Things had started getting serious but then...'

'James?'

'Yes.'

'That was him?'

Emma nodded with a sigh. 'He's still angry.'

'You haven't told him? Oh, Em, the poor guy. He should know.'

Her jaw tightened. 'It was better this way. You agreed, remember? And so much time has passed, I don't think it's worth dredging up what's been and gone.' She crossed her arms. 'He's got a kid now, a little boy.' Regret twinged inside. She'd always thought he'd make a great father.

'Does he have a wife or partner?'

'Don't know. I didn't see anyone, just his mum.'

Barbara drew her eyebrows together. 'It can't be coincidence, him being here. You should seriously think about talking to him, get things out in the open.'

Mum and her signs. She was always looking out for serendipitous moments and situations that supposedly aligned at the perfect time, which we were supposed to recognise, then act on, to ensure our lives orchestrated themselves into a harmonious symphony. Little miracles, she called them. She would probably buy a lottery ticket if some sort of numerical coincidence presented itself to her. *I saw the numbers 126 on a car's number plate, and now I've randomly checked my watch and it just so happens to be 1:26! It's a sign! Jackpot here we come!*

Emma managed a small smile. They sure could do with a lottery win right now. Her parents had a lot of equity in the holiday park to draw on if needed, but the aim was to sell it so they could retire. They'd had a good run, not as long as they'd thought, but they'd loved keeping this place going. As soon as the construction of the extra two cabins and games room was complete, they'd be able to put the place on the market and enjoy a financially worry-free retirement. But it wasn't like they were just selling a house, it was a whole way of life and it could take a while to find a buyer.

'I'll be busy working tomorrow till Saturday, might not get much of a chance. He leaves Monday,' Emma said. A breeze whooshed past her and she almost lost balance.

'You'll have weeknights, and then Sunday. Don't let him leave without seeing if you can resolve things. I know it seems easier to keep a secret the longer time goes by, but some secrets are meant to be told.'

'Then they wouldn't be secrets.'

'Exactly. Think about it, okay?' She placed her palm on Emma's cheek.

'I'll think about it.' *I've thought about it. Now, time to move on...*

The light snap of a screen door nearby turned Emma's focus to the reception office. The petite Amelia emerged carrying a pile of towels, her Tarrin's Bay cap on her head. 'Hi, Barbara. Emma. How's Don?'

'Fine, thanks. All going okay in the office?' Barbara planted an 'everything's great' smile on her face.

'Yes, don't you worry about a thing. Emma and I have got it covered, haven't we?' Amelia replied.

Emma nodded in confidence. The business perhaps, but her personal life? She sometimes wished she could take a vacation from it and have someone else handle her dilemmas for a couple of weeks. *Wanted: reliable employee with a caring nature who likes a challenge and is capable of managing daily personal crises and complaints from dissatisfied persons (namely, ex-boyfriends), while maintaining a professional and confident persona and staying sane. Apply within.*

A telephone rang and Amelia turned around, her silky, black ponytail swishing swiftly like a flamenco dancer's skirt.

'Oh.' She turned to Emma and held up the towels. 'Would you mind taking these to a guest while I grab the phone?'

Emma took the towels. 'Sure, which cabin?' *Please not number one, please not number one.*

'Number two.' She smiled and dashed to answer the phone.

Phew. Number two she could handle, but number one... She wondered how she'd get through this week with James here. Maybe he wouldn't need any assistance and she'd only see him on check-out. Oh, no she wouldn't. He'd be checking out Monday and that was her day off, along with Sunday. It was possible they could go the whole week without bumping into each other. Possible, but unlikely.

Emma left her mother to walk a while on the beach with her mobile gripped in her hand in case of emergency, and headed along the pathway to deliver the towels to the guests in number two.

She passed children having fun on the playground equipment on the grassed area next to the sand, and thought of her students. Her ex-students. She missed them, but it was good to have a break from the responsibility of looking after twenty-four children every day. A mother took hold of her two children's hands and ushered them onto the sand towards the water, while a boy of about five kept losing his hat when he went down the slippery slide.

Emma's gaze returned to the path in front of her, and she almost bumped into James. He stepped off the path, his body stiffening. She stopped and looked at his son and wanted to smile. He had his father's nose; strong and definite, a nose that said: *you can trust me.* 'I didn't know you had a son,' she said before she could stop herself.

James slipped his hands in his pockets. 'There's a lot you don't know.'

21

'It's Jackson, right? Your mum told me outside your cabin, before I knew she was your mum.' *God this is awkward.*

'My son is not your concern.' He wore a frown as expertly as his casual but classy cargo pants and fitted white t-shirt. His hands not budging from his pockets, she couldn't help but be drawn to the corded muscles and veins of his forearms, and further up, the firm, rounded muscles of his biceps. Jackson ran circles around him, holding onto a small red device of some kind. He pressed it and it made a laughing sound, contrasting with the mood of the moment. 'It looks like you have a delivery to make.' He gestured to the towels, then turned away and took hold of his son's hand.

She stood still for a moment. It was bizarre seeing James with a son. She wondered if Jackson had a middle name starting with J too, like James. *James John Gallagher.* JJ, she used to call him sometimes, but only when she was feeling flirty. It had been a long time since she'd felt flirty with anyone; the idea of it was as foreign to her now as the idea of being able to escape overseas on an adventure. It simply wasn't the right time anymore. So much for her careful planning.

Emma continued along and walked up the steps of cabin number two where a woman sat on the chair, her pregnant belly bursting beneath the fabric of her dress. 'Hi, you needed some extra towels?' Emma smiled.

'Yes, that was quick, Thanks! I'll just...' She gripped the sides of the chair in an attempt to lift herself up.

Emma held up a hand. 'Don't get up, shall I put them inside?'

The sound of a toilet flushing made her wait, she didn't want to invade their personal space. A man with dangly, dark curls emerged and greeted her. *'Bonjour, mademoiselle.'* He smiled.

'*Bonjour,*' Emma replied, her smile widening. 'I've taught a bit of French to first-graders when I worked as a teacher,' she added.

'Ahh, wonderful!' he said. 'You've been to France, no?'

Her gaze dropped to the floor. 'One day.' She handed him the towels, and he went back inside.

'Thanks again,' the woman said. 'I'm needing a few extra lately to roll up and put either side of my body in bed, helps support this lump of a thing!' She patted her stomach.

'Not much longer to go?'

'Seven weeks, though I don't know how much more I can handle.' She sighed. 'My blood pressure isn't behaving. I've been instructed to take it easy and rest until delivery.'

Emma eyed the pile of books beside her on the table. 'I take it you've got a bit of reading planned to pass the time?'

'I've come prepared.' She patted the books. 'But I'm getting a bit bored. I have to keep reminding myself I can't do what I used to do, and I've been told I should take advantage of the peace and quiet now while I have it.' She gave Emma a curious glance. 'You got kids?'

Emma shook her head and glanced away. 'No. Wasn't meant to be, I guess.'

'Oh, there's still time. You can't be much older than thirty.' She smiled.

'Thanks for the compliment, but I'm thirty-seven.' Emma smiled back. 'Is there anything else I can help you with?'

'Not that I can think of. I'm all set for an adrenaline-filled adventure holiday right here.' She patted the arms of her chair.

Emma chuckled. 'I hope you enjoy your stay. Call reception if you do need anything, or give me a yell if you see me slacking off around the grounds.' She winked.

'Ha, will do. Thanks...' She drew out the word.

'Emma.'

'*Emma.* Thanks. I'm Lizzie.' She held out her hand.

'Nice to meet you.' They shook hands. Emma stepped off the porch and walked back the way she came, in a much better mood than she'd been on her way to the cabin.

She approached the playground at the end of the walking track and slowed a little. The colourful structures stuck out amidst the beauty of the natural environment of grass, sand, trees, and flowers. So did the person standing there. James' arms were folded and his back was to her. He focused on his son playing; not on the climbing equipment, but underneath it. Jackson pressed his finger into the artificial spongy ground that her parents had installed around the playground last year to protect kids from injuries. James was like a military guard, still and strong, ready to intervene and protect his son from any danger that might arise.

When another child climbed up the equipment, Jackson moved away to another area. Two girls about nine or ten chatted loudly as they swung in circles around the poles holding up the tall cubbyhouse. One of them released a high-pitched laugh and Jackson clapped his hands to his ears and grunted. He moved away again and flapped his hands as though shaking something repulsive from them. Emma stopped, watching him. She knew instantly. She'd seen kids like Jackson before, had worked with them when she was employed as a teacher's aide and then as a special needs teacher. Her heart filled with warmth at the sight of the sweet little boy who was now smiling to himself and making lulling noises. Then her heart deflated when she realised James had caught sight of her, and she felt for him. Because she knew now, that he had a lot more on his plate than just the history of their sudden breakup.

24

James knew. He knew Emma was watching Jackson and noticing that he wasn't like other kids. When she'd caught his eye her face had been softer than before, and then her cheeks flushed and she walked off.

He didn't want her pity. Heck, he didn't want anything from her. Except an explanation. Just the truth, then he could forget all about her and get on with his life.

The young girls chatted again, saying, 'OMG, OMG! No way, really?' and, 'That show is totally the best.' Their rapid-fire conversation was barely understandable, but they were mighty excited about something as they hung from the horizontal bar with their hands and jumped off, then sat on the ground cross-legged to play a clapping game. At their repeated clapping and loud laughter, Jackson covered his ears again. He released a hand briefly, and pressed it: the screaming button. *Crap.* The girls' heads flipped to look at the boy, their mouths open. They laughed again as he pressed it a second time. 'That freaked me out!' one of them said. Then they resumed their (loud) conversation.

'Girls, be quiet, will you? I'm trying to read,' said a woman sitting at the nearby picnic table, barely looking in the girls' direction. They continued. 'Seriously, cut the chatter will you? Geez.'

James cleared his throat and gripped his biceps as his arms sat crossed on his chest. So the volume was irritating Jackson a tad, but the girls were happy and they were talking, there was nothing wrong with that. In fact, he felt like going up to the woman and shaking her, exclaiming, 'Your kids are talking, it's a freaking miracle! Look! Pay attention, do you have any idea how lucky you are?' He shook the image from his mind. The mother wanted her kids to shut up. He just wanted his child to speak. One word, anything. A swear word for all he cared.

Unintelligible sounds Jackson could make, but never a proper word. If James could wish for anything it would be to hear his son say, 'Dad'.

Just once. Please, just once.

CHAPTER FIVE

'What do you mean he can't have any ice-cream?' Martin Gallagher held the melting scoop over a bowl.

'No dairy. Jackson's been on the gluten- and casein-free diet for just over two weeks now,' James explained.

'Surely a little bit won't hurt?'

'No, Dad.' He moved his father's hand away from the bowl and scooped fruit into it instead. Jackson took the bowl and carried it to the floor in front of the TV where a Wiggles DVD was playing. 'If I'm going to give the diet a proper shot he can't have any at all. I've done my research, and if it might help him I want to do it one hundred percent.'

Martin held up his hands and sighed.

Why can't he let me do things my own way?

'I've heard it's helped a lot of kids,' Lizzie said.

James appreciated her support. 'It has, and Jackson's already sleeping better. I've also joined an online group of parents who are following the dietary approach, so it's good to have some hope.'

'He doesn't seem to mind anyway.' Lizzie cocked her head to where Jackson sat, nibbling his fruit.

He'd never liked ice-cream anyway, too slimy, but there was no need to remind his dad of that. The only fuss he'd kicked up was not being able to have a cup of milk before bed anymore, but the last few nights he'd been okay without it. And changing to gluten-free bread was relatively easy; there were quite a few options these days and James was pleased he'd worked out a list of suitable foods his son could eat.

'Fruit for dessert isn't the same without something else like ice-cream or custard.' Martin kept trying to make his point.

Now James was the one sighing. 'He doesn't even need dessert; none of us do, really. It's just a socially constructed habit carried down through generations. Food is food, doesn't matter what time of day you eat what.' He drummed his fingers on the table.

'Don't let Bella hear you say that,' his mother commented, glancing at the wooden urn above the kitchen cupboards.

'Nonna would only want Jackson to be healthy and happy,' James stated.

His mother nodded, her lips clamped.

His father got up and poked his head inside a cupboard. 'Did we bring any chocolate sauce?'

Marie Gallagher took the opportunity to cast a glance towards her son, telling him not to counter his father's opinions right now. The funeral had only been last Friday and he was still grieving over the loss of his mother, naturally. They all were, but it was harder for Martin, he was the only child left after his sister had died young. Only James and Jackson to carry on the family name now, and Lizzie's future child, but James doubted his son would ever have a romantic relationship in life. His chest folded in on itself with sadness. He knew he'd be caring for Jackson for the rest of his life. While other parents waved their children off to university or to get married, Jackson would still need help with daily living.

Many people on the autistic spectrum went on to lead relatively normal lives, but for James, his life plan was set. Whether a woman would ever be part of that plan he wasn't sure. Would anyone really want to be with him, to hand over their dreams for a lifetime of responsibility? Even if Jackson did get good results with various treatments, the underlying condition was too severe in his case. But there was always hope. Even if only a little. You could never tell what might be around the corner.

When the *Big Red Car* song came on the DVD, Jackson got up and copied the movements of The Wiggles. His body was able and willing to learn, but expressing himself verbally was a different thing altogether. Speech therapy had helped him make some sounds, but it was like trying to get blood out of a stone. The music therapy had proved better, at least he was happier in those sessions, and his Sound Machine was both a huge blessing and an occasional burden.

'Do you know if reception has fishing rods for hire?' Martin asked, having given up looking for chocolate sauce. 'I'd like to do some fishing while we're here.'

'Um, not sure,' James replied. And he sure as hell wasn't going to go in there and ask Emma.

'I'll check tomorrow.'

'You're probably better off going to the marina, Dad.' James scratched his head.

'Yeah but that's a long walk, I'll see if they have the basics while we're here.'

Marie Gallagher eyed her son. 'Darling, who was that woman you spoke to earlier? You said you'd tell me later.'

Oh man, not now.

'What woman?' Lizzie perked up, and André leaned forward on the table.

He shrugged. 'Someone I used to know.'

29

'More details please.' Lizzie eyed her brother with her interrogation stare.

James sighed. 'Emma Brighton, if you must know. We dated before Jackson was born.'

'Hang on, before Jackson's mother came on the scene?' Marie asked, and James nodded his confirmation. 'Oh, so she was the woman you'd mentioned a few times, when your father and I were living up north? The one you'd said things were working out well with?'

'Yes, Mum, and the one who left without any good reason,' his voice hardened. 'Would you like me to draw a timeline of events so you can all get a detailed history of my failed relationships?' James turned his head to the side.

'Honey, don't get upset. We're just concerned,' his mother soothed. 'She seemed so... nice, when I spoke to her.'

Lizzie looked at her mother and then at James. 'Is she staying at the cabins too?'

'No, she's running the place for her parents for a while,' James replied.

'*Emma*, you said?' He nodded. 'Brown hair, sort of a caramel colour?' Lizzie ran a hand over her own dark hair. 'Nice smile, good teeth?'

'Um, I guess so?'

'Well, unless there's another Emma, I believe I met her today,' Lizzie said. 'She brought me some extra towels.'

Ah, towels. That would be her. James recalled crossing paths with her on the way to the playground.

'She seemed lovely, but... she just left you without explaining why?' Lizzie's face creased with confusion.

James nodded. 'She said she was going to work at a school in Melbourne, but I found out that was a lie and she was actually in Sydney. She didn't give us a chance to talk or say goodbye, just said her piece and left in a hurry.' James raised his hands and let them fall to his side.

Lizzie shook her head. 'If I'd known, I wouldn't have been so nice to her.' She crossed her hands over the top of her belly.

'Maybe there was good reason?' André proposed. But he loved everybody.

James shrugged. 'It doesn't matter if there was, the point is she didn't have the decency to tell me the truth.'

'Maybe she'll tell you now, while you're here,' Marie said, before popping a strawberry in her mouth. *Emma's* strawberries.

'I already asked her. She's even less keen to talk than she was five years ago. She's obviously moved on.'

James glanced at his father, leaning on the kitchen bench. 'I'll go to reception and ask her about the fishing rods, and maybe I'll tell her my name, see if she squirms.'

'Martin, don't play games! We'll go to the marina instead and leave the woman alone,' Marie decided.

'No.' James sat up straight. 'I'll go. I'll go to reception and ask about the fishing rods. She deserves to feel awkward, and she'll have no excuse to walk away if she's working.' New resolve cleared his head. 'One way or another, I'll get the truth out of her before we leave this place.'

After waiting for an appropriate time to pull Jackson away from his DVD (you'd be asking for trouble if you interrupted The Wiggles mid-song), James unlocked the door to his cabin and Jackson rushed inside. He made an urgent '*mm*' sound, which James knew was code for toilet time. He went to follow his son into the bathroom to help him out, but was met with the door in his face. *Oh. This is new.* Since Jackson had finished toilet training six months ago, after he turned four, he normally left the door wide open and needed a little help with his aim, but tonight it seemed he wanted privacy. James shrugged and turned away, then returned to wait by the door in case his help was needed.

The toilet flushed and running water could be heard through the door. Then silence. He waited for Jackson to come out but he didn't. Deciding to give him some independence while it was being indulged, he listened through the door. A clang sounded — the stainless steel rinsing cup and toothbrush holder? Water ran again, and then, *was he actually... brushing his teeth?* James couldn't help himself, he inched the door open and peered through. Jackson was on the step stool in front of the mirror, his mouth open wide, rubbing the toothbrush strategically up and down his teeth. James always did this for him, and was often met with much defiance.

James stepped into the bathroom quietly, a huge grin stretching into his cheeks. He wanted to take in this milestone but at the same time didn't want to disrupt his son. 'Good on ya, mate,' he whispered. 'You're doing an excellent job.' He wanted to pat his back but resisted. *Let the boy finish.*

Jackson rinsed the brush under running water and placed it back in the holder, moving it into proper position, then sipped from the cup and spat the water out. He repeated this twice (*'three times, buddy, just to be sure'*), returned the cup to its position alongside the cup holder, then wiped his mouth on the towel.

For a brief moment their eyes met, but Jackson quickly reached into his pocket and pulled out the Sound Machine. He pressed a button and applause exploded from the device. It was the button James pressed for him whenever his son achieved something, and now, he was recognising the achievement on his own. Warmth flooded James' heart.

Jackson laughed, put down the machine and clapped his own hands. James joined in, laughing, then bent down and hugged his child. Jackson's arms stayed by his side, but he didn't pull away. James kissed his son's forehead and ruffled his hair as he stood straight again. 'I'm so proud of you, Jax. Good work.' James pressed the button and Jackson guffawed, clapping his hands hard.

Just when it's easy to think there's no progress, something happens, and hope is restored. James turned around, as if to double-check no one else was there and had witnessed the simple but profound moment. He wanted to say to someone, 'Hey, did you see that? Jackson brushed his teeth BY HIMSELF!' But a hollow sensation swallowed his joy for a second. The space behind him was empty, a void of unfulfilled possibility. No one was here to share in this moment, or future moments like it, and he would have to get used to it.

He returned his focus to the happy face of his little boy, now adjusting the hand towel as perfectly as he could manage it. James' smile widened, erasing the emotional turmoil from before. This is what mattered, this is what he lived for now: his son's happiness. He would get an answer out of Emma somehow, he could try some of the techniques he'd learned in law school, but then he would leave the past where it belonged. It was time to focus on the future, for father and son.

CHAPTER SIX

B y eight the next morning, construction workers were already well into their workday, busying themselves with the new cabins and games room. Emma ducked over to the construction zone for a closer look.

'Morning, Emma,' said Bob, the builder. Yep, his name was Bob, and he was a builder. Emma had made a joke the first time she met him, comparing him to the children's television character. Bob laughed it off, and no doubt was the butt of all jokes on a regular basis. To amuse Emma, whenever she walked past or came to visit he'd start humming the *Bob the Builder* theme song. She liked to start her day by going past the construction zone, it put her in a good mood.

'Working hard, I see.' She smiled.

He tipped his hard hat like the perfect gentleman. 'No other way to work.' He smiled. 'Roof will be installed next week, by the way.' He gestured above the soon-to-be games room.

'Oh good, let's hope the weather stays clear then.'

'Nothing but blue skies ahead, I hear.'

She gave a nod. 'I'll leave you to it. Have a good day.'

'You too.' He waved, and Emma walked off. Despite the

blue skies forecast for early March, there was no way to find out her life forecast. But grey clouds were certainly hanging overhead.

Emma unlocked the reception office and entered, flooding the room in light with a quick tug of the cords on the blinds. A small posy of flowers sat happily in a vase on the counter, and Emma smiled. Amelia always left something on the counter at the end of her workday on Mondays; flowers, chocolates, a post-it note with a smiley face on it... small gestures that helped start the work week off right. Emma planned on leaving a gift of her own on Saturday afternoon for Amelia to find Sunday morning. Something to say thanks for all the extra help she'd given over the past month. She just had to decide on the perfect gift.

The computer powered up and she checked the bookings for the next week. And the check-outs for Monday. Martin Gallagher from Welston had booked three cabins for seven nights. Cabin one for James Gallagher, cabin two for André and Lizzie Renault. *Lizzie.* The pregnant woman she'd spoken to yesterday. Emma remembered then that James had a sister. She'd been in primary school when they'd been in high school and they'd never met, and when James had moved back to Welston to open his law practice after living in Sydney, his family no longer lived in town.

Did Lizzie know who she was?

There were three guests checking out this morning, and three checking in this afternoon to take their place. The cleaners would be in at ten o'clock to prepare the cabins. Emma ran through her mental checklist. Running the holiday park was a nonstop business. There were always comings and goings, maintenance and repairs of the cabins and the grounds, cleaning galore, enquiries and bookings, and marketing and administration. The job was never boring, though could get overwhelming sometimes.

Emma checked the answering machine and returned a few calls, then confirmed internet bookings that had come in overnight. The place booked out months in advance, a year or so for the beachfront cabins. The rental caravans were easier to book, often taking short notice reservations for people needing cheap, emergency accommodation, while others brought their own caravans and booked a patch of ground to park their van.

The office door jingled and a young, tanned, and rosy-cheeked couple walked in. Emma flashed her best feature — so she'd been told — her smile, and stood tall behind the counter.

'We're just checking out,' the woman said. 'Sadly. This place is so peaceful.'

Emma had thought so too, until yesterday. 'I'm glad you liked it. How was the cabin?'

'Very impressive,' said the man. 'And thanks for the bottle of wine and fruit basket you left in the room for us.'

They must have been the honeymoon couple who'd checked in on Saturday night after hours. As she did for all guests expected to arrive after five, she left the cabin key with the local Mexican restaurant up the road who were open late, seven days a week.

'Oh, you must be Mr and Mrs Granford,' Emma said, remembering their name from last week's booking schedule. 'Congratulations!' She held out her hand and shook each of theirs. 'Are you heading home or is the honeymoon continuing?'

Mrs Granford smiled wide. 'It's not over yet.' She leaned in close and planted a noisy kiss on her husband's cheek.

'We're heading further south to tour a few wineries, enjoy the fresh coastal air.' Mr Granford spoke in a way that seemed like they hadn't a care in the world. A pang of jealousy irritated Emma, and she mentally scolded herself for it. She was lucky. Damn lucky. Just because life had presented her and her family with a few challenges didn't mean she had it tough. There was always someone worse off. But occasionally, she couldn't help but feel like she was missing something, and waiting for the day when she could do things she wanted without having to structure her life around other priorities and responsibilities.

'Sounds fabulous,' Emma said. 'Thanks for making the cabins part of your journey.' She took their key and filed it away in the locked drawer, then settled their account. As was policy for all newlyweds, she gave them a ten percent discount voucher for a future stay which, given their long waiting lists, expired in two years time.

'Thanks,' the woman looked at Emma's name tag, 'Emma.'

'My pleasure. Hope to see you again.'

They walked out all relaxed and smiling and glowing, and Emma was glad that she was able to be a vehicle for someone's happiness, if only in a small way, by providing a nice place to stay. She missed that about teaching; seeing the happiness on a child's face when they achieved something, or when she made a funny joke in class. Other people's happiness fuelled her own. In fact, she didn't know if she could have true happiness in her own right without helping it blossom in another person. Part of her people-pleaser personality, she guessed. It was just the way she was wired, and the way she'd been brought up. Look after others, do what's right for them, and life will reward you.

When midmorning rolled around, she was about to boil the kettle for a cup of tea when the door opened. James entered the office, his son by his side, carrying a pink owl. If it wasn't for the fact that it would feel awkward around James, she would have knelt in front of the boy and asked what the owl's name was. Instead, she glanced at James then looked away, pretending to busy herself behind the counter. 'How can I help you?' she asked in a polite but measured tone.

'I could answer that another way, but I'm here to ask if you have any fishing rods for hire. For my dad.' His measured tone competed with hers.

'No, sorry.' Emma tucked a strand of hair back underneath her Tarrin's Bay cap. 'The general store up the road has fishing bait and tackle, but the marina in the heart of town will have everything you need. Here.' She plucked a fishing brochure from a display stand and handed it to him. She glanced at his hand when he accepted the offering, remembered that same hand caressing her face, his thumb running across her lips...

Emma took a calming breath and forced herself to remain focused and emotionally unaffected. She was in work mode, and had to stay that way till five pm.

'Thanks,' he said. Jackson put the owl on the floor and spun it around in circles, the boy making rolling 'l' sounds. 'I also need a hat. For my son.'

'Of course. Right behind you.' Emma stepped out from behind the counter and pointed to the revolving rack in the back corner. 'Forget to bring one, huh?' What was she doing, making small talk with him when he clearly wanted anything but?

'No,' he snapped, and Emma lowered her gaze. 'I brought one, but Jackson...' James ran a hand through the thick, dark waves of his hair. 'If you must know, he half-flushed it down the toilet.'

Emma bit her lip to stifle a laugh, then cleared her throat. 'Oh. Right. Do you ah, need any assistance with plumbing?'

James waved away her concerns. 'No, I got it out. Threw it in the bin. I think it was a bit tight for him, he has a few sensitivities with things like that.' James put his hands in his pockets and shifted his weight to one foot.

'I understand. Well, there should be some here that are a bit roomier for a boy his age. Let's see.' She turned the rack around and appraised the options.

'Jackson, do you want to pick a hat?' James' voice took on a lighter tone, a tone she'd never heard before. His son stayed put, not acknowledging his dad's question. James gently grasped his son's hand and led him to the stand, pointing. 'Look, hats! Want to get a new hat for your head?' He patted Jackson's head, which was covered in a mop of waves like his father's, though longer. James picked one and held it out to Jackson, but his son pushed it away and grunted. 'Not that one? Okay. This one?' He held out another and got the same response. 'You need a hat, buddy. Stops you getting sunburnt.'

Emma knelt before him, not too close, but enough to establish her presence. She patted her own hat. 'I've got a hat,' she said. 'See? Want to touch it?'

Jackson glanced her way but didn't make eye contact. Emma took her hat off and put it back on again, demonstrating how it worked. Then she took a risk and put it on the owl's head. She knew it could go one of three ways:

1. Jackson would laugh or be perfectly okay with his toy wearing someone's hat.

2. He would completely ignore it.

3. He would chuck a fit and have a meltdown, and Emma would have two reasons to feel guilty around James.

Luckily, he chose number one. He patted the owl's hat, took it off and put it on his own head, then continued playing with the toy.

'You want a cap instead, huh?' James asked, plucking one from the rack. The boy pushed it away. He grabbed his dad's hand and made an urgent straining sound, pulling him towards the door. 'Hang on Jax, we have to give the hat back and choose another one.'

Emma flicked her hand. 'It's okay, he can have mine. I've got a couple of spares.'

James looked troubled. 'No, that's okay. I'll get him to give it back. Give me a few minutes.'

'No really, take it. It's his.'

He took his wallet from his pocket.

'James.' She held out her hand to decline his offer of payment and their eyes met.

'Well, thanks. I'll give it back when we check out.'

'It's okay if you don't.' Was she trying to somehow make up for ending their relationship by giving her ex-boyfriend's son a free hat? Ridiculous. A moment of awkwardness hung in the air when neither appeared to know what to say, then James turned for the door. Emma felt the need to say something. 'Is... is there anything else I can help you with?'

James looked her in the eye again. 'Not unless you have something to tell me?'

She opened her mouth but no sound came out, and she adjusted her ponytail.

'Didn't think so.' He walked out, leaving more emptiness in the office than had been there when she arrived.

CHAPTER SEVEN

'Looks like we're going for a walk,' James said to his father. 'No fishing rods, eh? Did you talk to Emma?'

He nodded. 'Not about the past, just about hats.' He pointed to Jackson's head, covered with the Tarrin's Bay cap that was a little too big for him. He didn't care. Whatever worked. It did feel kind of weird though, knowing it was Emma's.

'I was worried he might come back with a pink one,' Martin said.

James frowned. 'So what if he did?' Gender-specific colours were not worth getting concerned about; there were more important things to consider in child rearing. If his son was made happy by playing with a pink owl, then that was perfectly fine. And if he'd wanted a pink hat, well, so be it.

'Just saying,' Martin replied. 'Maybe it's time to give him a few more boyish things and experiences. Take him fishing, kick a ball around, you know.'

'I'd love to do those things with him, Dad, but he wouldn't sit still for fishing, and all he does with a soccer ball is roll on top of it.' James chuckled, even though his father's comment was a bit annoying. Boy things. Like doing them would somehow make his son whole and *normal*. The sooner his father accepted that his grandson wasn't going to be like James had been as a boy, the better.

'Are we heading into town?' asked Marie, emerging from the cabin wearing jeans and a drapey white shirt flapping in the breeze.

'Yes,' Martin replied.

'You coming too, James? Will Jackson be alright?' his mum asked.

'Hope so. Worth a shot, and the walk might use up his boundless energy.'

Marie checked in on Lizzie and André to see if they needed any supplies from the shops, then the group of four walked along the coastal track towards town, crossing over into the street as they neared. They walked past Tarrin's Bay Medical Clinic, an old weatherboard cottage that had been renovated and looked crisp, clean, and comforting. A small town medical practice was no doubt busy, he could see a row of waiting heads through the windows. It reminded him of his old law practice in Welston. He'd done well, but sadly, had to hand over the reigns and sell the business to someone else. His attempt to return to work part-time after Jackson's birth had resulted in a very unhappy little boy. A nanny was out of the question, Jackson wouldn't settle with anyone but James or his grandparents but he couldn't exactly hand over the parental role to his mum and dad, they deserved to enjoy their hard-earned retirement. James knew being a single parent would be a complete lifestyle change, but he'd gone into it willing and able, knowing his son's mother would never be back on the scene.

They turned into Park Street, the main street of town, planning to get a coffee before buying things they needed and hiring fishing rods. They passed a takeaway food shop, a restaurant, an old-fashioned bookstore, and approached a busy café with alfresco dining.

'Café Lagoon. I've heard they have good coffee.' Marie eyed the menu on a stand out front.

James remembered coming here years ago. He looked at Jackson who'd done well to cope with the walk and the sensory stimulation that abounded in the street. His face was tight though, and he gripped Owly close to his chest. He made soft, high-pitched noises, and James knew they wouldn't be able to sit in the café. 'I'll get something to take away and find a quiet spot in the park. But you two go in if you like.'

'Oh, no, dear, we can't do that. We'll join you outside, won't we Martin?'

His father didn't look overly pleased, but agreed.

They approached the counter where three staff members bustled about, and a young man came up to the cash register. 'Hi, mate, what can I get for you?'

'I'll have a cappuccino, and can I get a freshly squeezed juice for my boy? Apple and raspberry, thanks.'

'Sure thing. Does the little man want anything to eat as well?' The barista eyed Jackson and smiled.

'Oh, no, he's on a special diet. Unless you have anything gluten- and dairy-free?' Worth a shot. So far, his attempts to buy things at cafés had met with the discovery that there was the odd gluten-free item, but usually things weren't also dairy-free.

'Yes, we do actually.' Jonah — according to his name tag, pointed to the cake display. 'Apple and berry crumble muffins. Would he like one of those?'

James shrugged. 'We'll give it a try. I'll have one too. Take away. Thanks.' He smiled.

'No worries.' The young man exuded a calm but vibrant enthusiasm.

'Mum, Dad, what do you want? I'll get it all on my card.'

'You sure, honey?' asked Marie.

James nodded, and his parents placed their order. Jackson tugged on James' hand and he knew he'd have another few minutes before he got distressed.

'Open for dinner, are you?' Martin said, on looking up at the blackboard menu and café information.

'Sure are, till late every night. No rest for me.' Jonah grinned.

'We should pop in for dinner, love, what do you think?' Martin turned to his wife.

Marie nodded. 'Tonight, or later this week?'

Jonah raised his eyebrows. 'Well, if you come in on Friday, you'll need to reserve a table. There'll be some live music. I think it'll make for a memorable night,' he said.

That counts me out, James thought. But most nights he was too tired to go out anyway, so a home-cooked dinner in front of the TV had become the norm. Though it would be nice to have someone to share it with occasionally.

'Oh, sounds wonderful! Let's book in, Martin.' She rested her hands together on the counter. They put their names down and Jonah said he'd see them on Friday, and gave James a sticker of a smiley face in case Jackson wanted it.

Even though Welston was a smallish city, nothing beat a true-blue small Aussie town like Tarrin's Bay. The local business owners and staff were always friendly, and the air seemed full with peace and acceptance. Two things that scored high on James' list of values nowadays.

If it wasn't for Emma, he'd possibly consider moving here. But if she was going to hang around long-term, it could get awkward. Welston was great, but maybe it was time for a change of pace. He could go up north where his parents had lived for a while when he'd been at university in Sydney. Or he could go further south. Wherever he decided upon, he'd have to decide soon, because with Jackson turning five at the end of the year he'd need to figure out his options for education. He'd wait till he was six before trying some sort of formal schooling, but next year he hoped to try him out at a small or special needs pre-school and give him some experience being around other children, though the idea terrified him because he knew what he was like. Anyway, there was no need to decide immediately, he needed to enjoy a few days away and clear his head. Though how he would do that with Emma in the same vicinity he had no idea.

They crossed the road, Jackson stepping cautiously on only the white stripes of the crossing, and entered the green expanse of Miracle Park.

A miracle would be nice...

They sat at a picnic table and Jackson gulped down his juice. He picked at the muffin for a while, until he must have decided he liked it because he took a huge bite and James had to remove half of it from his mouth to prevent him choking.

'It's all or nothing with this guy,' James joked.

'If he has half the appetite you had at that age then he'll be fine,' his mother said. 'Bottomless pits, boys' stomachs.' She shook her head with a smile.

James patted his. 'Too right.' He bit into his muffin and revelled in the alternating soft and crunchy texture, the warm sweetness reminding him of Nonna Bella's home-baked goodies. Something he'd never have the pleasure of enjoying again. 'Didn't Grandpa John propose to Bella here in this park?'

Martin shook his head. 'Apparently, this was where they had their first date. He made a wish on her behalf in the Wishing Fountain. He proposed at the lookout near the beach, the one near Tarrin himself. That's why we're spreading her ashes there on Sunday.'

'Oh. I didn't realise,' James replied. 'I just thought it was her favourite place.'

'It was. Because of what it meant to her,' Marie said.

James wondered if he'd known enough about his grandparents. Had he been a devoted enough grandson? Should he have taken more time to listen to their stories and learn about their past while he was busy working hard at school, surfing, going on dates, and then working hard, yet again, at university?

It was only after becoming a parent himself that he'd realised how important family was. Sure, they were annoying at times, but the reality was; he wouldn't have coped with raising Jackson if they hadn't moved back south to be near him. He was lucky. His parents were there if he needed them, though he didn't like to admit he needed anyone.

I can do it myself, he'd told them when the reality of being a single parent became apparent.

And he could, but everybody needed a little respite now and again. And now, he realised, he craved more than just the odd bit of time out. The desire for good conversation, a few laughs, and good company inched its way into his mind. The last time he'd had that was a few months ago, when he'd caught up with friends in Sydney before Christmas, leaving Jackson with his parents. In the past, fun and freedom had been a regular occurrence, now they were as elusive as the unspoken words from his son's mouth.

When Jackson's appetite had been taken care of, he left Owly with James and ran over to the Wishing Fountain. With one hand holding his Sound Machine (laughter button on repeat) and one hand on the fountain's rim, he ran around in circles, mimicking the laughter from his device.

'Don't get dizzy, Jackson!' Marie called out.

The boy stopped every now and again to jump in the air, then run around in the other direction, tracing the rim with his hand.

Forget about getting dizzy, James was more concerned with getting the Sound Machine wet. Heaven forbid if anything should happen to his son's most prized possession.

'Cool!' A boy of about eight came up to Jackson, pointing to the machine. 'Can I have a look?'

Jackson ignored him and stood still, looking at his machine, pressing different sounds.

'Is there a burping sound?' the boy asked, laughing. He tried to take a closer look, and James instinctively stood, ready to intervene if necessary. 'Oh look, there is!' the boy pressed the burp and a revolting belching sound emerged.

Damn it, why did he have to do that? The burp was *never* pressed. Jackson hated it with a vengeance. A few people walking by turned their heads to see who had been so vulgar, not realising it was a recorded sound, and the boy laughed heartily. Jackson grunted and stamped his feet.

'Don't you think it's funny?' the boy asked, and pressed it again.

Jackson lifted his hand and gave the boy an almighty push, squealing from the effort. The boy stumbled backwards a little but didn't fall.

'Jackson, no. Come here.' James swooped in and took hold of the machine, pocketing it, then picked Jackson up. 'Mustn't push people.' His four-and-a-half-year-old body wriggled beneath his father's grasp.

A woman approached, checking that her son was okay, then caught James' glance. 'Doesn't your son know not to go around pushing other kids?' she huffed. 'Disgraceful. He needs to learn some discipline.' She shook her head.

'I'm really sorry, he didn't mean it, it's just that...' He was about to explain his son's condition but she'd already walked out of earshot, tugging her son along with her. James sighed, and Jackson wriggled free. What would he do when his son was too old and big to be carried? He was already getting heavy.

Jackson pounded James' pocket with his fists, and James gave in and handed back the machine, but led him to the picnic table where Marie wore an expression of concern and Martin wore one of... embarrassment.

'Should have stayed at the cabin,' James said, frustration hardening his voice. Would he ever be able to take Jackson somewhere without him having a meltdown? This one was only small compared to others, but in public even the small ones seemed huge. He was doing everything he could for his son's growth and wellbeing, but sometimes it didn't seem enough.

When Jackson had calmed down and was having a private moment with Owly, James checked his emails on his iPhone. He scrolled through the usual unimportant delete-worthy ones, and his finger hovered above one with the subject: VIP package enquiry.

He pressed it open and read it. He'd put an enquiry form on his website a couple of months ago to take expressions of interest for his new law business training package that he planned on launching soon, when he could spare the time to finalise the details. This potential customer had looked at his available programs for law graduates wanting to start their own firm, and said he didn't want any of them. He wanted the best package available, and when would it be ready please?

James didn't think anyone would want it. He'd be charging a bucketload for it as a high-end product for lawyers to maximise their profits through learning the foolproof management systems he'd developed, and marketing techniques to rise above the pack. His other self-study programs taught the same things, but this one was to include personal coaching, on-call access to him to help implement the systems, and an annual retreat for members only. He'd come up with the idea to leverage his knowledge and experience when Jackson's high level of care required him at home more than the office. It had been a blessing in disguise, and last year he'd out-earned his income from when he was in practice, yet he was working fewer hours. It was something he could do at home, around Jackson's needs, while still paying the bills and having plenty left over. Other law professionals had caught on, asking how he had done so well in his business in such a short time, so he thought his skills might be worth charging for.

James considered what to say in his reply. He didn't have a set launch date in mind, and the plans had been delayed with all the family upheaval of late, but maybe it was time to put the next level of his business in motion and give him something else to focus on besides Jackson. His existing products were all automated and earned him passive income. But he still needed to keep his finger on the pulse and maintain connection to the industry, not to mention give him some much-needed intellectual stimulation.

He thumbed in a reply on his phone's screen:

Thanks for your enquiry. The VIP package will be launching within 48 hours.

What was he doing? Was it really ready to sell? He'd done the work, but needed to get some of the technical things sorted out and commit to a schedule for the coaching and annual retreat. That was what was holding him back. He'd done occasional workshops to teach the basics of his program, selling his packages at the end of the event, but that was only a day being away from Jackson. This would be longer, though only once a year, and he'd have to arrange babysitting during his coaching sessions in case Jackson needed attention during them.

It didn't sound professional to have a screaming child in the background of a business call.

He looked at his parents, sitting here in the park with him, loyal and devoted. Then he looked at Jackson and a future of never-ending appointments and programs and health care needs flashed before him. He was financially stable already, but the extra money from this program if it really took off would be phenomenal. And he'd still be there for Jackson the majority of the time, so there was no need for guilt. He needed a new challenge, and there was obviously demand for his services. Yep, he just had to trust that it was the right move. If he waited for perfectionism he'd be waiting a long time.

James reread his reply and nodded to himself. Then he hit 'send'.

CHAPTER EIGHT

Emma pressed 'post' on the Tarrin's Bay Beachside Cabins Facebook page, and the photos of the construction works appeared on the screen.

'Bob our Builder is working hard as you can see! Stand by for an announcement next week regarding advance bookings for our two new cabins.'

Bob had given her permission to post the picture and his name, all for the sake of marketing. He said maybe having his picture on the internet would help him find a wife, and suggested to Emma that when her time was up running the cabins, she could perhaps produce a TV show called *The Builder Wants a Wife*. 'Farmers have all the luck, why not builders?' he'd asked. The guy was in his late forties and divorced; his wife had apparently not been suited to small town life, while Bob wouldn't live anywhere else.

Emma liked the appeal of city, country, *and* coast. She was flexible, though since moving back here the bay was starting to cast its spell on her. There was nothing like going to sleep and waking up to the constant hum of ocean waves, instead of tooting horns and ambulances. And, there was nothing like a lunchtime walk along the beach.

She grabbed her lunch bag and a towel, turned over the sign on the door that read 'gone fishing, back at 2pm', and headed towards the beach.

She hooked her shoes under two fingers and stepped onto the soft, warm sand that was like a carpet of clouds. Being the middle of a school day, the beach was quiet, only a few holiday-goers and locals wandering about and enjoying the water. She laid down her towel on a raised patch of sand near some rocks, and sat cross-legged, tearing the wrapping off her homemade chicken and roast vegetable wrap, courtesy of last night's leftovers.

The breeze tickled her face and although pleasant, foretold of cooler weather coming in the next few weeks as autumn kicked in. She glanced up to the right at Tarrin, the natural rock formation that resembled a man's face. He gazed across the horizon just like her, and he'd adapted to the winds of change without falling down, just like her. He was the perfect example of strength and persistence, of staying true to yourself and facing challenges head on. His face, formed a long time ago from bursts of waves licking at his rocky skin, and years of saltwater spray sculpting every tiny detail, was probably still changing; morphing into a slightly different appearance, but you could never tell. Like a person you see every day, so you don't notice ageing, Tarrin would always be Tarrin: tall, strong, and proud of his homeland.

When Emma finished her wrap she got out her sketchbook and pencil, and smiled. Since taking up drawing again a few years ago, she'd remembered the joy it brought her. She'd cast it aside when childhood's transition into adulthood brought with it ideals of 'doing better things with her time'. But now, more than ever, she knew that doing something purely for the joy of it was enough of a reason to do it. If not a damn good reason. Life was too short and precious not to use the gifts you'd been given.

She studied the incline of the headland that was home to Tarrin, and the shapes of the rock face surrounding him. She brushed the pencil across the paper in a sweeping motion, capturing the framework of the landscape. The sound of the pencil scratching across the paper brought back memories of silent moments with only her drawing material for company, when her heart would tell her hand how to move, what to draw, and how to create something to visually represent what she needed to express. If emotions were lines, or colours, or shapes, then she'd given birth to many over the past few years. It always surprised and delighted her what a blank piece of paper could turn into. One day she'd do something with all the drawings she'd filed away in desk drawers, but didn't know what.

As Tarrin grew to life on the page, she smiled at a seagull that had approached to steal a few crumbs from her lunch. It flew away, swooping through the sky, and she ached for that kind of freedom.

After a few more minutes of sketching she put her book and pencil away, promising to return to it another day, and stood, stretching her arms up high. She had time for a short walk before she'd have to get back to the office and await the afternoon check-ins.

Emma glanced across the beach to check if James was around. There was a man in the water, but not the same build as James, and there were no little boys Jackson's age. She tilted her replacement cap a little to the side to protect against the glare above the water, and walked along the shore, water lapping at her heels. A large beach umbrella was propped up on the sand ahead, bare feet crossed over each other beneath it. When she neared, she prepared a friendly smile, but then her smile twitched.

'Oh, hi Lizzie. How's the book?'

Lizzie looked up from behind the open book and her smile flattened out. 'It's fine. Thanks.' She returned her gaze to the pages.

She knows. James must have told her about me.

Awkwardness replacing the peace from her short break, she said, 'I'll leave you to it', and walked forwards.

'I hope it was a good reason,' Lizzie called after her.

Emma stopped, turned, backtracked a little. 'Sorry?'

'Why you left my brother in the lurch.'

If only she knew.

'I... I did what I thought was right, at the time.' She scratched her cheek.

'I? What about him? Why didn't you stop to think about what was right for him?'

I did, Lizzie, I did. That's exactly why I left him, it was for the best.

Emma adjusted the strap of her lunch bag across her chest and turned in the direction she'd come. 'I'm sorry, I can't discuss this. I have to get back to the office.' Emma stepped forwards again, then added, 'Enjoy your afternoon.'

Enjoy your afternoon? The woman had just had a go at her and she was adding pleasantries to an unpleasant conversation?

Emma's response was met with silence, and a smidgen of guilt rumbled in her belly. She hoped Lizzie's blood pressure wasn't climbing right now, she was supposed to be taking it easy. But in truth, her issues with James weren't Lizzie's concern. It was in the past, between her and him, and that's where it would stay. She shouldn't have to feel bullied into explaining something that had taken more guts to deal with than she'd ever thought she had.

So much for the beach walk. She felt exposed out here now, like a lone seashell washed up on the shore. She wanted to return to the safety of routine and confinement in the office where no one could question or judge her past decisions. But she should have walked the outer perimeter of the park grounds instead of cutting through it, because before she had realised, her past was standing in front of her. Again. James stood on the sand, his back to her, trying to coax Jackson from the green grass and onto the crumbling sand. The boy stood rigid like Tarrin, unwilling to move.

'Jackson, it's nice and warm. It will feel nice on your feet, and then we can make a sandcastle. Yeah?' He picked up a clump of sand and let it run through his fingers.

Jackson strained, his fists tight and his neck taut. Emma knew that kids on the autism spectrum often had heightened sensory sensitivities. Sand wasn't an uncommon phobia. The texture, the uncertainty of support underfoot. It was too unpredictable and different to solid ground.

'C'mon mate, just for one second, then we can go back on the grass.'

Jackson took something from his pocket and pressed it, a scream emanating which made Emma flinch. James gave up and returned to the grass, patting his son on the back and saying, 'It's okay, another time. It's okay.'

Emma knew she should walk straight past without him seeing her to avoid any further uncomfortable confrontations, but that need to help others weaved its way to the surface. 'You could try putting his favourite toy on the sand,' she said. *Damn it, Emma!*

James spun around at her voice. 'Excuse me?'

'To help him see that there's nothing to be afraid of. Or you could even get a tray and fill it with sand, keep it inside somewhere he'll get used to seeing it, so he can practise stepping in and out while still having his regular environment around him.'

James' eyebrows rose. 'You're giving me parenting advice?' He planted his hands on his hips.

'No, just offering some tips that might help. I've known kids like Jackson before.'

A big crease formed in James' forehead. 'Don't even think you can begin to know anything about him. You met him a day ago. I've been raising him on my own for four and a half years. You don't know anything about him. Or me, anymore.'

Emma bit her lip, which she should have done before deciding to speak. 'Sorry, I was only trying to help. I'll just go then, shall I?' She marched across the park. When she turned to the left to follow the path back to the office, she slid a glimpse towards the playground. James was now as still and rigid as Tarrin. But he was watching her. His eyes followed her, she was sure, all the way back, until she was out of sight.

Emma turned the sign on the door, sat behind the reception desk and checked for messages. Then she opened an internet window and found her favourite travel blog. She forced her interactions with Lizzie and James from her mind and focused on the beautiful pictures of Tuscan vineyards and Parisian moonlit streets. They held a magic she had yet to experience, a thrill she wanted to indulge. If she could, she would teleport to Europe right now and sit at a café eating local cuisine and sketching, pouring herself onto the page. But instead, she was sitting at work, behind a computer, trying her best to pour her grief and guilt back into the deep, dark pit where it belonged, so she never had to feel it again.

CHAPTER NINE

Emma had done her best to hide the following day. She stayed in the office as much as possible, and thankfully there were no extra towel requests from any of the Gallagher family. While checking a cabin up the end of the park near James' cabin, she spied them getting into a car; Jackson with his pink owl and her cap, and James with a backpack. She'd thought for a moment they might be leaving early on account of her, and felt a twinge of sadness and guilt. But later she'd seen Jackson playing in the garden near the playground, crouching down next to the bushes as if he was talking to the bright, dangly fuchsias that decorated the area. She could glimpse the playground from her window and occasionally cast a glance that way. Her insides twisted with contradictory urges — to seek him out, and to turn away from him. It had been a battle she'd dealt with in the past, but was now re-enlisted in.

After finishing work, taking the washing off the line and putting everything away, she made her way over to her parents' house for dinner. Her mother looked thrilled to see her, no doubt needing the extra company and set of hands. 'Come in, darling, I'm just serving up now.'

'Thanks, Mum.' At her mother's insistence Emma sat at the table, pushing her brown hair off her shoulders. She hadn't had to do that in a long time, but now that she was growing her hair long again, she noticed the unfamiliarity of the simple gesture. She leaned towards her dad and gave him a kiss on the cheek. 'How are you today?' she asked.

'Same old, same old,' he said gruffly, shrugging. 'At least I have a live-in nurse to care for me.' A small grin tugged at the corner of his mouth.

Barbara Brighton sighed. 'I'm more than that, dear.'

'I know, but you're not just my wife anymore. It's just the way it is.'

Emma was still getting used to her father's direct and honest remarks. He'd been nothing but courteous and respectful all his life, but now was less empathetic. It wasn't his fault, and they both knew to try not to let anything he said get to them.

'Smells good.' Emma studied the bowl of chicken and mushroom risotto that her mother placed in front of her, speckled with herbs and pine nuts.

'Eat up while it's warm,' Barbara said. She reached over to help her husband but he held out his good hand.

'I've got it.' He picked up the spoon. Emma had given her mum a cookbook called *One Pot Wonders*, so she could make as many meals as possible that Don would be able to eat on his own with one hand. He had minor use of his left side, but it was too weak to be consistent.

'Make sure you use your left a little too, give it a workout like the physio said. Otherwise it will weaken even further.'

'Yeah, yeah,' he mumbled, spooning risotto into his mouth.

Barbara turned her attention back to Emma and plastered a smile that Emma knew was partly forced. 'So, all going okay with you?'

'Everything's under control.' She nodded. Except when it

came to her personal life. 'Bob's ahead of schedule too, with all the great weather we've had, so we can start thinking about a more concrete plan for selling the place soon. Maybe we should bring in some stylists to fancy up the cabins, plant some new shrubs along the pathway...' Ideas ran through her mind.

'Yes, I guess so.' Barbara sighed again. 'It seems like such an effort to think of all that right now, though.'

'I know. It's okay, I'll come up with lists of what we need to accomplish and take it from there.' It'd be like working on her teaching schedule — a list of specific tasks to achieve a desired outcome. And the sooner the place was ready to sell, the sooner she could move on with her own life.

Clang! Don's spoon fell to the floor. He went to lean over to get it but could only tilt as far as the wheelchair would let him.

'I've got it, Dad.' Emma picked it up and wiped it with the napkin hanging from his collar.

He ripped the napkin off. 'I don't need this wretched thing, I'm not a baby.'

'I know, Dad, it's just...'

'No,' he said, putting the napkin on the table.

'Okay,' she said softly. She exchanged glances with her mother, knowing they were both thinking the same thing: he'd need to change his shirt by the end of the meal. His lopsided chewing made for lots of dribble and spills, but he was too stubborn to accept it yet. Understandably. He'd been an active man until the stroke, and it was bound to make him frustrated and upset.

Their prediction had proved correct by the time they'd finished eating, though he simply wiped at the glob of rice and oil on his shirt. He'd have to change into pyjamas soon anyway. Emma wondered how much longer her mother would cope, and whether they would need to finance some extra help in-house. A nursing home was out of the question at this stage, he wouldn't allow it, and he wasn't so disabled that it was a significant need. Maybe he would get better, maybe his mobility down the left side would improve with the physio. If he stuck to doing the exercises.

'So I guess there's no chance you might want to take over the holiday park long-term?' Barbara suggested with a small chuckle.

She hated to break her heart, but no. At least not now. Maybe after she'd had her European adventure she might feel differently, she might be ready to settle down and keep the family business running, but now wasn't the time. And a place like this — it was best run by more than one person; it was a perfect 'couples' business', but she was about as far away from being part of a couple as she was from Paris.

Emma tilted her head. 'Not at this stage, Mum. Sorry, I know it would be easier, but think of the sale price you could get. If it goes for a nice sum you might be able to pay for some help around here. And once it's sorted I'll keep coming back regularly, of course.'

'Why don't you try to keep it going a bit longer, Barb?' Don said. 'You love the place. I'll be okay, and like Em said, maybe we should hire someone to do a few things.'

'Oh I couldn't, Don. Not now. We need to focus on getting you used to... to...'

To living out the rest of his life in a wheelchair. To never going hiking in the Rocky Mountains. To never swimming in the ocean again.

Emma's heart sank.

'Well, we need to deal with where things are at right now. And we might need to move. This place isn't best suited to our needs anymore.'

'To *my* needs,' he corrected.

She was right. The two-storey house wasn't the most

suitable for a wheelchair, her dad having to live downstairs, much smaller than the upstairs, which had been designed to maximise the view.

'Still, there's no rush to sell, right? Why not see it through for a bit longer?'

'Don, my decision is made. Besides, I'll have more time to spend with Emma, and being retired will be good for us.' She took a sip from her glass.

'Emma needs to live her own life, Barb. And it's not like she'll be able to give us any grandchildren to keep you occupied.'

Barbara's spoon clanged against the bowl as she placed it down. Emma felt a dull thud in her chest and her jaw clenched.

'Don, that was uncalled for,' Barbara said.

'Well it's true. And you need to get over the fact that you'll never be a grandmother, and Emma will never be a mother. It's a simple fact.'

Emma covered her mouth, willing the hurt and sadness to stay within and not unravel her composure. Barbara's eyes became red and glossy.

She'd tried. She really had. But she couldn't take anymore, not tonight. Emma's chair skidded as she stood, and Barbara followed suit.

'Em, it's okay, he didn't mean it,' her mother said.

Emma shook her head and clamped her lips tight, turning to the kitchen counter to grab her bag.

'Wait, sweetheart, don't go. We haven't had dessert yet.'

'I can't... I...' Every word hurt to release, and if she tried to talk any further her words would morph into tears, and she didn't want her dad to see her cry.

'C'mon, love. Don't miss dessert, it's the best part of a meal,' he said.

Emma had always considered good conversation the best part of a meal, but tonight, it was sadly lacking.

'Thanks for dinner,' she said curtly. 'Goodnight, Mum. Dad.' She pecked her mother briefly on the cheek and retreated towards the door.

'Emma!' Barbara called out, but Emma was already halfway down the ramp.

She couldn't get inside fast enough. A sour, salty taste worked its way up her throat. Her lips still clamped tight and her heart pinching with each beat, she flung her bag onto the couch and went into the bathroom, turning on the shower. As it heated up she stripped off her clothes and let them fall into a limp pile on the floor. Standing in front of the mirror she avoided her own stare. Instead, her eyes turned downward to her stomach. She ran her shaking hand tentatively across the dull, purple-grey scar, her heart aching like it once had, at the deep, dark emptiness within.

After drowning her tears with the hot stream of water for what felt like hours, Emma stepped out and dried off, and she knew what had to be done.

She had to tell him.

She changed into trackpants and a long-sleeved t-shirt, and tied her wet hair haphazardly into a bun. It was late, but there was no way she could sleep tonight, feeling like this. Her dad had hit a nerve, a raw nerve, and although he meant no harm, it had hurt her. He was right, though: it was a simple fact, and she did have to get used to it. But maybe she wouldn't be able to if she didn't tell the one person she'd ever really loved what had happened.

Should she just turn up at his cabin? She didn't want to

disturb Jackson, who was probably sleeping. James might even be sleeping too, God knew he probably needed as much as he could get.

She could call the landline of cabin number one, but again, it might wake Jackson.

She could wait till tomorrow, but she'd have a restless night and be tired for work, and most importantly, she might lose her resolve and change her mind.

She withdrew her phone from her bag and pressed 'contacts'. She still had his number in there, had never been brave enough to delete it. Would he still have the same number from over five years ago?

Her gaze hovered over his name: James Gallagher.

She focused on each letter intently until they no longer resembled a name or a word, until they held no meaning, just like she'd done back then to try and forget him. But as soon as her focus returned it was there again.

James Gallagher.

The man she'd once thought she'd be with for life. Even though their relationship had been short, it had been intense and wonderful. The man who had been filled with hopes and dreams for his life, and who now barely resembled the guy she fell in love with. Did she do that to him?

She shuddered. She thought she'd be helping him by leaving, but did it really turn out that way? He'd said Jackson was four and a half, which meant whoever the child's mother was, he'd hooked up with her not long after Emma had left him. Was his son the result of a rebound fling? And where was the mother now?

Emma realised that even though James was the one who needed answers the most, she needed them too. She took a deep breath and pressed 'text message', then typed:

> James, is this still your number? It's Emma.

Her heart pounded as she waited, and waited, and waited. Had he looked at it and was wondering whether to ignore her? Or did the number now belong to someone else?

She put the phone in her pocket and poured a glass of water, though she probably needed wine. As she brought the glass to her lips her phone beeped and vibrated and she jumped, spilling some water on the table.

> Yes it's me. Why?

She typed back:

> I'm ready to tell you. Can we meet?

Waiting again, she thought he'd decided not to reply, but he did:

> I'll wait outside the cabin.

Emma slipped on her runners and locked up, sliding the phone and keys into her pocket. The park was quiet, serene, but it was about to get an injection of tension and who knew what else. She had no idea how he'd react. She didn't care that her hair was still wet or that she had no make-up on, she was simply going to tell him the truth, then leave. Again.

She made her way around the meandering concrete pathway at the back that weaved between cabins and gardens, the sounds of late night television and chatter filtering through the walls of the cabins. The constant whoosh of the ocean muffled the beating of her heart, and served to remind her that no matter what happened, life moved on. Things didn't stop for anyone. The ocean would be as ever-present as it had always been, and it gave her a sense of comfort that some things, at least, never changed.

Rounding the corner, she walked up to the back of cabin number one, where only a dim light shone through the closed curtains of the main bedroom. James' bedroom, no doubt, unless Jackson had bagsed it and left his father to sleep in the single bed of the kids' room. James would do something like that, she was sure of it. He would make a sacrifice, no matter how small, for someone else. And that was one of the reasons she'd done what she'd done. She hadn't wanted him to sacrifice anything for her back then, but he would have. If she'd let him.

Emma edged around to the side of the cabin, dark except for the hint of moonlight skidding off the ocean's surface and onto the shore, the white cabin walls reflecting its glossy tone. He was there at the cabin's side, sitting on the bench seat flanked by two potted plants, the kitchen window above it. His elbows rested firmly on his knees as he leant forwards, twisting his hands together.

'Hi.' Emma approached. James stood, slid his hands into his pockets. Their eyes met. 'Thanks for, for um...'

'Just tell me.' He crossed his arms.

Right. No messing around then.

Emma took a step closer. James didn't budge. 'Back when we were together, when everything was going so well and it looked like things might become more... permanent, something happened.' She cleared her throat. 'I didn't want to worry you, didn't want to burden you, but I knew I would never be able to give you what you wanted, so I left. To make it easier.'

'Easier? For you or me?' he said.

'For both of us.'

His eyes scored her like lasers, honing in on the truth that lay beneath, waiting to extract it.

She ran a hand over her wet hair, the coolness echoing that which emanated from him. 'I'd been having some... problems, with my health. Women's stuff. It was embarrassing, it's not exactly something a woman wants to talk about with her boyfriend.' She lowered her head. 'But when I went to my specialist, expecting a simple change in medication or maybe a small procedure to reduce the symptoms, she found something.'

James narrowed his eyes and tilted his head, and it appeared like he was holding his breath, waiting for the truth to come out.

Emma gulped. Her legs weakening like a deflating balloon, she moved to the bench and sat, gripping the armrest. James stood in front of her, arms still crossed, eyes still anticipating her revelation.

'It wasn't common for someone my age, but the evidence was plain to see.' Emma took a deep breath, though it felt like no oxygen had entered her lungs. 'I had aggressive cancer in my uterus.' The words felt foreign to her now, whereas once they had been so familiar. Like James; familiar and part of her one minute, foreign and far removed the next.

'Cancer? What? Are you...' James stepped closer and his hand stretched towards her for a split second, before he stepped back again and stiffened.

'I'm okay now, in remission,' she reassured. 'But back then, I didn't know what might happen and didn't want—'

'Why the hell didn't you tell me?' James' voice was high-pitched.

'James, I was going to, but that night I went over to your place, your friend's kids were there and you were having so much fun. And right after we'd had that *talk* too, and I just couldn't. I couldn't do it, I'm sorry.' She hung her head and rubbed at her neck.

'But I don't understand, I mean, why, what—'

'I'm broken, James.' She instinctively clutched her stomach. 'It's gone, all of it. I had a hysterectomy, followed by chemotherapy. That day, I'd found out that not only would I never carry a child, I could potentially...' she couldn't say the word. 'That *survival* wasn't guaranteed, as the cancer had spread. Our relationship was just warming up and I didn't want to put that on you. I didn't want your life and dreams to be affected by my problem, didn't want you to... to see me go through that.' Her chin quivered and she clamped her lips tight. 'I knew if I left then, you'd still have a chance. With someone else. You always wanted to be a father, and I wasn't about to rob you of that opportunity.'

'Christ, Emma.' James ran his hand through his hair, shaking his head. 'And you're sure things are okay now?'

She nodded.

'I would have helped you, can't you see that?' He glanced up at the cabin then lowered his voice, no doubt not wanting to wake Jackson. 'I would have been there for you!' He flung his hands in the air.

'I know you would have, and that's why I had to go. I could barely handle the effect on my parents, I didn't want you to suffer too.'

'But I did, Emma. I suffered!' He jabbed at his chest with his finger. 'Because you left!'

The pain of her impossible choice resurfaced, and her chest ached. 'But it would have been easier than the alternative and you know it,' she replied. 'Look, I know I hurt you, and I'm so, so sorry, but my head was in a spin. I was feeling all range of emotions, and I did what I thought was best at the time. I didn't want you feeling obligated to hang around.'

'I would have *wanted* to be around.'

'You say that now, but if you'd known what I went

through...' Emma gripped the armrest even tighter. 'Would you have really wanted the stress? The uncertainty? To know your chance of becoming a father had gone down the drain? To see my depression after the operation when it took every last bit of courage I had just to get up in the morning? To watch me puke my guts up and become a thin, hairless shadow of the woman I'd once been?' Emma's voice rose and shook and she clutched at her chest as it pulsed with the painful memory. The world around her seemed to spin, James becoming a blur in front of her, until everything sharpened when James' hands grasped her by the arms and wrenched her upright.

'You could have died, Emma! And I wouldn't have known. Why didn't you trust me to be there for you, to deal with it?' He lowered his face so it aligned with hers, and although it hurt like hell to look into his laser eyes, she did, acutely aware of the intensity of his emotions boiling up inside. For a moment she wanted to collapse into him, to let him support her body weight and carry her away, to surrender. But like she'd done that night, she closed her eyes to that image and cast it aside.

She pushed his hands off her and stood tall. 'I was confused, okay? I was worried. I was scared out of my mind. I thought if I took you out of the equation things would be easier to process. I would just focus on my treatment with my family by my side, and you would get over your broken heart and move on.' She flung her hand towards the cabin. 'And by the looks of it you did. And you got to have a child, see? That wouldn't have been possible if you'd stayed with me.'

James opened his mouth to speak but closed it again.

Silence bristled the hair on her arms as she tried to think of how else to explain her decision, to rationalise it, to make him forgive her, even though she wouldn't blame him if he didn't.

'I can't believe,' James' voice quietened, as though he'd lost all his energy, 'I just can't believe you went through all that. While I was busy hating you, you were busy...'

'Being sick.'

'Yes.' He shook his head, then met her eyes. 'You always loved kids.' She nodded, and he studied her face, as though gradually understanding what might have gone on in her mind all those years ago. 'I'm sorry about... the fact that... you can't...' He sucked in a deep breath and glanced up at the midnight blue sky.

There was no nice way of saying it.

'That I can't have children,' she did the job for him.

He shrugged in resigned agreement.

'I've had some time to get used to the fact.' She shrugged too. 'But I didn't see the point in both of us missing out. I wanted you to have that chance.' She inched closer to him, desperate to cradle his cheek with her hand but holding strong to resist.

With his short, high breaths and tight jaw he seemed to be doing the same thing, battling with his urge to comfort and his urge to stay strong.

'James, I hope one day you'll forgive me,' she whispered. 'I just did what I felt I needed to do.'

He held her gaze, stepped a tiny bit closer, his hand rising up in front of her. It trembled, and his Adam's apple bobbed as he gulped. Then he stepped back and looked away. 'No. No, I'm sorry, but no.' He crossed his arms. 'You should have told me, Emma. I thought our relationship was strong enough to share a challenge like that, but I guess I was wrong.'

Her heart dropped. 'But James, don't you see?'

'No. I appreciate you telling me, and I'm really glad that you're okay now, but that's it. I need to move on. I have responsibilities now, I can't let the past creep back into my life.' He turned away in the direction of the front of the cabin.

'Wait, James!' Emma stepped forwards.

James turned around briefly, gesturing to the cabin. 'My son is sleeping, so if you don't mind, I need to get back inside.' He stepped onto the porch and out of sight. The screen door closed with a hollow slap and Emma flinched.

Unable to walk away, she wilted onto the bench and dropped her face onto her hands, tears slipping between her fingers, and regret seeping between the cracks in her heart.

James stepped into the darkness of the cabin and quietly inched open the door to Jackson's bedroom. His son's breaths came slow and deep, and he was grateful he hadn't woken to the sounds of their argument. He closed the door slightly, leaving a gap of light, and paced the living room, not bothering to turn on a lamp. *Cancer? She'd had cancer?* And he'd thought she'd perhaps met someone else and didn't have the guts to tell him. He rubbed at his jaw that held day-old stubble and something inside twinged at the thought of how Emma's diagnosis must have scared the life out of her. Regardless, she should have told him. They were a couple. Couples shared things — good times and bad. They'd only been together for a couple of months but they'd known each other before, at school. It wasn't like they'd just met and started dating, it had been a long time coming; a slow build, and everything had been heading in the right direction, or so it seemed.

James gently slid aside the kitchen curtain and peered below. She was still there, sitting on the bench seat, her head in her hands. He had to stay strong and stand his ground. She'd been through worse. She would recover, and any minute she'd probably wipe her eyes and head back to her cottage, ready to get back to normal.

Before he changed his mind he released the curtain and went to sit on the couch, but it only reminded him of that talk they'd had the night before she'd left him, when they'd snuggled together in his dimly lit living room and talked about life. *Their lives...*

'*What's your dream, James John Gallagher?*' *Emma had asked, her finger tracing his hairline and her sweet scent intoxicating him.*

'*Simple, really. A satisfying career, financial freedom, the woman of my dreams, and passing my superb genes onto my offspring.*' *He'd chuckled, but he'd actually meant it. That was what he wanted from life.*

'*Kids, huh?*' *she'd asked, teasing his neck with her lips.*

'*I'd love them. Couldn't imagine not having them, to be honest.*' *And then he'd threaded his fingers between hers and squeezed the softness of her hand.* '*Can you imagine little Jameses and Emmas running around? I can.*'

'*Is that right, JJ?*' *She'd giggled.*

'*It couldn't be more right.*' *And he'd poured forth all his feelings for her and their impending future together into one unforgettable kiss, and what would turn out to be their last one...*

James stood abruptly, shaken from his flashback, but clear-headed for the first time since he'd arrived in Tarrin's Bay. Emma hadn't been selfish, she'd been self*less*. She'd tried to spare him the sadness of feeling what she was already feeling: loss, grief, for the children that hadn't been born yet, and never would.

She thought she'd be taking away my dream.

James dashed to the door and flung it open, grabbed the side of the doorframe for leverage and swung himself off the porch. The seat was empty. Like he'd thought, she'd pulled herself together and gone home. He ran to the back of the cabin and saw her figure walking quickly in the distance. He wanted to run after her, but couldn't leave Jackson. He wanted to call out, but it would wake Jackson and probably other children in the park. He pulled his phone from his pocket and texted:

> Come back. Please.

He watched her figure stop and look at her phone. Then she turned around, and although they couldn't see each other's faces, James knew she was torn. She just stood there.

He texted again:

> I'm sorry. I understand now.

She looked at her phone again, then put it in her pocket.

'C'mon, Emma,' he whispered.

She swivelled to the side, looking over her shoulder towards the safety of her temporary home, then looked again in his direction. She took a slow step forwards, then another, and another. James ached to be next to her, to comfort her.

Emma walked slowly, and when she reached the space between his cabin and the next, the moonlight caught her face. Regret and surrender shared space in her eyes. When she neared, he closed the gap with two steps of his own, and lifted his hand to the curve of her cheek. This time it didn't falter.

'James—'

'Shh.' He ran his thumb gently across her bottom lip.

Her wide, red-rimmed eyes gazed into his with their history of pain and suffering. It broke his heart more than it had been broken by her departure. Heat stung the backs of his eyes and his hand tingled at the soft, long-forgotten familiarity of her skin. His left hand tangled gently with hers and he squeezed it softly as if to say, 'It's okay, everything's okay'. He ran his hand up her arm and around her shoulder, dropping his other hand to match and pulling her body close to his. A slow sigh escaped her mouth and warmed his neck, like she'd been waiting to release her breath for all these years. He spread his palms across her back and pressed firmly but gently, encasing her with his support and understanding. He wanted to let her know with all of his being that he was here and she would never have to bear a heavy load on her own again.

CHAPTER TEN

James watched with pride as Jackson prepared his own breakfast the next morning. His son climbed on the bar stool next to the kitchen counter and tipped gluten-free cereal into a bowl. Some of it toppled onto the counter and the floor, but James didn't clean it up. He'd do that later. It was more important that Jackson was learning some independent skills. When he'd filled the bowl (a little *too* full) with rice milk, James pressed the applause button on the Sound Machine and Jackson got so excited he accidentally bumped the bowl and liquid splashed onto the counter and his hand. Jackson's smile turned downwards and he squealed with irritation, his face becoming red.

'Here, buddy.' James swiped his son's hand with a tissue then carried the bowl to the table. One step at a time. He didn't want to risk his son dropping the bowl and having a meltdown after his achievement of getting his own breakfast. It would probably scare him off trying again. Jackson sat at the table, a cushion underneath him to lift his body higher, and gobbled mouthfuls of cereal.

James fried two eggs and made himself a bowl of cereal as

well, joining his son at the table, though he was now almost finished. His mind flitted to the memory of Emma last night, her deep brown eyes and the trauma they'd held over the past few years.

He couldn't believe he finally knew. He knew why she had left him.

It was surreal, and he'd been angry for so long he wasn't used to feeling anything different. He understood now, but part of him still hurt. Like ripping a Band-Aid off, the damage had been done, but he needed a little time for the rawness of it to heal and settle. He still wished she'd told him, but last night when he'd realised and fully understood the reason why she hadn't, his anger had floated away like a dove released into the sky.

This changed everything.

No longer was he just here to say goodbye to Nonna Bella, to launch his online program, and to spend time outdoors with his son. The strong urge to reacquaint himself with Emma rippled through his bloodstream. He had to talk to her again, while he was here, while the chance lay open like a diary waiting to be filled with memories and dreams. He wanted to know more about what she went through, how she had coped, and if she had to have any ongoing treatment. He wanted to do the things he would have done back then if he'd known, provide support, though several years too late. But he also didn't want to burden her with bad memories. She might not want to talk about it.

The bouncy spring sound broke his thoughts as Jackson bounced with his Sound Machine on the couch after finishing his cereal. 'Jackson, not after breakfast, matey, you might throw up!' He stood and pointed to the toys on the floor. 'Time for a puzzle?' Jackson pressed the spring sound again and continued jumping around, James shaking his head. 'Well in that case, *I'll* do the puzzle, all by *myself.*' James sat on the floor and rearranged the wooden shapes, putting some into the correct spots and pretending to forget where the others were supposed to go. 'Oh no! I can't do it! If only I had someone to help me.' He made fake, frustrated grunt sounds as he held the pieces in the air, wondering where to put them. Jackson leapt off the couch and grabbed a puzzle piece from his father's hand, putting it in the correct position, followed by the others. Jackson pressed the applause sound and laughed, then tipped the puzzle over and started again from the beginning.

James chuckled and returned to his (now cold) eggs and cereal, eating them quickly. He was anxious to finalise his VIP program to be launched, but first, he needed to do something. He put the dirty bowls into the dishwasher and got his phone from his pocket.

> Are you free for lunch?

He texted. He turned on the kettle while he waited and spooned some coffee into a mug.

His phone beeped.

Yes, 12:30.

James smiled, typed back:

> My cabin?

See you then. I'll bring the food.

He pocketed his phone and checked his watch. Depending on how Jackson went today, he should be able to get a decent amount of work done before lunch. His parents could help, but he didn't want to bother them too much. He was used to working sporadically around Jackson's needs anyway. He'd promised that customer that the program would launch within forty-eight hours, which would be by tonight. And he never went back on his word. Besides, he wanted to get it done and dusted ASAP so he could focus for the rest of the week on his new mission: getting to know the only woman he'd ever truly loved, all over again.

———

Emma snapped the lids tight on the plastic containers of leftover risotto her mother had brought over this morning as a peace offering after her father's hurtful comment. When Emma told her mother about telling James the truth, Barbara had clasped her hands together with a smile and said, 'See? Sometimes what we think of as upsetting leads to something we need. If Dad hadn't said that, you might not have told James.' Now Emma could turn it around; anytime her mother had to put up with her husband's unfiltered remarks, she could remind her that 'maybe it is leading to something you need, Mum' and give her a little wink.

Emma put the two containers into a tote bag, along with a bottle of juice and a punnet of strawberries. She'd remembered how Jackson had eaten one eagerly and wanted to bring something he might like. She drew in a deep breath, nervous for some reason. One minute she'd been avoiding James and keeping her long-held secret, and the next, the secret had jumped ship and she was about to have lunch with him.

Emma's phone pinged with an incoming email. Jen, on her lunchbreak at school, had replied to the email Emma had sent her last night:

OMG. I can't believe you finally told
him. Good on you! How are you feeling
about it now? I swear, I got tingles
when I read how he just embraced you
like that. Em, that's so beautiful. See
— I knew he would understand. I bet it's
a big relief. What happens now? Are you
going to spend some time with him?

So many questions. And no answers. But tingles, yes, tingles. It had felt so good to feel his hand on her face again, his arms wrapped warmly around her. She didn't know what she was going to say in her reply to Jen yet, but she'd figure it out. Sometime. If only the answers would fall into her lap. Would James leave on Monday and that would be the last of it? Would she ever see him again? Did she *want* to see him again?

Yes.

Emma grabbed her bag and walked out the door with her head held high. There was no need to feel nervous, James had forgiven her. She walked along the pathway past the playground and the cabins, smiling at people as she went by. There was a beach umbrella on the sand like before — Lizzie on her grand adventure. She wondered if James would tell her the truth. She wouldn't mind, and hoped she would feel differently about her once she understood. But it felt strange to know that someone else knew what had happened. Just when she'd been ready to say goodbye to her past for good, it was now returning to her in full force. Life had a funny way of surprising people.

Emma walked past cabin number three and caught a glimpse of James' mum and dad through the open door. They cast a wary glance then looked away. Great. They hated her. And James had obviously not told them the reason she'd left him. She hurried along and stepped onto the porch of cabin number one. Jackson's Sound Machine greeted her with a bouncy sound, then he pocketed it and tossed his pink owl in the air repeatedly.

James approached the doorway. 'Come on in,' he said with a small smile. It probably felt foreign to him.

'Thanks.' She smiled back and held up the food offering. 'Risotto, hope that's okay.'

'Sounds good.' He accepted the bag and placed the containers on the table.

'I brought strawberries for Jackson, thought he might like some.'

'He'd love them, thanks.'

Their casual, pleasant conversation was a stark contrast to yesterday's heated and emotional one.

'Does he want some risotto too?'

'Oh, um...does it have any cheese in it?'

'Yes, parmesan.'

'Oh, not to worry, he'll just have his usual. Jackson's on a dairy-free diet at the moment, and gluten-free.'

'Oh right. Allergies?' she asked.

'Not exactly. It's a common diet used for autism, so we're giving it a go. Early days yet, but so far so good.'

Emma recalled hearing something about it in the past with some of the kids she'd taught. 'Something about the food affecting their brain?'

'Yep, the proteins. They can bind to the opioid receptors in the brain and mimic some of the symptoms of being on drugs like morphine.'

Ah, morphine. She remembered that well. Although it had been wonderful, she hoped she'd never need it again in her life. 'Sounds like you've done a lot of research.'

'I have. A lot of late nights.' He nodded, then spread some peanut butter on what she presumed to be gluten-free bread.

'Here, mate. Eat up.' He placed the plate on the table and Jackson came over and grabbed one of the triangles. 'I'll just heat up the risotto.' He placed it in the microwave and they waited the incredibly long time for it to beep. James pressed open the door when it showed two seconds to go. She held back a laugh. She *always* did that.

Soon they were seated at the table like old times, side by side, eating food.

'So, what do you do now?' she asked, then hoped it didn't sound rude. He raised a son on his own, that's what. 'I mean, are you a full-time dad?'

He took a sip of juice then answered, 'I stayed in law for a while, but it got too hard with Jackson, so I had to get creative. I produced a self-study program for up and coming lawyers to teach them what I'd learned in regards to setting up a practice; systems, admin, marketing, all that. It went better than I expected.'

'Wow, that's great, James. And you did all that from home while looking after Jackson?'

He nodded. 'I've learned to switch my attention from one thing to another quite quickly.'

'Oh yes, I remember having to do that with teaching, a ton of kids asking you things all at once, I got good at multitasking.' Was she comparing teaching to parenting? She wished she hadn't now. James obviously had a lot more to handle than she had, and for him it was 24/7.

James' head lowered, then he glanced up at her. 'I'm sorry, Emma, about...you know. I still feel bad, I can't begin to know what you went through.'

'It's okay.' Her heart softened at his kind words. 'Thanks for understanding.' She wanted to touch his hand, show her appreciation but didn't want to overstep the mark.

Jackson picked up a DVD and held it up, making an urgent

sound to his father. 'You know how to do it, mate. Put it in the DVD player.' He pointed, then looked at Emma. 'I'm trying to teach him some independence.' She nodded. Jackson opened the DVD case and held it out to the player. 'That's it, press open.'

He tapped at the device then managed to find the open button, squealing when it opened. He placed it in and with an emphatic push, the disc disappeared inside. The Wiggles appeared on screen and Emma smiled. 'What did parents do before technology, huh?'

'I have no idea.' He smiled and gestured outside. 'Shall we sit out on the porch?'

They got up and moved outside, the breeze wafting over from the ocean, Wiggles music their lunchtime soundtrack.

She wanted to know something, but didn't know how to ask. *Might as well just blurt it out.* 'So, um, is Jackson's mother around?'

James rubbed his jaw. 'Ah, no. To put it bluntly. She's never met him. I mean, obviously she did, but only briefly and then the nurses took him away.'

Whoa.

'She didn't want him. But I did. Simple as that.'

'Gosh, James, I'm so sorry.'

'It's okay, it's better to have one parent who's committed than two if one of them isn't into it.' He shrugged.

Emma was amazed. He'd given up his career to raise a child. And one with special needs at that, though he obviously hadn't known it at the time. She couldn't imagine Jackson's mother carrying a child to term and not wanting it. She'd kill for that chance.

James didn't want to tell Emma the full story, at least not right now. It could upset her, and it sure as hell upset him every time he thought about how he'd almost lost his son. He glanced through the window at Jackson, standing on tiptoes and moving along to the music on the DVD with a small smile on his face. Although he hadn't ever imagined his life would turn out like this, now he couldn't imagine it being any other way.

James returned his attention to Emma as she ate, her lips sliding over the silver spoon as she elegantly devoured the risotto. He never thought he'd be sitting here with her like this, he always thought his future would involve relaxing lunches with the mother of his child. But Stacey wasn't the woman for him. Never had been. Except for that one night when for a few hours the pain of losing Emma had been diluted and overpowered by the intense rush of lust and passion...

'C'mon, man, she's gone. You've given it a few weeks, it's time to move on.'

Gary was right. If she'd wanted to change her mind she would have done it by now.

'Two nights in the city, you can crash at my place. A party is just what you need.'

'I'm not exactly in the partying mood, but okay. I'll stay.'

'Once the crowd arrives you will be. Just like old times!'

James sighed. Those old times felt so long ago, and to be honest, he didn't know if he wanted anything resembling those days again. He'd grown up. He wanted more. But Gary was a permanent twenty-one-year-old in a thirty-something's body.

'I'll finish up at work and then I'll head up. See you in a few hours.'

He'd arrived to Gary's inner city apartment with a bag of spare clothes, the most basic of toiletries, and a heavy heart that took all his effort to heave it up to the fifth floor. Dinner and drinks tonight, a harbour cruise tomorrow, and then Gary's famous first-week-of-December Christmas party that had become an institution among his law friends.

By the time Saturday night had rolled around, James had loosened up. It had been good to get away, if only for a couple of days, to give him a fresh perspective. And God knows he'd been burying himself in work since she'd left so he didn't have to bury himself in the hurt. But if he kept going at this rate he'd burn out like a wildfire with no more ground to cover.

After reminiscing with old friends, a few others arrived at Gary's apartment to join the party. A colleague of Gary's had brought a mate and his girlfriend who was a singer and actress. And the girlfriend had brought a friend.

Stacey.

Also a singer and actress, she had just moved to Sydney to perform a major role in a musical that was starting in January.

'And you are?' she'd asked, when he'd shaken her hand after Gary's colleague introduced her and his girlfriend. Her green eyes were like emeralds, enticing him with a hypnotic sparkle. He wondered if they were coloured contact lenses, they were so bright.

'James.' He offered a brief smile, not the slightest bit interested in flirting.

'I knew a James once,' she said. 'He wasn't the nicest guy, but maybe you'll change my opinion of the name after tonight.' She winked, and James had resisted rolling his eyes. Great. A woman on the prowl. Just what ne needed, another potential heartbreak.

But her charm and wit had gradually chipped away at his icy heart, as had the alcohol he'd been drinking, and she became interesting. And sexy. With a great dancer's physique from years of ballet, she'd opted for musical theatre instead of dance, and her enthusiasm for her upcoming foray into show business was alluring.

When half the partygoers had left, Gary promised he'd shout

a round of drinks at the bar on the corner of his street, which had been the hub of many coming-of-age milestones during his university days. Karaoke dares, the-world-is-my-oyster business discussions, and the odd drunken kiss with random strangers.

James, Stacey, Gary, along with his colleague and girlfriend took a seat at a low round table surrounded by lazy armchairs and a bench against the wall. Their discussions ranged from who made the best cocktails through to the potential for opening up a bar of their own one day to enjoy in their retirement. Stacey and her friend Belinda talked about their theatre training and experiences, and even did a little duet, while a small crowd had formed around them. Her voice was delicious. James found himself increasingly attracted to her beauty and talent and drive. He had that same drive for his career and life in general, and he liked that she 'got him' and he 'got her'.

'Anyone else feel slightly old?' Gary asked, looking around at all the younger people who were just getting their Saturday night started, while the ones with families were heading home.

'Speak for yourself!' Stacey said with a laugh. 'Look at them, most of the crowd have their eyes glued to their new phones.'

James laughed too. 'They're probably posting on Facebook about how much fun they're having socialising.'

'I don't even have Facebook yet, is it really that great?' asked Gary.

James hadn't gotten into it either. Didn't have the time or inclination.

'Or they might be texting their friends instead of walking around looking for them,' she said.

'Okay, now I do feel a bit old.'

'Oh, no, we can't have you feeling old!' Stacey sidled up next to James. 'Give me your number.'

He was going to ask what for but she'd already slipped her hand into his pocket and grabbed his phone, then added herself as a contact, and retrieved his number too.

She tapped away at her phone and James' mobile beeped.

You don't look a day over twenty-five ;)

He glanced up from the screen and into her emerald eyes, a sneaky smile creeping up one corner of his mouth. He almost replied in the regular, spoken way then stopped himself and looked back at his phone.

Neither do you.

Her reply:

Maybe I'm not.

His reply:

Age is all in the mind anyway.

Her reply:

I know what's in my mind, and it's got nothing to do with age.

James gulped.

What has it got to do with?

He stole a glance at her as she thought up a response, her dark hair falling over one shoulder like a casual, friendly hand, her cheeks an earthy pink. An automatic hint of desire wafted through his body and it both annoyed and exhilarated him.

It's got everything to do with you.

He stared at the words for a few seconds, scared that if he looked up at her he'd launch himself at her with a ferocious kiss. Damn, this mixture of heartbreak, alcohol, and hormones wasn't doing his self-control much good.

'You two are as bad as everyone else,' said Gary, and not *knowing how to respond to her text message James distracted himself with a completely opposite topic of conversation with Gary's colleague, which helped settle his urge back to the pit of where it belonged.*

Many flirtatious glances and half-smiles followed as the

group chatted and laughed and drank, and by the time most were ready to head home, James was only warming up. He'd already joined Stacey in a (pathetic, on his part) duet of some song he'd forgotten as soon as they'd finished, and she seemed just as keen to keep the party going as he did. Gary had been right; this night was just what he needed.

'I'm gonna get another drink,' James said to Gary, patting him on the back. 'I'll get a cab later. Anyone else for another?' He glanced around, their faces slightly blurry under the dim light of the bar and his inability to stay focused.

'Me!' Stacey flung her arm in the air like she was answering an important question in science class.

'Sure you don't want to get in the cab with us?' asked her friend.

'Nah, I'm not ready for beddy-bye's just yet.' She laughed and snorted, which would normally have made James cringe but only made him burst out laughing and give her a high-five.

'Not that kind of beddy-bye's anyway,' she mumbled.

'Don't worry, I'll make sure she gets safely home before I head back to Gazza's.' James promised, waving the party-poopers off.

'Ur so nice,' she slurred. 'James is now my favourite name.' She used her finger (complete with sparkly nail polish) to write his name in the air in front of her. 'James. J-A-M-E-S. I'm such a good speller.' She laughed again and doubled over, and James led her by the elbow to the bar where they enjoyed a final drink and some more ridiculous conversation.

In the cab on the ride home on the way to Stacey's flat, James' phone beeped.

You gonna walk me inside?

He exchanged a blurry glance with the woman seated next to him whose free hand rested on his thigh.

I promised I would get you home safely, *he replied, amazed that his spelling was intact, but then realising that maybe he just thought his spelling was intact and it really wasn't.*

He paid the driver and got out of the car with her, and the driver asked, 'You want me to wait while you walk her inside?'

James paused, looked at Stacey who was having trouble standing on her heels. 'No, I'll get one a bit later.'

He walked up the steps with Stacey and into her building, and followed her straight into her bedroom. She pushed him onto the bed, unzipped herself from her dress, and crawled on top of him.

Emma became a distant memory as he gave in to his moment of weakness, waking the next morning with not only a shocking headache, but a vague concern that he'd forgotten one very important precaution. He was more worried about the risk of an STD, thinking she may have been on the pill, but a few tests gave him the all clear. A month later he found himself having a serious conversation with the woman he barely knew who'd given him the night off from his grief.

'More juice?' James asked Emma, holding up the bottle.

'Yes please.' Emma held her glass under it as he poured. 'Jackson seems to be enjoying those strawberries.' She cocked her head in his direction.

'Thanks for bringing them.'

She smiled.

They chatted about small things for a while, until Emma turned her wrist. 'I guess I should head back soon.'

He'd forgotten it was a workday for her, just when he was starting to relax around her again and enjoy the peace of the beachfront while Jackson was occupied. He had a sense that he didn't want her to leave. Then again, he still had to finish his work for the day too.

Emma stood and took her containers and bag, then crouched down near Jackson. 'See ya, little man.' She smiled and waved, even though the boy didn't respond. Emma didn't seem offended in the slightest. Of course she wouldn't be.

'Thanks for lunch,' James said.

'Thanks for...' Emma stalled. 'Thanks.'

He knew she meant more than just the use of his cabin and his company.

He walked her out and as she stepped off the steps and onto the path, he had a thought.

'Emma?' he said, and she glanced up at him with her beautiful brown eyes. 'I'm having a barbeque here tonight. With my family. Would you like to join us?'

She glanced away then back again. 'Oh. Well, that would be nice. Though...' She gestured discreetly to the next cabin. 'I don't think your sister is very fond of me,' she whispered.

James leaned on the porch railing to get closer to her. 'Sorry, they knew about us. But I'll tell them they have no need to hold a grudge. I mean, I won't tell them the details, I'll just say we've worked things out and there's no hard feelings. That okay?'

She nodded.

'It won't be an issue. Six thirty?'

'Deal. What can I bring?'

'Just yourself. I've got this one covered.'

'She's having dinner with us?' Lizzie asked, as James met her and André at the door to their cabin after they'd returned from lunch on the beach.

'Yes. Everything's okay now, I'm not angry with her anymore.'

'Just like that?' Lizzie raised her hands.

'Just like that.' No point telling her the details and how he hadn't accepted her apology at first.

'Wonderful! The more the merrier, yes?' André smiled, and stepped aside for Jackson to rush past him and into their cabin.

'So what was her excuse?' Lizzie wouldn't let up. She was the type that needed full, expository details of every given situation in order to feel satisfied.

'Whose excuse?' James' mother approached, followed by his father.

Lizzie turned around, the arch in her lower back getting more pronounced with the increasing weight of her belly. 'Emma's.'

'You've talked to her?' Marie came up the steps onto the porch, and James nodded.

'So what *was* her excuse?' Martin crossed his arms.

'Look, it doesn't matter. I just wanted to let you know she'll be joining us for the barbeque tonight. Be nice to her, okay?' James went into his sister's cabin to deal with a brief Jackson issue (no DVD's in cabin number two — disaster!), and when his son was occupied with pulling tissues repeatedly out of the tissue box and placing them in a neat pile, he found that his whole family had migrated into the living room.

'So she *did* have a good reason for leaving suddenly?' Marie asked. She shared a similar curiosity to her daughter.

'Geez, can't anyone trust me when I say it's all sorted?' He plonked himself on the couch and flipped open a tourist magazine, though the content might as well have been a medical textbook; he wasn't paying attention.

'It's just such a change to go from being so upset with her to inviting her to dinner,' Marie said.

'I agree,' said Martin.

'And isn't it better that we know so we don't accidentally say anything wrong tonight?' Lizzie would probably start using her 'delicate condition' to get the truth out of him next.

'Was it another man?' asked Martin.

'No!' James stood and tossed the magazine on the coffee table. It landed with a slap, startling Jackson. 'Sorry, buddy.' He walked to the kitchen counter and leaned on it, his body tired from all the drama and the afternoon slump dragging him down.

'For heaven's sake, just tell us, we're your family!' Lizzie said.

'She had cancer, okay? Cancer with a capital C! Happy now?' He shook his head and turned away, grabbing a glass and filling it with tap water. Silence. 'What? You do know what cancer is don't you?' He sculled the water, wishing it were beer.

'Cancer? But why... how did she...' Marie's face creased with confusion and concern.

'She can't have children. Because of the treatment she had. And she didn't want to burden me with that and get in the way of me having my own. So there. That's the big secret.'

Martin leaned a hand on the kitchen table, while Lizzie took a seat next to James and André rubbed her shoulders.

'She still should have told you,' Martin said.

'Dad, please. She knew I wouldn't leave her side and that's why she couldn't tell me.'

'Goodness me.' Marie touched a hand to her heart. 'The poor lass.'

Lizzie clasped her hands over her belly. 'Crap. And while I was being nasty she was probably looking with envy at this huge lump I'm carrying.'

'Wait, what do you mean you were being nasty?'

'She was walking on the beach and came up to me. But I fobbed her off. God I'm an idiot.' Lizzie lowered her head.

'Great. No wonder she was worried about accepting my dinner invitation.'

Lizzie groaned with apparent regret.

'I still think she should have explained her reason for leaving. I'm sorry for her, but still. It's always best to be honest.'

James didn't bother rebutting his father's comments. He wasn't exactly the king of empathy.

'Martin, just think what the poor girl must have gone through. She must have had a thousand fears running through her mind at a time like that.' Marie came up to James and placed her arm gently around his back.

Jackson pressed the screaming button on his Sound Machine and though James was used to random loud sounds invading his eardrums, he flinched. 'Better go. Looks like the tissues have run out.' He went to the floor and shoved all the tissues back in the box then placed Owly in front of his son. 'Time for Owly's nap at our cabin?' He flattened his palms together and tilted his head, resting it on his hands in a sleeping position. Communication with Jackson had to be visual, and sometimes he had to draw pictures or use pre-printed flash cards to help his son understand daily routines.

Jackson made a 'shh!' sound with his finger over his lips, cuddling Owly close to his side. He'd started doing that lately whenever he wanted his favourite toy to have a nap.

'I'll fire up the barbeque at six.' James stood.

'I'll help,' said André.

'I'll be the one hiding behind the potted plant,' Lizzie said. 'Though it will look like more of a garnish in front of me.'

James chuckled, glad that his sister had lightened up and could see the humour in the situation. Some days humour was his only saviour. He stepped towards the door, then glanced at his dad with a hopeful expression.

Marie must have noticed. 'We'll make her feel welcome, won't we Martin?' she sidled next to her husband and grasped his arm.

'See you tonight,' Martin replied.

James marinated the chicken tenderloins and put them in the fridge, and checked that the sausages were defrosting at a suitable rate on the kitchen counter near the sink. Then as Jackson supervised Owly and adjusted his blanket, James sat at the table with his laptop and mentally turned on the work switch in his mind.

Right. Time to get this sorted.

He proofread the web copy on his sales page, checked all the links were working, added the buy now button code into the HTML of his website editor and made sure the check-out system linked properly to his PayPal account. He then crafted a launch email to send to his database, utilising the copywriting skills he'd learned in the marketing course he'd done, the same skills he'd teach to clients of his program. It was amazing how a simple but significant change of words could mean the difference between making a sale and not making a sale. Just like with law, when he'd learned how to give a closing statement, words were everything. But more than that, the way the words were said and the emotion behind them were crucial. It wasn't about deceiving people, it was about connecting with them to help them find what they were looking for, whether it be the truth, a solution, or an opportunity to improve their life and business. He'd felt the emotion behind Emma's words last night. She had connected with him, got through to him, even if it had been a bit delayed. Yes, words were very important, and he hoped he'd get the chance to say the right ones with Emma this week.

James hovered the cursor over the 'send' button. Click. Email sent. Product launched. Now to see if it would take off. And now to see where the rest of this week would lead him in the unpredictable, ever-changing journey of his life.

CHAPTER ELEVEN

There was nothing quite like the enticing smell of an Aussie barbeque. The aroma of spices, onions and meats cooking on high heat became stronger as Emma walked the pathway to James' cabin, each step bringing both gladness and apprehension. Glad things seemed to be okay between her and James, and apprehension that his family might not be as forgiving.

The sky was still bright blue and wouldn't get dark for another hour or two thanks to daylight saving. People in the distance walked slowly along the shore as many often did at this time, for pre-dinner exercise, though she wasn't sure strolling counted much as exercise. There'd be yoga on the beach tomorrow evening. Emma decided she might give it a try. She hadn't done a yoga class in a while but the few that she had done she'd found both relaxing and invigorating.

'Good evening.' James looked up from his barbeque duties and a thin haze of smoke wafted around him.

'Hello. Hi, André,' she said, catching the eyes of both men on the porch.

'We're enjoying our stay very much,' André said. 'You have a beautiful place here.'

'Glad to hear it.' She smiled and made her way around the porch to the steps, meeting James at the top.

'I've got this,' André said, and James put down his tongs and wiped his hands, then held a hand out for Emma to welcome her inside.

'This is Emma,' he said.

His mother smiled and approached, holding out her gentle hands and clasping Emma's between them. 'Nice to officially meet you, Emma. I'm Marie.' Her eyes held understanding and kindness in their soft gaze.

She knows.

'And this is my husband, Martin.'

James' tall father stepped forwards and held out his hand, taking hers and giving it a firm, confident shake. 'Hello.'

'Hi. Thanks for letting me join you all for dinner.'

'It's our pleasure,' Marie said. 'You may have met Lizzie already?' She gestured to her daughter seated at the table.

Gulp. 'Yes. How are you, Lizzie?' Emma held out a hand so Lizzie knew she didn't have to get up from her chair to greet her.

'Tired but good.' She smiled. 'Thanks for the extra towels, by the way.'

'No worries. Anything else you need just let me know.'

'Thanks.' Her smile arched into her rosy cheeks and she fidgeted with her beaded necklace.

She knows too.

Had James told them the details of her secret?

Jackson burst out of one of the rooms and ran towards the front door. She thought he was going to run outside but he banged on the wall next to the door with his palm, then spun around and ran back down the hallway and banged the back wall, then hurtled back again, making a 'vvv' sound, complete with a spray of spittle.

'Jackson, not too loud,' Martin said.

'It's okay.' Emma flicked her hand. 'I used to teach a classroom full of kids. I learned to become immune to loud noise.' God, was she calling Jackson *noise*? She hoped it didn't come out the wrong way. 'Hi, Jackson.' She waved as he rushed past her and banged the wall.

'Would you like a drink?' James gestured to the kitchen counter. 'Wine, juice, beer, or lemonade.'

'Lemonade, please.' Though the wine might calm her nerves, she didn't want to loosen up too much and lose her cool. Better to have the wine with dinner.

James handed her the sparkling liquid and handed drinks to his family members.

'So,' Emma said, trying to think up some small talk to break the ice. 'What brings you to Tarrin's Bay?'

She was met with silence and awkward glances between the family. James spoke up. 'It's my — *would* have been — my Nonna Bella's birthday this Sunday. She loved Tarrin's Bay so we booked the cabins ages ago, but unfortunately she's not with us anymore.'

Oh crap. Forget about breaking the ice, she'd shattered it.

'Well, she is in a way.' Marie pointed above the kitchen cupboards to a wooden urn that was definitely not part of the cabin's decor.

'Mum,' groaned Lizzie. 'No need to show her.'

'We're spreading her ashes on Sunday afternoon, at the lookout near Tarrin,' James said.

'Oh gosh. I'm so sorry, I had no idea.' Emma felt like pulling her shirt up over her head.

'It's okay.' James smiled. 'So, um, how's your dad?'

Nice change of subject, one tragedy to another. 'Good.'
Sort of.

'Oh yes, we heard you're running this place for your parents. They live nearby?' Marie asked, eyebrows raised.

'Yes, just up the hill overlooking the beach.' She gestured in the general direction.

'Well then, perhaps you'd like to invite them for dinner too? There's plenty of food, isn't there James?'

James scratched his head. 'Um, yes there is...'

'It's okay, I think they already have dinner sorted,' Emma said. 'And Dad, well, he's in a wheelchair so it takes a bit of effort to get him places.' Not to mention the fact that he'd make for an uncomfortable dinner guest and would probably tell each person exactly what he thought of their clothing, hair, and attitude.

'Sorry to hear that,' Martin said. 'Was he in an accident?'

'Dad.' Lizzie covered her face with her hand. She was dealing with a lot of embarrassment today.

'He had a stroke recently; hence I've taken over things for them. At least until they can sell the park.'

'What a lot you've had to deal with,' said Marie. 'I mean, having a family member go through such a challenge. Must be a lot for everyone.' She lightly touched Emma's arm.

Yep, she definitely knows.

'Selling this beautiful place?' André poked his head around the door from outside. 'Maybe we should buy it, *ma cherie*!' He winked at his wife.

'I think we should save our money for this little rascal, I'm sure he or she will suck our bank account dry!' She chuckled, then glanced at Emma and covered her mouth.

She definitely knows too.

'Anyway, um.' Lizzie pointed outside. 'I might go sit out

there in the fresh air.' She pushed herself up and waddled to the porch, James holding the door wide for her.

'Let's all head outside,' Marie suggested, clasping her hands together.

Emma stepped outside and as the family hovered around the sizzling barbeque to observe the cooking progress, Emma sat next to Lizzie in a wicker deck chair.

'Emma, I'm sorry I was rude the other day,' she said. 'I was just—'

'Don't worry about it at all.' Emma held up her hand. 'Seriously, it doesn't matter.'

'I was just looking out for my brother, I remembered how upset he was when your relationship broke up, and...' She shook her head. 'Oh, I should just learn to keep my mouth shut.'

Emma placed her hand on her arm. 'Let's start fresh, shall we?'

Lizzie met Emma's gaze and nodded, then leaned a little closer. 'James told me. I hope that's okay; we kind of forced it out of him. I'm so sorry about what you went through.'

'We?'

'Yeah, everyone knows. Sorry.' She shrugged.

Wonderful. Though after being in hospital she'd gotten used to the fact that her private parts were up for public discussion.

'But he didn't tell us the type of cancer, just that you...' She glanced down at her belly and shook her head again. 'Oh Geez, I'm sorry.'

'Lizzie, it's okay. *I'm* okay. It was endometrial — *uterine* — cancer. I don't mind you knowing because, well, we're both women and I know you'd understand.'

Lizzie clamped her lips together in an apologetic smile, then something happened that surprised Emma. Tears welled up in

Lizzie's eyes. 'I can't begin to imagine, I mean...' She wiped at the corners of her eyes.

Emma dug into her pocket for a tissue. 'Here,' she said.

'Thanks, gotta love these hormones!'

'Everything okay?' André asked.

'Yep. Damn onions.' Lizzie laughed, and André returned to the barbeque with James.

'I like your necklace.' Emma pointed to the long, colourful beads.

'Thanks. My hubby brought it back from his last trip to France. Spoils me rotten, he does.'

'He seems really sweet.'

'He is. I'm a lucky woman. Very lucky.' She looked down at her belly and her eyes became glossy again.

'Okay, people, eat up.' James stepped aside. 'What can I get for you, Emma?'

She stood and eyed the tender, steaming meats and colourful salads.

'A bit of everything?' he asked.

'That sounds good to me.' She smiled, her tastebuds eager. 'Looks delicious.'

He placed a selection onto her plate and she grabbed a knife and fork and napkin from the side table. Martin carried out the extra folding table from inside and set it up on the porch, making room for everyone.

'I'll get Jackson's, you eat first, darling.' Marie took a plastic plate and filled it with food. 'All suitable for him, I gather?'

'Yes, all gluten- and dairy-free. Except the bread rolls.'

Marie took the plate, and James loaded another for his mother. 'I'll eat inside with Jackson, he's not great with a crowd,' said Marie to Emma.

'It's okay, I understand,' she replied. Marie went inside and sat Jackson on the table, then started cutting up his meat.

They sat around the two tables on the porch and dug into the balsamic glazed chicken thighs with rosemary, thin lamb sausages with browned onions, and the sweet potato salad, fried rice, and bread rolls.

'So, Emma,' said Martin. 'You're a teacher? Have you taken some leave while you're helping out here?'

Emma swallowed her mouthful of food and dabbed her lips with a napkin. 'Yes, I'm actually on leave until next year. I'd planned it a while ago and Dad's turn just happened to occur around the time I left.'

'Right.' He took a sip of beer. 'So what had you planned to do for the year, before your dad's stroke?'

Man, he was almost as direct as her father. Must be the lawyer in him, like James, though she assumed he might be retired by now.

'Dad, she probably just wanted some time off to relax,' said Lizzie.

'True, but I'd actually been about to book a European holiday when I got the call about Dad. So my trip will have to be postponed, I'm afraid.' Here she was, telling people she barely knew something she hadn't even told her own parents yet.

'Oh that is a shame!' André said. 'I hope you will be able to make it over there one day.'

'I'm sure I will. Dad's getting a little more used to his situation each day, and Mum is getting the hang of things. Once I know they're settled and have all the help they need and the place is sold, I'll reassess.'

James took a sip of wine. 'Where would you go?'

'Paris, Tuscany. Maybe London too.'

'I can advise you on lots of beautiful, hidden places to see in Paris,' André said with a smile.

'Thanks. There's a lot I'd like to see, and I always said I'd do it one day. I figured now was the perfect time. At least, it was, but life tends to surprise you and change your plans sometimes.' She exchanged a knowing glance with James.

'It sure does,' he said.

'I've learned to be flexible,' she added, then took another mouthful of food.

'I'd love some flexibility around now,' said Lizzie. 'Enough to put on my own shoes would be handy!' She laughed.

'That's what you've got *me* for,' said André, leaning over and kissing her on the lips. God he was sweet. She was right, she was very lucky indeed.

James noticed the romantic moment too and cleared his throat, and Marie came back outside, taking the spare seat next to her husband.

'How did you two meet?' Emma asked the soon-to-be-parents.

'It was like a fairy-tale,' said Lizzie. 'I was in Paris for a conference, and I met him at the hotel. He was staying there too.

'Oh, so you weren't living there, André?'

He shook his head. 'No, I had moved to Australia as a teenager, but was back home for a family wedding. The weddings in Paris are not fancy, it's really just signing some papers at City Hall, but we hired a function room in the hotel for a small family gathering.'

A wedding in Paris... Emma's mind wandered.

'The hotel had double-booked our rooms,' Lizzie added to the story. 'Obviously we didn't want to share with a complete stranger, but by the end of the day we'd exchanged numbers and had a nice conversation while waiting for our rooms to be sorted, and the rest is history!'

Lizzie's life seemed more amazing by the minute. Emma tried to quell the annoying touch of envy that surfaced in her chest.

Marie glowed, her hands clasped together under her chin. 'Such a lovely story. More romantic than how we met, right Martin?' She nudged him.

He cleared his throat. 'I'll have you know that meeting your future wife while analysing a lengthy terms and conditions statement is quite romantic.' Was that a brief smile? He didn't appear to be the smiley type, but maybe he was just cautious.

'Mum and Dad met in the university library,' explained Lizzie.

'That's right,' said Marie. 'I was a librarian, you see, until my retirement a couple of years ago. I was young and studious, working in the university's library, and along comes equally studious and dashingly handsome law student Martin Gallagher.' She smiled and nudged him again, and he held his drink up to hide his face. 'He made everything seem so fascinating, even that wretched terms and conditions he was analysing. Every time I have to agree to one I always remember that day.'

Emma smiled, trying to imagine them as young and in love. 'That's a lovely story too.'

She didn't remember the exact day she met James in high school, probably because they didn't officially meet, she just knew who he was and would occasionally pass him and his crazy, mop of wavy hair in the halls.

A moment of silence hung in the air while they chewed their food, and Emma wondered if James was also thinking about their past. Did random thoughts of her ever pop up into his mind like they did in hers? Or maybe he just focused on the present and the future, as parents of young kids often do.

'Hey, Emma, has anyone said you look a bit like that actress, oh what's her name?' Lizzie circled her hand in the air, scrunching up her face. 'The one that was in, oh what was she in?'

James chuckled. 'Been working on your memory skills, have you?'

Lizzie nudged him. 'Baby brain is what it is. At least I have an excuse.'

'Hey, my memory is perfect, thank you,' he said.

Don't I know it.

'Oh! I know!' Lizzie clicked her fingers. 'Kate Beckinsale.'

'Oh, I think I know her, she was in... you know, that one with...' Marie said.

'Yeah, I know what you mean but I can't think of the name either!'

'Like mother like daughter,' Martin said. 'Now that's given me an idea. Remember we used to play that Celebrity Head game with Bella? We should play it tonight, as a little tribute.'

'Oh that's a lovely idea, Martin,' said Marie.

James ran his hand over his head. 'We don't have to, we can just have conversations over food like regular people,' he said.

'Boo to that, I wanna play!' Lizzie slapped the table with her hand.

James shook his head, and eyed Emma with an apologetic but resigned look on his face.

'I'd love to play the game, and honour your Nonna.' Emma smiled. Sometimes a break from having to keep thinking up topics to discuss was welcome, and games provided a structured way to lighten the mood. Plus she had good memories of her own family trying to lighten her load by playing them between chemo treatments. To her, doing things like that was what regular families did.

'Then it's settled. I'll get the materials after dessert.' Martin clapped his hands and stood.

While everyone ate dessert, James put Jackson to bed. Emma had wandered inside at one point to refill some drinks and overheard him reading to his son. She couldn't make out all the words, but the tone and softness in his voice made her heart melt. Though she couldn't see through the gap in the door, she imagined he was sitting on the side of the bed, Jackson tucked up under the blanket with Owly, and James' strong but tender hand rubbing his son's back. She got some ice from the freezer just so she could hang in the kitchen a while longer and listen to him.

A deep longing rose within and she sighed. She'd never allowed herself to consider feeling anything again for him, but now, having told him her secret, she wasn't sure if those rules applied anymore. How on earth would she handle things now? She still couldn't give James any more children, though she wondered if he would realistically want more with the high demands already placed on him. Things had changed since the night she left him, but one thing hadn't. And though she tried to quell the resurfacing attraction and unbreakable connection she felt with him, she couldn't help but hope that there could be a chance for them to be together again. A chance for her to make it up to him.

The door to Jackson's bedroom eased open and James emerged. 'Oh. Hi. Didn't know you were in here.'

'Just refilling some glasses. You want one?' She held up the bottle.

'Nah, I'm good.' He glanced towards the porch outside where Marie had lit citronella candles to ward off the evening mosquitoes. 'Has my dad got everything set for Celebrity Head?'

'Yep. Just waiting on you.' She smiled.

'If it's too weird for you, they won't be offended if you don't want to play. Don't think you have to stay.'

Emma shook her head. 'No, no. I want to. Weird is good.' She smiled. 'Unless it's too weird for you?' She raised her eyebrows and shifted her weight to one foot.

'No, I'm fine. It's... nice, having you here.' He slipped his hands into his pockets and rose slightly on his toes.

Emma scratched her head. 'Um, thanks. I guess we should...' She gestured outside.

'Yep. Let's see if you're really Kate Beckinsale.'

They returned to the porch and took their seats, Martin with a pile of post-it notes and pens in front of him on the table. 'Righto. I'll pass these around, and you have to write a celebrity or character's name for the person next to you. I'll start.' He wrote on a note and stuck it to his wife's forehead.

Marilyn Monroe.

Everyone smiled. Marie wrote one for James:

Hugh Jackman.

And then James looked at Emma with an inquisitive look in his eyes. 'Who shall I make you?' He tapped the pen against his chin. 'I know.' He covered the post-it as he wrote, then patted it onto her forehead. Emma smiled and glanced upwards, wondering what name he had given her. At least it hadn't resulted in an eruption of laughter; everyone seemed keen to keep poker faces so as to not give anything away.

Emma eyed Lizzie with a smile, then wrote the first name that came to mind.

Kate Beckinsale.

She hoped it wouldn't be too obvious.

'Ha!' André said, then covered his mouth.

'Oh no, what hideous creature have you made me?' she teased.

'Not hideous at all,' said James, and Emma wondered if he generally liked the actress or if he was alluding to Emma looking like her, and therefore giving her a compliment.

'Shh! No hints!' Marie waved her hand over the table.

Lizzie wrote Steve Carell on André's post-it, and André wrote Hannibal Lector on Martin's. Emma assumed that they must have a good father and son-in-law relationship for him to get away with that one.

'I think our guest should start,' said Marie. 'Emma, I take it you know how this works?'

She nodded. 'Okay. Am I female?'

'Yes,' they all said.

'Am I an actress?'

'Um, not exactly,' James said. 'No. Officially, no.'

Damn.

'My turn,' said Lizzie. 'Am I female?'

'Yes.'

'Am I an actress?'

'Yes.'

'Am I hot?'

'I can't answer that, you're my sister.' James chuckled.

'Yes, you are, *ma cherie*.' André leaned in for a kiss.

'So I am?' Heads nodded. 'Right. Am I blonde?'

'Hold it right there!' James shot up and dashed inside, then returned a moment later with Jackson's Sound Machine. He closed the door to the cabin to reduce any noise, then pressed the *ba-bow* game show sound which indicated an incorrect answer.

Emma laughed. Boys and their toys. Her ex-students would have loved that machine, though she was sure they'd take it upon themselves to give the rude sounds a workout.

'Ha, I take it I'm not blonde?' Lizzie twirled her hand towards her husband to pass the game on.

'See, I knew you'd have fun, James,' said his father. He shrugged, then pressed the laughter button. It was good to see

James enjoying himself after all she'd put him through and the angst of the first few days.

'Am I female?' asked André in a high-pitched voice.

'No.'

'Glad to have that confirmed. Your turn, Martin.'

'Am I male?' he asked.

'Yes.'

'Am I talented in what I do?' He raised his eyebrows.

Emma exchanged glances with the family, Marie scrunching up her face. 'Some would say so,' Marie said. 'I guess you could be considered a good cook!'

'Oh. Am I a celebrity chef?'

Laughter filled the air, and not from the Sound Machine.

Hannibal Lector's Cooking Show — giving you a hand in the kitchen...

'Well, am I?'

'Um, that would be a big fat...' James said, then pressed the *ba-bow* button.

'I'm confused.' Martin scratched his head, and Marie patted his back in pity.

After Marie asked if she was female and an actress, the obvious first questions, she asked if she was still alive.

'Sadly, no.' said Martin.

'Trust you to give me a dead person!' She whacked him on the arm.

'Finally, my turn.' James rubbed his hands together and asked the usual first questions, then asked if he was hot.

'Smokin',' said Lizzie. 'But it's weird saying that to my brother.'

Weird or not, it was true. In both cases.

'Am I American?'

Emma took hold of the Sound Machine and pressed the incorrect button.

'Bugger.' He snatched the machine back from her and gave her a teasing look. 'Let's see how long your reign is, Em.' His relaxed expression became stiff, and Emma's mind went blank. *Em.* He hadn't called her that since...since the good old days. By the look on his face he had realised the same thing. It was as though the hurt and pain from the past five years had evaporated and they were back in old times, but with a fresh perspective.

'Um, let's see,' she began. 'If I'm not an actress, then am I a character?'

James pressed the clapping button.

Character, character... it had to be someone well known. Someone James would know that I know...

'Am I a young character?' she asked.

'Yes.'

She had a thought. A memory. She could be wrong, but...

'Am I Hermione Granger?'

'How the hell?' Lizzie exclaimed.

James pressed the applause button again and everyone added their own real applause. 'Nice work.'

'How did you get that so soon?' asked Martin.

Emma had wondered whether to keep digging with questions first, but the memory of when she watched the first Harry Potter movie with James when it was on television gave her confidence. *She had said to him that night, 'If I could be a fictional character, I would be Hermione Granger.'*

'Why?' *he'd asked.*

'So I could put a spell on you.'

'You already have,' *he'd said, before leaning close to her and planting a delicious kiss on her lips.*

'Just a hunch,' Emma replied to Martin's question. She stole a glance at James, whose familiar look in his eyes told her he remembered that night too.

'So, game is over, yes?' asked André.

'No,' said Martin. 'Emma may have won but we still need to ascertain second and third place.'

'Okay then, let's see if I can guess which hot actress I am.' Lizzie rubbed her hands together.

'Do you mind if I use your bathroom?' Emma asked James, gesturing behind her.

'Technically it's yours,' he replied. 'Go ahead.'

She stood and left them to discover their temporary identities, and tiptoed past Jackson's room to the bathroom, though James had said he didn't wake as easily as he used to. She pushed open the bathroom door and as she stepped inside, her gaze focused on something on the floor. A smile eased onto her face as a warm, satisfied sensation embraced her from within.

On the bathroom floor was a plastic tray filled with sand.

James had taken action on her suggestion to help Jackson get used to the feeling of sand underfoot, even though he'd told her off for offering such advice. Stubborn sweetheart.

She peered outside the bathroom door for a moment and watched him from behind as he played the game with his family. He pressed the Sound Machine at his sister who, like Marie had done to her husband, whacked him on the arm. Emma grinned. Ridiculous games and mild violence — signs of a happy family.

The feelings she'd tried to quell earlier rose to the surface, and she recognised them for what they were. There was no hiding from it. As much as she was scared to step back into this world with James, she knew what the alternative was like and she no longer wanted it.

Damn it, she still loved him.

CHAPTER TWELVE

J ames didn't know what he loved more, the refreshing sensation of the salt water enveloping his body as he swam, or the fact that he no longer chose to hold onto the hurt and frustration caused by Emma leaving.

With each stroke through the water, he pushed further towards a greater feeling of relief, but as waves tumbled around him and pushed him backwards, he was reminded of his fears. His doubts. His insecurities.

Emma's already moved on. Now that she's cancer free she obviously wanted to have some freedom, travel, see the world. Not commit herself to the responsibilities and challenges his life would offer her. She'd had enough of those, and he didn't want to burden her with any more.

Under the water, all sound muffled and he thought that if Jackson would go in the water he would probably like the sensation, the numbness of it. But swimming lessons hadn't proved effective yet. He was hoping he could try them again when they got back home.

Home. Where *was* home, really? Was it an actual place or

was it a place *within* him that when he felt like he'd arrived there, would be with him anywhere he went?

Emma was probably finding her home too.

James surfaced and allowed the buoyancy of the waves to lift him effortlessly up and down, ebbing and flowing like the breath that swirled in and out of his lungs. He smiled as he remembered waking to two sale notifications in his inbox. The VIP program had started. Two clients, ready to go. If it were to really take off he would like at least six clients as a minimum to form a solid networking mastermind group to share ideas and successes. The high price meant he would likely not be bombarded with orders, and should it take off more than expected he would have to cut off the numbers at some point, otherwise the coaching sessions would take up too much time.

James dove under the waves again, each burst of energy through the water clearing his mind, calming the never-ending thoughts and worries that swung from one topic to another. He'd never been able to calm his overactive mind, but getting into the water helped somewhat. Even though the movement was constant, water grounded him.

Emma used to ground him too.

But now she had the potential to shake the ground he stood on.

He moved towards the shore until his feet met lumpy sand beneath him, and he walked out of the water.

Speak of the devil. Emma was heading in his direction, but she had her head in a book as she walked.

'Good book?' he asked when she neared.

She stopped abruptly. 'Oh. Hi.' She lowered the book and slipped it into her bag, then took off her sunglasses. 'Not bad. Have you been for a swim?' she asked, then shook her head. 'Oops, I think the answer is obvious!'

James chuckled. 'And if my powers of deduction are intact, I'd say you are on your lunchbreak?'

'Correct.' She smiled. Her eyes lowered for a moment then connected with his again. Was she checking him out? It *had* been a while since they'd seen each other. He would have reached for his towel but it was further up on the beach.

'Thanks for last night.' She swiped a strand of hair from her face and tucked it beneath her cap.

'It was fun,' he replied. 'And I'm sorry about your dad's stroke, I hope he's managing okay.'

She shrugged. 'Taking it day by day. I'm sorry about your Nonna. I think it's lovely what you're all doing here for her.'

'Thanks. In hindsight I think it would have been easier arriving on the weekend, spreading her ashes, and then having our week-long break. There's sort of this... uncomfortable anticipation hanging over our heads. Dad's trying to keep busy with activities and overeating to keep his mind off it, I think.'

'Understandable. How's Jackson coping? Did he know your gran well?'

Emma's concern for his son was admirable. He had barely thought about how it might affect Jackson, as the boy had never gotten close to Bella so James just assumed he wouldn't have felt much difference with her not being around anymore. 'He's been okay. We visited her, but he's not too good with nursing homes and hospitals so it was always a challenge. I think it's the smell or something, and the narrow corridors. Last time he was there he had a meltdown, so I had to alternate visits to Nonna with my parents so one of them could be with Jax.'

A thin crease formed in Emma's forehead. 'There must be so much you have to think of on a daily basis, to help him.'

James nodded, scratched his head. 'Oh, and, thanks for the suggestion of the sand tray. It occurred to me after you left that you probably saw it in the bathroom last night.' His cheeks warmed. 'Sorry I fobbed off the suggestion at first. But it made sense when I'd had a chance to think, so—'

'James, it's okay, you don't have to explain,' she said. 'And give it time, it might take a little while.'

'I've started putting Owly in there, to see if that helps him.'

'Good idea.'

James glanced into the distance at the row of white-walled cabins with their blue roofs, each slightly different but essentially the same, like human beings. From a distance, Jackson was just like any other child. Close up, the differences showed.

'Are you okay?' Emma asked.

'Huh? Yeah, fine.' He rubbed at the back of his neck, his gaze lowering to the damp sand beneath his feet. Why did she have to ask that? She had this way of getting people to open up to talk about what was on their mind, and he'd bottled up so much for so many years he was desperate to let at least some of it out. He exhaled loudly. 'I just wish I could do something as simple as make a sandcastle with my son, you know?' A lump formed in his throat.

Emma gave a small nod, remaining silent, a cue to continue.

'When he was born, I had these grand ideas of things I'd want to do with him, to teach him. Milestones to celebrate together. Most of those have gone out the window now.' Why was he saying all this? She couldn't have children and here he was talking about his parenting challenges.

'Oh, James.' She touched his arm and he felt the water transfer to her fingers.

Her softness made him stiffen. He didn't want comfort, he just wanted to let a few thoughts out of his head. 'Ah, but he's a good kid. I guess there'll just be different types of experiences to enjoy with him.'

'True, but there's nothing wrong with feeling sad about

what might have been. Believe me, I've been there, in my own way.'

Of course. She got it. She knew what it was like to have grand ideas of how life would be, only to have life turn things upside down and give you something you didn't expect.

James didn't know how to respond. When he was about to change the subject and comment on the beautiful weather, she lightly cupped his elbow. 'C'mon,' she said.

He drew his eyebrows together in curiosity. 'What are we doing?'

'We're going to make a sandcastle.' She grinned. She placed her bag on the ground, rolled up her pants and sat, then gathered up clumps of sand. 'Well c'mon, give me a helping hand.' A smile tweaked at the corner of his lips at her teacher-like voice. 'I want to check out your construction skills.'

'I don't think they'll be as good as the guys you have working for you.' He cocked his head towards the new cabins.

'Bob and the team? I bet you can outdo them when it comes to sandcastles.'

He laughed and knelt on the sand. 'Bob? And he's a builder?'

'Yep, and quite proud of the association with the children's character.' Emma patted the clump of sand in front of her.

James pressed the sides of the clump together, forming walls. 'Let's go for a square shape.' He flattened the sides into corners, while Emma worked on the other side of the clump.

'Triple decker?' she asked, adding another clump on top.

'For sure.'

They formed a square shape on the second level then James gathered up a pile of wet sand for the third level. They pressed and patted, smoothed and sculpted. While working on the top level their fingers brushed against each other, speckled with grains of sand.

Emma took her hands away. 'You do the top.'

He finished the top of the sandcastle, then ran his finger around the perimeter of the bottom level. 'We have to have a moat, right?'

'Every good sandcastle needs a moat.' Emma drew a door shape into the side of the castle, then added a flat stick to be the drawbridge.

They scooped out sand from the tops of each level, making a floor and walls. James became lost in the moment; the satisfying warmth of the sand on his hands, moulding to his touch, felt therapeutic. So he wasn't doing this with Jackson, but he never thought he'd be making a sandcastle with Emma. The kindness of her initiative added to the warmth spreading inside him.

'You're doing a good job, James.'

'Thanks, what can I say?' He held up his hands in front of the sandcastle.

Emma smiled. 'I mean, with Jackson. You're a good dad.'

Oh. He swallowed. 'You can tell, just from a few days?'

'I've met a lot of parents, observed their kids. You're doing great. Trust me.'

He bit his lip. Was he really? He still couldn't budge the feeling that there was always more he could be doing. Not a week went by when he didn't do some sort of internet search on the latest autism research, or chat to other parents about what was working for them.

'Thanks Emma, that's nice of you to say.' He focused on one wall of the castle and took extra care to sculpt it into perfect shape. He watched as Emma did the same, and he wondered what it would have been like, what it *would* be like, if Jackson had a female around. Would things have been different if Jackson's mother had stayed? Or maybe they would be worse. He was glad in a way that he didn't have to share custody, didn't have to move Jackson from house to house or only see him on alternate weekends. He was one parent, the only carer for his son. 'Sometimes I feel like I have to be both father and mother for him. Like I have to give him double the love, because his mother didn't want him.'

James stopped and looked up. Did he say that out loud? He'd been so lost in his thoughts he hadn't noticed till the sound of his own voice in the open air had hit his eardrums.

He glanced down and Emma had stopped too, was looking right at him. 'You only have to be you. I think the love you have for him is more than enough.'

God, he wanted to take her hands in his and bring them to his lips. He wanted to wrap her in his arms again like he'd done that night she'd told him her secret. Bizarre, how only a few days ago, he didn't want to be anywhere near her.

'Can I ask, what happened to his mother?' Emma squinted as though her question might sting.

A few days ago he would have said, 'It's none of your goddamn business', but now, being in nature with the sandcastle between them and acting as a strange kind of safety barrier, he wanted to tell her. He wanted to let out his secret too. Something he'd never even told his parents. They knew what happened to Jackson's mother, but they didn't know the whole story. He'd never told anyone.

James placed a shell on the top of the castle, positioning it like a satellite, ready to pick up and transmit all his secrets to her.

'She's currently overseas. Working in musical theatre.' That was the easy part. But the memory, the *what if* that crossed his mind whenever he thought about the past always made him queasy. 'She chose her career over her son. She wanted an abortion.'

Emma flinched.

He knew it would trigger her. When she had so desperately

wanted a child of her own, knowing someone would have willingly given up the gift they'd received was bound to rattle her.

Just like it had rattled him...

New Years Day, of all days, was the day James' life changed yet again. Nursing a mild hangover from the previous night's celebrations, he'd woken to a text message from Stacey.

It wasn't a Happy New Year. Or Thanks for that night we shared last month, if you ever want to hook up again let me know. *Nope. It was a simple but profound message, straight to the point:*

James, I'm pregnant. It's yours. Don't worry, I'll deal with it.

Pregnant? Deal with it? What did she mean by that, that she would raise the child on her own or that she would...

No.

No way.

He called her straight away. 'We need to talk about this.'

'There's nothing to talk about, I'm not having the baby.'

The baby. Not hers, or his, or theirs, but the. *Like their child was some minor nuisance she could just cast aside.*

He convinced her to meet him in person to at least discuss the options, but her crossed arms, tight lips, and tired eyes told him it would be akin to convincing a jury to convict an innocent man.

'It's my baby too,' he pleaded. 'You can't just get rid of it without consulting me.'

'I had the decency to at least tell you. I could have just had the abortion and never told you, but no. I thought you at least had a right to know.'

'And I have a right to decide, too.'

'It's my body. And my job depends on my body. This is my big break, I can't do the role with a big belly.'

'It's only temporary, you can still do the role for a couple of months until you start showing, then your understudy can take

over, and by then you would have performed a lot of shows and
your name will be out there.'

She sighed. 'You don't understand.'

James glared at her. 'Oh I understand alright. You're about to
deny life to the child I'm willing to be a father to. How is that
fair?'

'What, James, you think we're just going to play happy
families? I made a mistake. We made a mistake. Let's just get it
over with and move on, back to our own lives.'

His life. Without Emma. And without the child who he'd
helped bring to life. It didn't seem right. Especially after he'd seen
what his sister had gone through over the last three years trying to
get pregnant. Not to mention the miscarriage. Who knew if
Lizzie would ever be able to become a mother?

'We don't have to play happy families. You go, live your
dream life. I'll take full custody.'

She laughed, which only riled him more. 'What? You think I
can't do it? Because I can. And I will.'

'James, James, you're a successful corporate man. A baby will
have you falling down that ladder of success faster than you can
say "objection!"'

He loved his career. But there was always this nagging
feeling that something was missing. There was something more
out there, waiting for him, even if Emma would never be a part
of it.

'So you're not prepared to make a few sacrifices for what,
seven months, to give a little kid a chance at a life?'

'It's not a little kid, it's barely the size of my fingernail. It's a
foetus, James. It's not fully developed. It's not like it'll feel
anything.'

Heat burned his throat and chest. 'How can you be so
insensitive?' he fumed. 'I'm all for women doing what they feel is
right for themselves, but not when the other person involved

doesn't get a say. Yes, we made a mistake. And we have to deal with the consequences of that mistake, not pretend it never happened. That's what adults do, they suck it up and deal with the consequences. Grow up, Stacey.'

She turned away and waved her hand. 'I don't have to listen to this. I'm outta here.'

'No, wait!' He grasped her arm. Appealing to her human nature wasn't going to work, she only cared about herself.

There was only one thing he could do...

'So how did you convince her to have the baby?' Emma asked.

James' jaw tightened and he wiped sand off his hands and stood, the sun burning into his bare back. He turned around to look at the water, knowing that every drop in the ocean was vital to the whole, every drop deserved to be there, just like every new life was part of the big wide world. He turned back to face Emma who now stood in front of him.

'I'm ashamed of what I had to do.' He lowered his head.

'You can tell me.'

He looked into her eyes and saw nothing but understanding and... love?

'I paid her off, Em. I bribed her. Money in exchange for my son's life.' He sat on the sand and rested his elbows on his knees. He gazed out at the vast body of water rolling and tumbling onto the shore, just like the memory of that day when he hadn't been sure if the life he'd helped create, even though unplanned, could be taken away from him without his consent.

Emma sat quietly next to him, matching his position, her elbow brushing against his. 'You did what you had to do to save your son's life. There's no shame in that.'

He was glad they were both looking at the ocean; eye contact right now would be difficult as his eyes became hot and moist.

'The whole time, I was worried she'd take the money and run, get rid of... have the procedure. It was only when Jackson was placed into my arms for the first time that I really felt secure in the fact that I was a father.'

'It must have been a difficult few months.'

'It was, and highly unconventional, to say the least.' He picked up a bit of sand and let it run through his fingers. 'I made her sign an agreement. As security. She would have the baby and take care of her health, and I would pay her more than she was getting for the show she was performing in. She sacrificed the chance of being asked back to do another season, knowing they could just take the understudy again, but she got it. She got right back into work after he was born, got into the Melbourne season of the show, like her stint in Sydney had been a brief flash in time. Like it never happened.'

'I'm sure, deep down, it was hard for her. I'm sure she felt some connection to the baby.'

James glanced at Emma. 'I thought she might too, but really, I doubt she did. She was detached the whole time, as though it was just another role she had to play. When it was over, she moved on.'

Emma's warm hand rested on his arm, gritty sand tickling his skin. 'I'm sorry, for my part in this. If I had been honest with you from the start, this would have never—'

'Emma, don't. Don't do "what ifs". Yeah, you're right, if you hadn't left, I would probably never have met her, and definitely wouldn't have had a one-night stand with her. But she gave me Jackson. And despite his challenges, you know what?'

'What?'

'I wouldn't want any other child but him.'

Emma's chest rose with a quick breath, and she threaded her fingers together as her elbows rested on her knees.

'The only thing I ever wished was that you were his mother.'

James swivelled towards her, took her hand in his. It trembled, and he steadied it with a rub of his thumb.

Their gaze broke and she looked at the ground. 'After the operation, I started believing that maybe I wasn't meant to be a mother, and that's why it happened. It was fate's way of telling me "forget it, girl, this gig ain't for you". I spent so long convinced of that fact, but now...' She looked back into his eyes. 'Now, I ache to feel that kind of love for a child. To be a parent. I still want it, I just don't know if it will be the same. Can I love someone else's child as much as I would have loved my own?'

'Of course you would. Parenting is more than genes. Stacey is proof of that. She carried the child for nine months and feels nothing. But you, you *feel*. You feel for everyone, You're the most loving, kind-hearted person I know.' He ran his finger across her cheek, hot from the sun.

She took her cap off and placed it on the sand, then checked her watch. 'I have to go back soon.'

Had he gone too far? He hoped she didn't think he was trying to find a mother for Jackson, he only meant that she would be a great mother to anyone.

'Do you have to get back to Jackson?'

'Soon. But I'm going to have one more swim.' James got up and stretched. Maybe the deep and meaningful was over.

Emma stood and walked with him to the shoreline. 'Well, enjoy. I guess I'll head back.' She gestured over her shoulder.

He wanted to see her smiling face again, wanted to lift her spirits. 'You mean you're not coming in with me?'

She raised her eyebrows. 'I'm in work clothes, I—'

James kicked at the wave rolling into the shore and splashed her with water.

'Hey!' She stepped back.

'What? It's only water, it'll dry.' He splashed her again.

A vengeful smile transformed her face and she kicked the

water and splashed him back.

'Oh c'mon, is that all you've got?' He splashed her again and she held out her hands and turned her head as water landed on her face.

She stepped into the water, her rolled-up pants tinged with dark patches at the hem, then reached down and lifted a large splash onto his face. 'Take that, hot-shot.' She grinned.

'Hot-shot? I'll give you hot-shot.' He slid one arm behind her back and one under her knees, lifting her off the ground.

She squealed. 'Put me down!'

He ignored her plea, waded into the water.

'James! I'm in my work clothes!'

'I'm sure you have a spare outfit to change into.'

'But why would I—'

He released his hands. Splash! She dropped into the water, flailing about and squealing. 'Oh you!' She got up and charged at him, pushing him backwards into the water, her body falling with his.

'Now you're just causing trouble for yourself!' He laughed.

She splashed more water on top of him.

'Ah, so refreshing, Thank you.' He basked in the salt water as it splashed and sprayed around him. Emma gave him a light slap on the arm.

'Be honest, you're having fun, right?'

She narrowed her eyes, but her smile gave him her answer. 'I didn't even bring a towel, I'll have to walk back to the office a sopping wet mess!'

'I've got one.' James gestured to the shore. 'But only one. You'll have to fight me for it.'

They stood face to face in the waist-deep water, eyes glaring, until Emma eyed the towel up on the sand, then made a dash for it. James chased, lifting his knees high to manoeuvre out of the water, laughing and running with her across the sand.

He got to it first and held it up in the air. 'First in, best dressed!'

'Hand it over, JJ,' she said, and they paused for a moment.

That's what she used to call him.

'Sorry,' he teased, wrapping the towel around his back.

'I know some karate.' She raised her arms and one leg in a fighting position, ready to pounce, and he laughed. He bet she didn't really know karate, but then again, who knew what else had happened in the last five years.

He ran his gaze over her glossy face, hair stuck to her neck, and her wet clothes moulded to her curves. She was beyond beautiful, and as she stood there in *Karate Kid* pose, utterly adorable.

James opened up the towel so that it spread out behind him like wings. 'There's room for two in here.' He stepped close to her.

She stiffened, hesitated, and he worried he'd gone too far. But then she stepped closer and he wrapped his arms and the towel around her, pulling her close to his body so that the towel completely enveloped them like a cocoon. What surprised him was that instead of taking the towel from him, she slid her arms around his wet back, under the towel, and hugged him. He moved the towel across her back and rubbed at her wet shirt, her hair, and touched the corner of the towel to her cheek. Then he unwrapped the towel from his body and wrapped it completely around her. 'Take it. I've got another one at the cabin.'

Emma held the edges of the towel underneath her chin as she smiled, stepped backwards a few steps, then turned away to walk back to work.

He realised in that moment that, unlike the towel, there was only one Emma. And he would like nothing more than to have her wrapped around him.

CHAPTER THIRTEEN

E mma scurried around the playground towards the reception office, hoping no one would notice her clothes were soaking wet beneath James' towel.

Damn. She turned briefly, remembering she'd left her cap on the beach. *Stuff it, I'll get it later.* She was about to enter the office when Bob appeared behind her with a sandwich in his hand.

'Hey, forget your swimming costume?'

Her cheeks warmed. 'I was just wading a little in the water but, um, there was a big wave, and...' She glanced down at her dripping body.

'Looks pretty calm out there to me,' he replied. 'Also looks enticing, maybe I'll cool off with a dip after work. Water nice?'

'Very. It'll be cooler later though, maybe you should have one now.'

'Nah, almost done with lunch, gotta get back to work or the boss might fire me.' He winked, meaning her.

'But what if the woman of your dreams is down at the beach right now and by waiting, you two will never meet and you'll spend the rest of your life searching for each other?' She smiled.

He glanced towards the ocean. 'Bugger. Now I'm torn.'

'Take a swim if you want, Bob. The boys will hold down the fort for another fifteen minutes I'm sure.'

'But won't I get a stomach ache if I swim after eating?' He chuckled.

'That's an old wives' tale.'

'Speaking of wives, if my dream woman *is* down there I'll just have to trust that she'll walk past the construction site afterwards. Destiny and all that.'

'My mother would believe in that, for sure. And you never know. If I see any suitable women I'll send them your way.' She winked back and unlocked the door to reception. Then she realised she should change out of her clothes, so locked the door again, going instead to her cottage to get a new outfit.

When she was back at her desk, she opened the email inbox on her phone. She still hadn't replied to Jen's message. She reread it and tried to think of a reply.

How are you feeling about it now? What happens now? Are you going to spend some time with him?

Confused. I don't know. Yes.

Her answers formed in her mind, but she would need to elaborate. She typed in a reply and filled Jen in on how she'd spent some time with James already — lunch, the barbeque with the family, and splashing around on the beach and embracing in a towel. What would be next? Would there be a next?

Jen, my mind is racing. I feel like I don't deserve to know him again, to be with him again, after hurting him like I did. But he seems to have forgiven me, in fact, it's almost like old times. We're talking, laughing even, and he's telling me personal things about his life. What do you think he wants? Just to make amends while he's here and then go our separate ways when he leaves in three days? I'm confused, I'm hopeful, I'm scared, all at once. He's not just James anymore, he's James and Jackson — a package deal. It's not something to take lightly.

I did realise something though: I still love him.

What am I going to do?

I've come up with three reasons why it's a bad idea to get involved with him again:

1. I was about to go travelling! I still want to. I can't start a relationship then disappear (again). And I can't expect him to hang around and wait for me to figure my life out (again).

2. I'm worried my deception will always hang over our heads, even though he says he understands.

3. What if I'm no good for Jackson? And what if James wants to have another child?

Maybe I should leave the past where it belongs, go overseas, and start fresh.

Emma hit 'send', then checked for any work emails and updated the Facebook page with an enticing picture of a hammock strung between two trees, overlooking the beach. Her email pinged on her phone. A reply from Jen already?

```
Hey hun,
   Quick reply as my kids are with the
teacher's aide while I escaped to the
bathroom. One of the darlings spilled
paint on me. Such joy.
   Anyway, if he's forgiven you, then
quit worrying. Go with the flow. Enjoy
reconnecting with him while he's there.
And in response to your 3 objections:
   1. If you still want to travel, then
do it. Otherwise you'll regret it. If
you're meant to be together, somehow it
will all work out.
```

2. Though he won't forget about what you did to him, he also won't forget about why you did it. Worry is wasted energy.

3. I only know what you've told me about Jackson, but I can't imagine any woman who would be better for him than you. And future kids? Maybe he doesn't want any, or maybe he would be prepared to adopt.

Okay, here's what I think you should do...

The door to reception opened and Emma glanced up from her phone, feeling like a schoolgirl getting sprung for doing something naughty when she was supposed to be working.

'You left this at the beach.' James held her cap in his hand.

Emma quickly closed her inbox. *Great timing!*

'Oops, thanks.' She stood.

James stepped forwards then glanced at one of the framed pictures on the counter top. 'Nice drawing, is that by a local artist?'

Emma scratched her arm. 'Um, actually, it's me. I did it.'

James' eyes widened. 'I didn't know you could draw. How did I not know that?'

'I used to do a bit when I was younger, but only got back into it a few years ago. I found it therapeutic.'

'Do you have many completed drawings?' he asked, his wet hair dangling across his eyes.

She nodded. 'Quite a few.'

'You'll have to show me sometime, when you're not busy working.'

Was that an invitation? Did he really want to see her drawings or did he just want to see her?

'That is, if you want to.'

'No, yes, I mean I'd be happy to. They're not totally amazing or anything, but—'

'How about tonight?' he said calmly.

'Tonight?'

'Yeah, you can do a little private art show for me.' He smiled. 'Drop in whenever.'

Did that mean right after work, at dinner, or after dinner?

'And if it happens to be around dinnertime I've got it covered, Mum made some kind of one-pot-wonder with last night's leftovers.'

Could he read her mind?

'But my parents are doing their own thing tonight, going out for a meal. So it'll just be us. And Jax.'

Emma wondered if perhaps this was some kind of test to see how she coped around Jackson the more time she spent with him. Was James sussing things out in case they resumed their relationship? She wished she'd had a chance to read Jen's advice before he came into the office and interrupted her emailing, in case it had crucial James Advice that would have been helpful to take into account.

'Sounds good. I'm doing yoga after work but I'll pop over after that.' Boy, were things getting busy. She'd hardly had any time to herself this week.

'Yoga aficionado *and* an artist. You're full of surprises.'

'Oh, I'm definitely no aficionado. Haven't done yoga in a while so I'll probably fall flat on my face or pull a muscle!' She shifted her weight to the other foot and grasped her arm awkwardly.

'I'll keep an icepack handy at the cabin.' He chuckled.

'Gee, thanks for the vote of confidence.'

'Best to be prepared. See you later.' He placed the cap upside down on the counter and walked out.

Emma lifted the cap and noticed something resting inside it. A seashell. The one James had used as the satellite dish on top of the sandcastle. Her fingers ran over the serrated surface, reminding her of the bumpy but beautiful ride their relationship had been. *Had* been. She held it to her ear, the vacuous whoosh filling her mind with memories of the past. Five and a half years. Where would she be and what would she be reminded of in another five and a half years if she held this shell to her ear again? Would this week be a distant memory, or the start of something new and wonderful?

Emma put the shell into her pocket. She'd put it next to the candle on her bedside table later on, and no matter what happened after this week, she vowed that the shell would serve as a reminder of forgiveness, understanding, and hope. If she never had James in her life again, at least she'd have that.

As Emma walked across the grass towards the beach for the free yoga session after work, she thought about what Jen had suggested in her email:

```
Okay, here's what I think you should do…
    Casually ask him what his plans are
for the future, get an idea of how his
goals and dreams have changed. But also,
enjoy the time you have with him while
he's there. Be in the moment and allow
yourself to feel, so you can see if
there's still something between you.
Feelings first, decisions later.
```

It was easy for her to say that, Jen's relationship with her boyfriend, Sean, was all about spontaneity and going with the flow, and despite their apparent commitment to each other, there'd been no talk of marriage or even living together. But maybe she was right. And barring tonight, there were only two more days to interact with James. Although half of Sunday would be out of the picture as she would be driving to Jen's birthday party in Sydney.

Feelings first, decisions later. Mantra for the week.

Right. Easy. Feelings had a mind of their own, decisions required more brainpower than she had right now. And right now, it was time to focus on the feelings of her muscles stretching and body bending, the ocean breeze refreshing her mind. That, she could handle.

Emma took off her shoes, stepped onto the sand, and walked over to the flat area of beach near the rock wall.

'Hi, Emma, right?' asked Chrissie the yoga instructor, as she turned her attention away from a couple of women.

Emma nodded. 'Hi.'

'Glad you could finally make it.'

Emma had chatted to her a couple of weeks ago and promised she'd join in the classes when she could.

The women introduced themselves to Emma and she told them she was running the cabins for the time being. 'Must be a great job!' said Louise, a middle-aged woman with long hair tied into a ponytail yet still reaching to her lower back.

'It's a beautiful place to be.' Emma smiled.

'Sure is. Especially with Chrissie's free classes here. They are an absolute godsend to me, gives me a break from my demanding children!' Louise rolled her eyes.

Emma's stomach twinged. She knew Louise was just making light conversation and that parenthood could be tough, but comments like this made her uncomfortable. She would love to have children to place demands on her. Because as well as those demands came loving moments, developmental milestones, laughter, bedtime cuddles, and... Oh, she couldn't allow herself to think of those things. If she had been meant to be a 'Louise', then it would have happened, and she never would have had the uterine cancer. Some things just weren't meant to be.

'Do you have kids?' Louise asked.

Oh, the dreaded question. Again. Why did it always come up when talking to other women? Why couldn't they ask things like, 'What do you do in your spare time?' or, 'Seen any good movies lately?' It was as though a woman's life in her reproductive years was defined by her ability or decision to bear offspring.

'No,' Emma replied. Conversation closed.

'How's your boy, Chrissie?' asked Louise, turning to face the instructor, and thankfully, avoiding any additional commentary on why Emma didn't have children and whether she wanted any in future.

'Kai is growing up very quickly, sometimes I think he's seven going on seventy!' She laughed, her blonde ponytail wafting in the breeze. 'He has a certain way he sees the world, and follows his own path. Tells it how it is too, doesn't worry if nobody agrees with him.'

Sounds like my father.

'He'll go far,' said Louise, and a few other people arrived on the beach for the class, two men included. One of them was quite young and attractive, and Emma found herself smiling at him. Maybe she should stretch her horizons a little and branch out, see the world and consider the possibility that there was someone else out there for her when the time was right. There was more to the world than James Gallagher.

The class began with a few rounds of Salute to the Sun,

though in this case, heading towards dusk, it was more like a Farewell to the Sun. Emma's body started out as stiff and uncooperative, but by the time they'd progressed to further poses, or *asanas*, it had loosened up a little. Except one side of her neck, which she must have slept on funny the night before as it had been bugging her all day with a dull ache. Before her five-year remission mark, anytime she had an ache or pain or sickness her mind would try to prepare her for the possibility of the cancer returning, though obviously not in the uterus, but there could have been metastatic cells that had been missed and taken up residence elsewhere. But now, she would have to push those automatic thoughts out of her head. It had been five years, she'd been given the all clear, and she needed to get on with her life without fear or worry. As Jen had said: worry is wasted energy.

Emma breathed deeply into each pose, imagining clarity and calmness filling her body with each inhalation. She noticed the young man, his lean, defined body effortlessly bending and twisting into position, and admired the beauty of his ability and physique. *Would James ever do yoga?* She couldn't really imagine him doing it, but then again, what did she know of him these days? She could definitely see him out there in the waves on a surfboard though, and had in the past, and she wondered how often he got to do that nowadays with his time taken up with his business and Jackson.

Chrissie helped Emma maximise the advanced poses she had difficulty with, though fatigue seeped into her muscles. She would have to do this more often to get back into shape and improve her flexibility.

Near the end of the class, Chrissie got a tall glass candle holder from her bag, and reached down to the small pink candle within it with a gas lighter, bringing the flame to life. She nestled it into a flat patch of sand. 'As we do our meditation to end the class, I'd like this light to be in honour of Maggie, a student of mine, who is no longer with us in body.'

Louise exchanged sorrowful glances with another woman. They must have known her. Maybe the woman had come to these classes too. Another student clasped her hands together in prayer and bowed towards the candle. Although Emma didn't know who Maggie was, she could feel the impact she'd had. Her life had been significant, memorable, she just knew it.

The group sat cross-legged on the sand in meditation pose, hands resting on knees with palms facing upwards.

'Now sit for a moment and focus on your breath, in and out,' Chrissie said softly. 'Don't worry if your mind wanders a little, just bring it back to your breath. In the words of one of my favourite songs,' she said with a smile in her voice, 'Just Breathe...'

Ah yes, the Drew Williams ballad, Emma recalled. Such a nice song with simple yet powerful lyrics. The song played in the jukebox of her mind...

Sometimes life gets away from you,

Sometimes life takes the joy from you,

But when things around you come crashing down,

And the past you'd rather forget keeps spinning you around,

There are three little things that you must do, to bring you back to you...

Don't forget to breathe,

Don't forget to cry,

Don't forget to take the time to do what's right, and bring your soul to life,

Don't forget to breathe...

That's what she needed to do: bring her soul to life. Take it out of the dark enclosure of fear and grief and finally let it run free. Do what was right for her, and enjoy the gift of life she'd been given a second chance with.

A sense of calm and peace washed over her with every breath she took and every caress of the ocean breeze. Everything would work itself out. All she had to do was stay true to herself and let things unfold the way they naturally would, however that would be.

When she opened her eyes and Chrissie bowed a thank you to everyone for attending, Emma approached the instructor. 'Thank you, that was really great.'

'I'm glad. See you again next week?'

'Yes, for sure.' Emma smiled, picking up her shoes. 'Do you mind if I ask, who was Maggie? What happened to her?'

Chrissie tucked a strand of loose hair behind her ear and lowered her head a little. 'She was a regular yoga enthusiast, that's how I met her. Sadly, she passed away a couple of weeks ago. Cancer. She'd beaten it once before, but the second time around it was too aggressive, though she put up a good fight.' Chrissie clamped her lips together and nodded in a resigned way.

Oh gosh. 'I'm so sorry,' Emma whispered. 'Second time around?'

'Yes, she'd had a good run for eight years, but it recurred in another part of her body, sadly. Only forty-two years old.'

Not fair. 'Did she have any...children?' Emma gulped.

Chrissie shook her head. 'Apparently she'd been planning them with her husband just before the first cancer appeared. Obviously the diagnosis changed those plans, and after her remission they decided against starting a family, partly because her treatment would have made it difficult, and partly because they decided to travel and fulfil their bucket lists instead,' Chrissie explained. 'They did become foster carers for a few years though, until...'

Until she was the one who needed care.

'I'm sorry if I've upset you by asking about her,' said Emma.

'Oh no, that's fine. I think it's good to talk about her, about people who've passed on. We need to remember them, and the positive things they did with their lives.' Chrissie's eyes seemed distant, as though remembering not only Maggie, but perhaps someone else.

'I agree. And it's lovely what you did, with the candle.' Emma gestured to the flame still alight in the candle holder on the sand.

'She loved candles. She actually gave me this one as a thank you for being her teacher.' Chrissie's eyes became glossy. 'So I thought it was the perfect choice for tonight.'

They stood and gazed at the flame for a few moments, transfixed by its sinuous flickering and golden glow. 'Well, I'll light one for her tonight too, as I read in bed,' Emma promised.

Chrissie smiled. 'Oh that would be lovely. How nice of you. Thanks.'

Emma smiled and farewelled the pretty teacher, then turned to walk back up the hill, her shoes hooked under her fingers. The blades of grass were cold underfoot where the shade covered the ground, and she shivered.

Don't forget to breathe...

She tried, but her breath caught high in her throat. Maggie had been a young woman like Emma. She'd been in remission like Emma. She'd given up the idea of having children, like Emma. And Emma hoped like hell that that would be where their similarities would end.

CHAPTER FOURTEEN

'Say Dad. Dad.' James spoke firmly and clearly as he sat next to Jackson on the floor of the cabin. 'D, Da, Dad.' He pointed to his own chest to indicate the meaning of the word.

Jackson only made his usual 'vvv' sound, like he was an engine about to speed up.

'Okay, let's try something else then.' He picked up a toy car and pushed it forwards on the floor. 'Vroom! Vroom!'

'Vvv,' Jackson said. He took the car from his father and turned it upside down, then tried to get Owly to sit on top of it but the toy kept falling over. Jackson's face creased with disappointment and he moaned.

'Owls aren't supposed to sit on cars. And this one is too big.' He picked Owly up and sat him on the couch. 'How about there?'

Jackson grunted and wrenched Owly off the couch, trying again to get him to sit on the upside down car.

James sighed. 'Oh well, gotta give you credit for your originality and persistence.'

When Owly fell off for the umpteenth time, James moved the car closer to the leg of the coffee table and put Owly on top, with the toy's back resting against the coffee table leg to support it. Bingo!

Jackson squealed and grabbed his Sound Machine, pressing the applause button.

Where there's a will there's a way.

Jackson arranged other cars in a semicircle around the owl, as though it was giving a concert. Then there was a tap at the door. *Emma already?*

He turned around and stood. His parents were at the door.

'Oh, hi. Off to that café for dinner?' he asked.

'Yes,' his mum replied. 'But we wanted to drop by first and have a quick chat.'

James slipped his hands into his pockets as his parents walked in. 'What about?' They didn't look like they were just there to chat about the weather or what they wanted to do for lunch on Sunday.

They sat at the table.

Quick chat? Yeah right.

'We've just been speaking to André,' Martin said.

'Is Lizzie okay?' Concern pinched his chest.

'Oh yes, she's fine.' His mum flicked her hand. 'But André is considering the possibility of taking a job opportunity in Queensland towards the end of the year.'

'Right. Well, that's good then. Though we won't get to see them and the new baby as much.'

'Exactly,' Marie said. 'Which is why,' she glanced at her husband, 'we've been thinking...'

Martin cleared his throat. 'We might move there too.'

'To Queensland? Aren't you all settled and happy in Welston?' An uncomfortable wave washed through him. He could get by without his parents around, but there were times when having them close by made things easier with Jackson, especially now with his new VIP program. What would he do for babysitting?

'Well yes, but a warmer northern climate would make your father's arthritis a bit easier in the winter months, and I want to be there to help Lizzie with the baby. You know how hard it is in those first few months.'

Yep. And not just the first few, James thought. He sat and leaned his elbows on the table.

'Now, I know you still need our support, and we want to be around for you and Jackson too, so we made a few enquiries.' Marie glanced at Martin again.

'Enquiries? About what?'

His dad cleared his throat. 'Turns out an old friend of mine owns a real estate agency up north, and when I happened to mention our family situation, he told us he has a grandson with autism too.'

'And?' James didn't like where this was going.

'He goes to a really good school there. A special school, tailored to these kids. Reg, my old pal, said his daughter is good friends with one of the admin staff there and could have a chat to you about the possibility of enrolling Jackson for the year after next.'

School. Queensland. Big changes. James wasn't ready for this. He just wanted to get through this week first, but knew he'd have to start planning schooling for Jackson and make some definite decisions. 'Hang on, shouldn't you have discussed this with me before making enquiries?'

'That's what we're doing now, and we only enquired about housing options which led to finding out about the school, so it all sort of fell into place.' His mum grasped his hand. 'Darling, I think this could be good thing for you and Jackson. A fresh start. And it would be great for us all to be together.'

'Your mother has a point. And now that your Nonna is... not around anymore, there's less need for us to stay here.'

'Less need? Jackson's going to have needs for the rest of his life.' He stood. 'I don't want to hold you back, you're free to go where you please, but now I'm starting this new program I'll need some help with him. It could take a while to find someone he's comfortable with.'

'So come with us.' His mother stood too. 'Leave the past behind and move on to a new place with new people and new opportunities.'

James ran his fingers through his hair. 'But Jackson, he likes it here. There's no way of knowing what he'd be like in a new environment. I don't want to upset him with too many changes.'

'I understand that, love, but now is the best time, while he's young and not at school. If you move earlier, you'll have time to settle him in before school starts.'

James paced across the room.

'Look,' his father said. 'Think on it. No need to decide right now.'

'I don't know if I could decide this week, let alone right now.'

'Okay. We'll leave it with you.' Marie patted him on the back. 'Just wanted to give you the heads up so you were informed, in case the topic came up with André.'

'Fair enough,' he said flatly.

'Right, well we better head off to dinner.' She took hold of her husband's elbow. 'We can talk more about it another time.'

He nodded and saw them to the door.

'Bye, Jackson,' Marie called. The boy continued playing with his toys. James' heart sunk at the resigned look of sadness on his mother's face. He knew she did her best to stay positive and accept him the way he was, but of course it still hurt that she couldn't interact fully with her first grandchild. No wonder she wanted to be close to Lizzie when her baby was born. It would be a second chance.

As his parents walked away from the cabin, so did a sense of security. Like he'd been abandoned, the way he'd felt when Emma left. Only now there was more at stake.

It wasn't that moving to Queensland was a bad idea, and he did need to look at all options for Jackson, but now, things had changed. Now he couldn't help but wonder if meeting Emma again had come at the right time. Now he had more to take into consideration before making any big decisions.

All thoughts of the conversation with his parents faded away when he opened the door to Emma later that evening. Her cheeks were rosy and hair was silky, framing her face softly and curving around her shoulders. Her sky-blue top formed a V on her chest, drawing his attention downwards.

'You look nice,' he said.

She tucked hair behind her ear. 'Thanks.'

'Yoga was good?'

'It was actually. Definitely got the blood flowing.'

'I can tell. You look all rosy and healthy.'

She smiled and lowered her head. Then he had an urge to do something. She might think it silly but the temptation was too great to resist. He held up a finger as if to say 'wait a sec', then picked up Jackson's Sound Machine. He pressed a button and a wolf-whistle pierced the air. He bit back a grin.

Emma's eyebrows rose and her mouth opened in surprise. 'Well, who needs words when we have that, huh?' She chuckled and her cheeks became even rosier.

'It definitely comes in handy sometimes, and not only for Jackson.' He placed it back down and Jackson pressed the same button, releasing another whistle into the room. James hoped he wouldn't get too used to that one and press it while they were out in public, in case random women thought he was whistling at them.

Emma stepped inside and walked over to his son. She placed a sketchpad and pencils on the floor. 'There you go. In case you feel like drawing.'

'That's nice of you. Thanks, Emma.'

'My pleasure. It's okay if he doesn't use them, just thought I'd leave them in case.'

'Judging by the fact that he once drew all over one of my important documents, I'd say he probably *will* be interested in them.' James gestured to the couch for Emma to sit. 'And what about your drawings, I take it you brought them?'

'Yes.' She withdrew some papers from her bag as they sat on the couch.

James placed them on his lap and studied them one by one. Some were pencil drawings, others watercolours. Some were simple doodles and others fully realised artworks. All were beautiful. 'Emma, these are amazing. I had no idea you could do this.'

His gaze lingered on one of a large, old tree beside a lake, its branches reaching out in all directions and a tyre-swing hanging from it. 'I love it.' It made him think of childhood, playing outdoors as a kid. Freedom.

'Thank you.' She smiled softly as he glanced her way.

'You could make a book of them all.'

'Like one of those coffee table books?' she asked, and he nodded. 'Maybe one day I will.'

'You should.' He looked at some more. 'Did you use anything as inspiration or draw them from your imagination?'

'A bit of both. Some were copied from pictures I found in

magazines, others I just let the pencil lead me where it wanted to go.'

'Go with the flow, huh?'

'Yeah. Go with the flow.' Emma looked off into the distance for a moment, as though that phrase meant something to her.

Did she want to go with the flow tonight, or did she have firm guidelines in her mind of how things would or would not unfold between them? James wished he could read her mind. But by looking closer at the drawings, it was as though he could get a glimpse into her heart, her soul even. Especially with the watercolours. The way the colours blended and contrasted in the same picture told of conflicting emotions, the curves and shapes of the brush strokes hinted at a delicate ebb and flow of those emotions, a sense of acceptance, but in some, also uncertainty and apprehension. The whole emotional spectrum was displayed in these drawings, and he felt privileged to be shown them.

He, too, felt conflicted. He was glad to not be consumed by anger and sadness anymore, and too much time had passed. He just wanted to spend time with her and see if their connection was still strong. So far, it looked that way, but it was early days. What if things didn't work out? What if she got scared and retreated again, hurt him all over again? He didn't know if he could bear that. Or worse, what if he wasn't enough for her? Life with Jackson would be a challenge, and to be honest, he wasn't sure he wanted a big family anymore. All his resources and strength were channelled to Jackson, and always would be. How could he possibly father another child, biologically or via other means, and still provide the same level of care for his son? Emma probably wanted to adopt a few kids now that she couldn't have any of her own, and if that were the case, then he would be no good for her. Maybe he *should* just up and move to Queensland.

'So, have you eaten?' he asked, aware that he was probably zoning out a little.

'I haven't actually.'

James stood. 'Time for the one-pot-wonder then.' He went to the kitchen and withdrew the casserole dish from the fridge, and scooped two servings into bowls.

'Jackson already eaten?'

'Yep.'

James microwaved the dinner and placed the bowls on the table.

'Thanks for this.'

'Don't thank me, thank my mum.' He grinned.

Jackson moved about the room for a while as they ate, then returned to the living room floor.

'How's your program going, the one you just set up?' Emma enquired.

James had the urge to check his emails again, but restrained himself. 'Good, thanks. Another sale came in today, which makes three. Doesn't sound like much but it is, and I only want a few clients for this particular program.'

'Congrats. Sounds like you're providing a needed service.'

'Hope so. Some think my stuff is unnecessary, a way to milk new graduates of their savings, but they can think what they want. I'm happy with what I've created and so are my customers.' He hoped he didn't come across as having a big ego, but he was just being honest. When it came to his work, he knew what he had to offer and offered it. The naysayers could get stuffed. His results in private practice spoke for themselves.

'I'm pleased for you.' A soft smile formed as she reached for her glass. 'It's good to help similar people with things you've learned. Maybe I should do something to help cancer survivors, or those going through treatment. Don't know what though.'

Emma. Always helping. It was a great idea, but he hoped

she would at least look after her own needs for a while. 'That's a great idea. But maybe you should... take some time for yourself first.' Maybe his question was really a way to see if she was keen to leave the past in the past and move on from his life.

Emma gave a subtle nod.

'Did you say you wanted to go overseas for a while?'

'I did. But I'll reassess after mum and dad are sorted with the cabins. I don't want to leave if I'm still needed.'

Something deep inside James said, '*I need you.*' He ignored it and took a swig of wine. He sensed Emma realised the double meaning in her words after she'd spoken, as she lowered her head and scratched her neck, though he doubted it was itchy.

'So, ah,' she said. 'When was Jackson diagnosed with autism?'

James thought back to his son's early years and the concern his mother had shown at her grandson's slow development. He hadn't been worried at first, he'd never had any other child to compare Jackson to, and he thought he was just a unique kid. But when he finally got him checked out and his mum's fears were validated, it was a shock. His son — autistic? He hadn't even known much about the condition, but the more he researched the more he realised the clues were spot on. 'About two years old,' he replied. 'He had further testing done later to determine how he was progressing, but it was pretty clear from the testing that he was on the spectrum.'

'Must have been a lot to take in.' Her eyes connected with his and her empathy soothed him like a soft blanket.

'It was. But things are better now that I know what we're dealing with and have had a chance to get him into various therapies. There's been a lot of support for him, it's been great.'

'That's great. And, um...' She bit her lip. 'Did his mother ever find out about the diagnosis?'

He wasn't expecting that question.

'Sorry, I should mind my own business.' She flicked her hand.

'No, it's okay. I don't mind talking about it with you. You're a good listener.'

Emma smiled and he felt like he could tell her anything, everything that was bottled up inside. She had that effect on people, on him.

'She knows. At least, I texted her to let her know. But never got a reply.'

Unlike the first time...

'Might as well,' said Lizzie. 'Even if I had given up a child, part of me would still like to know that they're healthy.'

'Okay. I'll do it.' James sent Stacey a text message the day after Jackson's first birthday:

Just letting you know he's well. Hope you are too.

She'd replied:

Thanks. I am.

And that was it. The last he'd ever heard from her. A year later when the diagnosis had come in, he'd felt alone and wished he could discuss the implications with someone apart from his parents and sister. His friends didn't understand. Part of him, although it was stupid, wished Stacey would have a massive personal transformation and change her mind and come back, if only to help with Jackson and to quench his painful loneliness.

But his next text message informing her of Jackson's diagnosis — just wanted to keep you informed — met with no reply. He'd sent a follow up — sorry if I've upset you, just needed to tell you. I don't expect anything. He'll be okay, I'll be okay.

But unless she'd changed her phone number, she obviously wanted to sever all ties. So he vowed never to contact her again.

'We'll be there for you,' said Lizzie when he'd told her what *happened. 'You can do this. You'll be the best dad for him. You already are.'*

And he'd leaned onto his sister's shoulder and let silent tears stream down his cheek.

'I'm sorry. Again. What you've done on your own is truly admirable.' Emma lightly touched his hand.

He simply nodded a thank you. He glanced towards Jackson as he sat there...drawing? James stood, ready to press the applause button on the Sound Machine when he realised what his son was drawing on. 'Oh no, Jackson!' He rushed to him and took the paper from his hand. Paper with one of Emma's drawings on it. Jackson screamed. 'You need to draw on blank paper, mate, not this.' *Holy crap.*

Though it pained him, he held up the picture to Emma who came to his side, Jackson still crying and trying to get the paper back from his dad. 'Jax, settle down please. Here. Draw on this.' He put a blank sheet in front of Jackson, but the boy grabbed it and ripped it with two clenched fists.

'Oh God, I'm so sorry Emma.' He shook his head. Her drawing of a skyscape with clouds and some kind of magical town built on them now had coloured streaks and squiggles across it.

Emma looked at it. 'It's okay, really. It doesn't matter.' She spoke loud above Jackson's noise.

'But it does. You put time and effort into these. God, I should have been supervising him better.' He moved her drawings to the kitchen counter. Parenthood was so embarrassing sometimes.

'No, I shouldn't have left them there. It's not your fault. And it's not Jackson's fault.' She touched his arm. 'Besides, it's good that he was using the gift I gave him, don't you think?' She offered a lopsided smile.

'Half of it, at least.'

'And it's only one of my many drawings. I won't miss it, seriously. In fact, I quite like the burst of colour he's added.' She tilted her head as she held it up in front of her.

Then she sat on the couch in front of Jackson and took one of the pencils. She added another streak of colour to her drawing, as Jackson watched. He leaned forwards with his pencil and drew a sharp, frustrated line on it. Emma then added another, as though they were lightning strikes spearing through the clouds. Jackson's cries turned into sniffles as he and Emma shared the paper, adding squiggles and lines and shapes and creating a colourful, chaotic mess. Then Jackson smiled.

God, how does she do it? She was like Mary Poppins meets SuperNanny. The woman could handle any childhood disaster.

James sat on the couch next to her, Jackson kneeling in front of them.

'I really am sorry,' he whispered, touching her hand.

'Shh,' she replied. 'Can't you see I'm having fun here?' She looked at him briefly and winked.

He couldn't help it. He leaned over and kissed her on the cheek.

She turned back to him. For a second he wished she'd turned her head just as he'd kissed her, so that his lips landed on hers instead of her cheek.

'Some things aren't worth getting upset about,' she said calmly, then resumed drawing with Jackson.

When the drawing had no more room for further vandalism, she asked James if he had any Blu Tack (which he did, it was holding a toy giraffe's head onto its neck after Jackson had snapped it). She stuck the picture on the wall at Jackson's height. Jackson patted it then pressed the applause button and Emma clapped too. He hoped it didn't mean his son would think it okay to draw on anything he desired, but right now, it didn't matter. She had taken what he thought was a terrible situation and turned it completely around.

Emma took a blank piece of paper and drew a circle on it, added two eyes, a nose, and then pointed to where the mouth should be. Jackson added a line elsewhere, then Emma slowly and gently touched the boy's hand, guiding it towards the mouth area. Jackson pressed down on the page and a wiggly, though definite line appeared, forming a smiling mouth.

Emma clapped and Jackson pressed the button again. Emma drew another circle with eyes and a nose, then pointed to the mouth area and waited. Jackson put the pencil on the paper again, making an arc for the mouth. James' heart melted. His son was learning something new. And for once, he wasn't the one teaching it. He leaned over and drew a circle himself, adding two googly eyes and a fat nose, then allowed Jackson to draw the mouth. Next, he drew only the circle, hoping that his son would add all the facial features. Instead, Jackson grunted at the picture impatiently, and James gave in and drew the eyes and nose.

'One step at a time,' Emma whispered, and he looked into her deep brown eyes with gratitude. Those words could apply to them as well.

'That's good advice,' he whispered back.

Jackson took hold of the paper and lay on his stomach on the floor, drawing his own things. James took another piece of paper and wrote on it: *thank you.*

He handed it to Emma. She wrote back: *you're welcome.*

He smiled and put pencil to paper again, but this time he drew. A stick figure in a skirt, a circular head, and long hair. He added a halo above her head.

'Guardian angel?' she asked.

He gave her the picture. 'You.'

Her chest rose sharply with a breath. She licked her lips

then drew another stick figure. With short hair, big biceps, and abs.

'Hugh Jackman?' he asked with a grin.

Emma shook her head.

'Your dream guy?'

She nodded, then wrote underneath the stick figure: *James*.

———

Emma waited while James gave Jackson a bath, supervised his dental hygiene (from outside the bathroom, apparently Jackson didn't want an audience), and read him a story and settled him for sleep. She had turned on the TV and kept the volume low, but couldn't concentrate on it, her mind filling with a warm sense of belonging. It seemed natural, being here with James, even with Jackson around. She was surprised how unaffected she'd been about her drawing being defaced, and seeing Jackson's excitement at learning to draw a smiley face had brought back memories of the satisfaction of teaching. But this was different, because he wasn't a student; he was the flesh and blood of the man she loved.

Deciding to postpone any important decisions until the time came for James and his family to go back home, Emma sketched to keep her hands and mind busy. An abstract arrangement of contrasting shapes, swirls and patterns. Maybe it was representative of her state of mind? When she'd taken up drawing during her treatment, she'd used it both as an escape from reality and a representation of reality — a way of expressing what was going on inside so as to not keep things bottled up. It was amazing how something unseen — an emotion or a thought about a situation — could *become* seen, through art. She'd liked knowing that she'd created something new. Maybe it was a substitute for motherhood — giving birth to something beautiful, something that came from her.

Emma tilted her head side to side, appraising her drawing, and added a few finishing swirls around the edges, then signed it *EB*. She placed the pencil and paper on the coffee table and leaned back on the couch. A dull ache formed on one side of her neck and she brought her hand up and rubbed at it. She pressed on the muscle with a circular motion, trying to break up the tension, and made a mental note to book in for a massage appointment on one of her days off.

'Do you need that icepack?'

Emma turned her head. James had come out of Jackson's room. He turned on the hallway light, probably in case Jackson needed to get up during the night, then turned off the living room light, adding a dim, cosy warmth to the room.

'No, it'll be fine. And it probably needs warmth more than cold. It's just a bit tight.' She rubbed at it some more.

James rubbed his hands together.

Hang on, is he going to...

Warm hands came down on the curve between her neck and shoulders, as James stood behind the back of the couch. He gently but firmly squeezed the tender muscles, his thumbs pressing into her skin, his fingers kneading. She tensed a little at his touch. 'Ooh, that *is* tight. Isn't yoga supposed to help sore muscles?'

'Yes, but I've only done one class. It might take some getting used to. And anyway, I was leaning over this paper and doing a sketch which probably didn't help my posture.' She gestured to the drawing on the coffee table.

His hands paused as he peered over. 'Nice. Does it have a special meaning?'

'Nope. I just let the drawing draw itself.'

'Well, tell the drawing it did a good job.'

'I will.' She smiled, though her back was to him.

James massaged her shoulders, rubbing them in firm rotations. Her tension eased and she took a calming breath. He found a tight spot between her spine and her shoulder blade and pressed into it with his thumb. 'Does that hurt?'

'No,' she replied. 'It actually feels good. Maybe you should become a massage therapist.'

'Nah, I'd get bored.' His hands stopped for a moment. 'I mean, not that I'm bored now! Far from it. I just mean that my mind would get, it would need...'

'I know what you mean,' she said.

He chuckled. 'Hang on, let me get into a better position before I pull a muscle from easing yours.' He came around the side of the couch and sat to the right of her. 'Turn sideways a bit.' Emma swivelled and bent her left knee so that it rested on the couch, the other foot still on the floor as though she was side-saddle on a horse. James shuffled around too, his hands on her back, pressing deeper and slower.

Holy moly, that feels good. Emma hoped she hadn't accidentally said that out loud.

'Is this okay?' he enquired.

'Um, yes. It's, ah, good.' She cleared her throat.

'Then I'll have to do better.'

'Huh?'

'Well, we can't have just *good*. What sort of massage therapist am I if it doesn't feel amazing?'

Oh, but it does.

He altered his movements, his hands taking on their own rhythm, and like the ebb and flow of the ocean his hands danced across the shore of her back, cleansing, invigorating, caressing. A tingling warmth spread across her skin, even more so when his hands moved up to her shoulders and gently slid underneath the neckline of her top. His skin, her skin, together again.

While his thumbs massaged the back, his fingers massaged the front, circling the roundness of her shoulders. Her hair that she'd swiped in front of one shoulder fell onto his hands. He gently guided it back, and with his finger he traced the length of a stray wisp from behind her ear, across the nape of her neck, and over her shoulder. His hand lingered on her hair, tingles shooting from her skin to her head as her hair shifted subtly like leaves in a breeze. He moved his other hand to her hair too, swiping it across to the side repeatedly, his fingers tangling gently in the strands and sending bursts of pleasure across her scalp.

Emma sighed. There was something so incredibly beautiful, erotic even, about someone playing with your hair. All tension evaporated and only a soft, sweet sensation remained, like she was floating among the clouds with tiny stars raining gently on her like a thousand magical sprinkles.

Then she felt something new. Warm breath, *his* breath, on the back of her neck. And then...his lips. She closed her eyes as his soft kiss from behind took her senses to another dimension. His lips trailed across her skin, an alternating treat of breaths and kisses, up the side of her neck, behind her ear. When he kissed the concavity between her earlobe and neck she practically melted. That was it. She couldn't keep her back to him any longer. As his lips continued their journey and moved to her cheek, she moved her head slowly to the side, seeking them out. Soon her chin was near her shoulder, her lips only a breath away from his. Caught in the transition of anticipation, she looked up into his eyes and saw confirmation of her own emotions mirrored back: he still loved her too.

His lips lightly brushed hers with the softness of a feather, as though each and every cell wanted to savour the moment before passion took control and overwhelmed them with its intensity. She breathed in, ready to exhale and surrender to her desire, aching to have his lips pressed passionately against hers.

As their lips touched again, a tapping at the door pulled her back. She flipped her head towards the door, and James stiffened, standing and clearing his throat. 'Huh?' he said, his voice heavy with unfulfilled need and confusion. He went to the door and Emma rearranged her hair back to normal position as he opened it.

'Hi,' Marie Gallagher whispered. 'Jackson asleep?'

Oh God, perfect bloody timing.

'Of course, it's getting late. What are you two doing here?' He opened the door wider and let his parents in.

'Gosh, it's a bit too dark in here.' Marie turned the light switch on and Emma blinked at the bright light. 'Oh, Emma. I didn't know you were here.' Marie's eyebrows rose as she noticed her in the living room.

'Evening, Emma,' Martin said with a nod.

'Good evening.' Emma stood and smoothed down her top. She felt like they were teenagers getting sprung making out.

'Sorry to drop in unannounced, but we were so excited.' Marie grinned.

'Well, *you* were so excited, I was simply...moderately pleased,' said Martin.

Marie held out her phone to James. 'Look. We got to meet Drew Williams!' She jiggled on the spot.

'Seriously, you'd think my wife was a starstruck teenager,' Martin said to Emma as he shook his head with a hint of a smile.

Emma moved towards the visitors and peered at the phone. 'Really?'

'Yes, he was a surprise guest at Café Lagoon, sang a few songs. No wonder the young chap — oh. What was his name again?'

'Jonah,' said Martin.

152

'*Jonah* had said we should come for dinner on Friday night!'

Emma smiled at the photo of Marie and Martin, a smile as wide as the Sydney Harbour Bridge plastered on Marie's face, and a...moderately pleased one on Martin's. Wedged between them was the good-looking, confident, smiling face of Tarrin's Bay born and bred international superstar, Drew Williams. 'Wow, lucky you! Is he still there now?'

'No, he loved us and left us after a few songs I'm afraid. But oh, what a treat!'

'He does have quite the singing voice,' Martin added.

'*And* he's incredibly handsome.' Marie fanned her face.

'Marie, he's practically the same age as your son, act appropriately.'

'Oh I am, honey, I am!' She fanned her face again. 'Don't you agree Emma?'

Emma nodded. Drew was many an Australian woman's fantasy — the down to earth celebrity who had a heart of gold. But despite this, if she could choose, she knew exactly who would win her heart, and he was standing right next to her, the heat from his hands still lingering on her neck.

'Well, good for you guys, glad you enjoyed the night,' James said. 'Did you get his autograph too?'

'You betcha.' Marie pulled out a signed postcard with a professional photo of Drew, guitar in hand, on the beach. 'If people had known he was playing, the café would have been swamped, I'm sure. Jonah said that he sometimes visits discreetly, surprising patrons with an impromptu performance and a free round of drinks.'

'Is he living here again?' Emma asked.

'Not sure, it's all a bit hush-hush, but some say he may have a house somewhere in the area.'

'Probably one of those rich ones up in the hills,' said Martin.

'Anyway, couldn't wait till morning to tell you. What have you kids been up to tonight?'

Emma looked at James and a silent awkwardness hung between them.

I was just about to get it on with your son.

'Um, Emma was teaching Jackson how to draw faces, and she brought some of her own artworks to show me.' James moved to the coffee table and showed them Jackson's handiwork, then Emma's.

'Impressive,' said Martin, eyeing the landscape drawings.

'Wow, Emma, you have quite a talent.' Marie touched her arm.

'Thanks.' She smiled.

They oohed and ahhed (well, Marie did) over the drawings, and James offered them a cup of tea.

'Oh no, we better get going, love,' said Marie. 'Talk more tomorrow.' She and her husband opened the door.

'And don't forget to think about that opportunity,' Martin said to James.

'Martin,' Marie whispered, giving him a light whack on the arm.

James' lips became tight and he scratched his head. 'Well, goodnight Mum, Dad.' He stepped onto the porch to see them off and Emma smiled and waved goodbye. They walked along the moonlit path to their cabin, and James stepped back inside.

'Sorry about that,' he said.

'It's okay, I can understand your mum's excitement.'

James slipped his hands into his pockets and swivelled side to side, seemingly unsure how to bridge the gap between where they had been a few minutes ago and where they were now.

Maybe some small talk would help. 'So, what's this opportunity your dad mentioned? Something for your business?' Emma asked casually.

James' lips became tight again and he twisted one corner of them to the side. 'Oh, nothing.' He waved her question away. 'Anyway, do you want a drink of something, or a snack?' He moved to the kitchen.

With the bright light filling the room and having just been in conversation with James' parents, the mood had now changed. Emma didn't know if they could recapture the purity and perfection of the moment between them that had now passed.

'Actually, I should probably head home. Working again tomorrow.'

James rested a hand on the kitchen counter. 'You sure?'

'Yeah, and I bet you need some sleep before Jackson wakes at the crack of dawn.'

He nodded. 'So you're off work on Sunday and Monday, is that right?'

'Yes.'

'Well, I guess I'll see you around. Tomorrow maybe.'

'Uh-huh.' She nodded, grabbed her bag and drawings, and stepped through the door when James opened it for her.

Should she give him a goodbye kiss? Or would that dampen the power of the one that had almost evolved into unbridled ecstasy only moments before?

She hovered on the porch, then the squeak of the door next door caught her attention. Lizzie emerged in her nightgown, stretching her arms up to the sky.

'Oh, hi guys,' she said. 'Just getting some fresh air before bed. You coming or going Emma?'

'Going.'

'See you later then. Sleep well.' Lizzie yawned.

'You too.' Emma stepped off the porch and gave a little wave to James. 'Thanks for tonight,' she said.

'Thank *you*,' he replied.

As Emma walked along the path, the salty scent in the air filled her nose, and the night breeze lifted all traces of James' warmth from her skin. Maybe it wasn't meant to be. It had felt so, *so* good, but maybe the interruption had been a sign, an obstacle, a 'hey girl what do you think you're doing?' from the universe. Maybe this weekend would simply be closure from her hasty departure five years ago. A chance to let any remaining embers of attraction run their course and burn out, to make way for new life, new flames, and — what James' dad had said — new opportunities.

CHAPTER FIFTEEN

Emma left the reception office just after twelve thirty pm, and glanced over at the park in case James was there with Jackson, but she couldn't see him. She made her way along the path and up the hill towards her parents' house. She would have to try and see James after work today, Saturday night. Two more days and he'd be gone.

'Hi, darling,' her mother said when she opened the door. 'You look lovely.'

'Oh, Mum, I look the same as I always do in my work uniform.'

'Exactly. Lovely.'

She kissed her mum on the cheek.

'Hi, Dad,' Emma said. 'How are you?'

'Bloody brilliant,' he replied. Emma didn't know if he was being sarcastic or not. 'How's construction going, is Bob behaving himself?'

'It's his day off, today. Saturday, remember?' she said.

'Every day is the same to me.' He flicked his good hand.

'Well, someone commented on our Facebook post about

Bob's photo,' Emma said. 'Reckoned he looked hot.' She laughed.

'Oh, that's good,' Barbara said.

'Why is it good?' her dad asked.

'Because he says he can't get a wife, and maybe Facebook will help,' Emma explained.

'Huh?' her dad said. 'How can he get on Facebook then?'

'What do you mean, Dad?'

'If he can't get wi-fi. How can he get on the Internet to access Facebook?'

Emma burst out laughing. Her dad's hearing issues were at least creating some light entertainment. '*Wife*, Dad, not wi-fi!'

'Oh!' Barbara laughed.

'I thought you meant he couldn't get Internet,' he said. 'Maybe he needs to go on one of those Internet dating things.'

'He says that's his last resort.'

'He ain't getting any younger,' Don Brighton remarked. 'Last time I saw him his wrinkles were giving mine a run for my money.'

'Dad!' Emma was glad Bob wasn't around to hear him.

'Anyway,' Barbara clapped her hands together. 'How are you going with James?'

'Um...' Emma replied. 'Well, we're getting along okay, so that's good.'

'Just okay?'

'Pretty good, then. His son is really cute.'

'What happened to the child's mother?' Barbara asked.

Emma's insides twisted. 'Um, let's not talk about that.'

'What should we talk about then?' her dad asked. 'I know, what do James' parents do?'

'Why?' And why were they so interested in Bob and James and James' parents? Were they trying to avoid another awkward discussion about the park and Emma's personal issues?

'Just making conversation. Are they retired?'

'James' dad was a lawyer, like him. His mum, a librarian.'

'Huh?' her dad said again. 'How does that work?'

'How does what work?'

'You know, did she have him via a test tube or something?'

'Don, what are you on about?' Barbara asked, her face creased with confusion.

'I'm all for modern day marriages, but I'm just wondering how they managed, with her being a lesbian.'

Oh no! 'God, Dad, I didn't say lesbian! I said *librarian!*'

Her mother lowered and shook her head. 'We will have to start speaking more clearly, love.'

Emma laughed again; she couldn't believe what she was hearing. Forget her artworks, maybe she would have to start documenting all these faux pas from her dad and put them into a book: *Post-stroke Humour.*

'Anyway, let's have lunch, shall we?' Barbara placed the cutlery on the table and they sat down.

After a relatively peaceful time eating lunch, her mum said, 'So, isn't it around the time to get your latest test results? Where are things up to?'

'I already got them, Mum. All good.'

'What? When?' Her mum placed her hand on her arm.

'All clear?' her father added. 'Well, that is fabulous news. Good to see those doctors are earning their ridiculously high paycheques.'

Emma smiled; glad her dad could have some good news. 'I got the results a month or so ago.' She leaned closer to her mother. 'Around when the, um...'

'Oh.' Barbara covered her mouth with her hand. She glanced at her husband then back again. 'When the stroke happened?' she whispered.

Emma nodded.

'Oh, love, you should have told us.'

'I couldn't, it seemed unimportant compared to what was going on.' Emma fiddled with her collar, heat crawling up her neck.

Barbara took her daughter's hand, tears welling in her eyes. 'This is wonderful,' she whispered. 'We need to celebrate. Did you have anything you wanted to do?'

Emma kept silent, and shrugged.

'What about a nice weekend away sometime, or a pampering day at the spa?'

Emma bit her lip. *Or a trip to Paris.*

'Is everything okay?' Barbara asked.

'Yes. It's fine. I was just, ah...'

'What are you not telling me?'

Emma took a deep breath. 'I was going to book an overseas trip, when it happened.'

'Overseas? And so you had to cancel your plans? Oh dear, sorry Emma.' She shook her head. 'And you've never been overseas. Why don't you still go?'

'I can't. I need to be here. You both need me.'

'Em,' she said. 'We can hire a park manager in the meantime, until we sell the place. We'll manage.'

'But they'll need training, and it'll cost more money. No. I'll stay.' She exhaled a short, sharp breath. 'You were both there for me when I needed you. I want to do the same. I owe you.'

She dared to glance at her father, whose eyes remained still.

'You don't owe us,' he whispered. 'We just want...' His eyes became glossy. 'We just want you to be happy.'

'Oh, Dad.' She leaned over and grasped his hand. 'I am happy.'

'But you need to experience the world. We've done that. You should leave us old withering codgers and go off on the trip of a lifetime.'

Emma laughed, and almost burst into tears at the same time.

'He's right, Em. Don't let life get away from you.'

She didn't know how to respond.

'And in terms of James. If you're meant to be with him, it will work out somehow. But don't hold back for him either, otherwise you'll regret it.' Barbara gathered the plates.

'Shouldn't I wait for a sign or something, Mum?' she asked.

Her mother shrugged. 'Stuff the signs in this case. Sometimes you just need to do what you need to do.'

What did she need? What did she want? Emma still had to figure all that out. Before her dad's stroke and reuniting with James it was easy: five years in remission — go overseas to celebrate. Now there were her parents to consider, *and* James. She didn't want to mess things up a second time with him.

CHAPTER SIXTEEN

A fter lunch, James took Jackson to the bathroom in the cabin and pointed to the sand tray against the wall.

'Let's try the sand again, yeah?' James already had bare feet, there was hardly any need for shoes around this place. He slowly stepped into the tray, his feet taking up nearly the whole thing. He exaggerated a smile. 'Ooh, this feels great!' He wriggled his feet and sand spread between his toes. 'Jackson's turn?' He stepped out and pointed to the tray.

Jackson gave a high-pitched sound then grabbed Owly from the vanity where he was keeping the soap company, and moved towards the tray. He gently placed the toy inside the tray, and he squealed and gripped his hands tightly together, then flapped them about. 'Ooo, ooo,' he said with his lips in a forced pout.

'That's it, good work Jackson! Ooo, ooo,' he echoed. Was he just making sounds or was he trying to mimic an Owl's night-time call? Either way it was all progress.

James bent down and moved Owly's tiny feet around as though he was enjoying the squishy feeling of sand. Then he pressed the applause button on the Sound Machine and added his own clap for the toy's accomplishment. Jackson squealed and jumped.

'Okay, now Jackson's turn.' He moved Owly to the side and gestured for Jackson to step into the tray. James lifted his own foot to remind him, then pointed to his son's foot. 'Jackson step in?'

Jackson edged closer and grabbed his father's hand, something that always made James proud. A simple touch evoked such strong paternal feelings for his boy. 'Yep, put your foot in.'

Jackson lifted his foot and James' anticipation lifted with it.

C'mon, buddy, you can do it.

Jackson stepped into the sand, one foot only, and gripped his father's hand tighter.

'It's okay, I've got you. You won't fall.' The boy stood rigid with one foot in and one foot out. 'Other foot now.' James tapped the foot that still rested on the bathroom floor. Jackson lifted it and stepped completely into the sand tray. His toes curled and clenched as though he was walking on broken glass. 'Good boy! Feels good doesn't it?' James smiled and encouraged him to move his feet, stepping on the spot with his own as an example. 'Stomp, stomp, stomp. Can you do that?'

Jackson didn't seem to understand but he looked down at his feet in the sand and made an 'ooo' sound again. He looked at Owly on the floor, then bent down and picked up a clump of sand and tossed it over to the toy.

James bit back a 'no'. He could clean it up. Mess was sometimes necessary for learning new things. As long as the plumbing didn't get clogged by large clumps of sand it'd be alright.

'Do you want Owly to join you?' James tried to let go of his son's hand but Jackson wouldn't release his grip, so James leaned over and picked up Owly. He handed the toy to Jackson who placed him on the sand next to his feet. Jackson's body seemed to buzz with the sensations, his muscles tense and corded through his skin, his cheeks flushed and eyes wide. Every new sensory experience was overwhelming for him. James had learned that autistics often absorbed a huge amount of detail from their environment, whereas others naturally filtered excess stimuli and retained only the vital pieces of information. For Jackson, every experience was full-on and could be difficult to process and focus on.

James took the Sound Machine from his pocket and pressed the applause for Jackson. 'Yay!' he said, then as Jackson relaxed a little, he let go of his hand and clapped too. Jackson stood on his own in the sand with Owly, his hands poised in mid air and his teeth clenched and jaw tight, but with a kind of smile.

James loved being around to witness his son's progress. What would happen if Jackson went to that school, would he miss out on seeing things like this? Would some stranger be the one to capture all his son's new milestones?

He laughed as Jackson bent down and picked up more sand, then tossed it up in the air. He hoped, though, that should they visit any place that had a cat litter tray his son wouldn't think he could just jump in at will and toss the granules all over the place.

James released a breath. One step accomplished, sand was no longer an enemy. Now to hope Jackson could handle walking on the real thing.

He went outside and led Jackson to the edge of the grass where the sand began to cover the ground. He stepped onto it and gestured for Jackson to come too. His parents approached, eyes eager to watch their grandson try something new. Jackson's face twisted into trepidation, but still James grasped his hand and tried to lead him to the sand.

'Ugh!' he grunted, his body glued to the spot. He pointed

back to the cabin, as if trying to compromise and use the sand tray instead.

Nope, not going to happen today.

James stepped back onto the grass and let Jackson run into the cabin by himself.

'Give it time,' Marie said.

Time, so much time.

He noticed his dad was holding a fishing rod and tackle box. 'You two off to catch dinner?'

'I am, but your mother thinks she'll get bored.'

'Yes, I think I'll do some reading instead. But why don't you go with your father, James?'

James raised his eyebrows and sussed out his dad's response. He couldn't remember the last time they'd done anything together, just the two of them. 'But Jackson, he'll—'

'I'll watch him. I can read here and there while he's playing.' Marie started walking towards the cabin.

'You sure?' he called after her.

'Yes, of course.' She waved.

James tossed her the keys in case they needed to lock up and go somewhere, then slid his hands into his pockets and looked at his father. 'So, whereabouts?'

'Let's go into the harbour. Might drive over instead of lugging this load all the way there. Plus we'll have to carry all the heavy fish back in the esky.'

'You sound confident.'

'Always.'

Forty-five minutes later, legs dangling over the pier, sun streaming across the horizon, they (meaning Martin) had caught a couple of bream. James had taken a walk up to the mobile kiosk at the marina to get two coffees, and as they sipped from the cardboard cups with plastic spouts, James finally relaxed. He wasn't used to sitting still, or gazing out at the ocean, he was always watching Jackson, helping Jackson, calling out to Jackson, or thinking about the next step for Jackson. It was like his nerves were on high alert 24/7.

He found his thoughts of what Jackson might be doing right now fading away. His mum would call if there was a problem. His thoughts now turned to Emma.

'Dad, did you always know you wanted to be with Mum? I mean, was there ever a time when you thought, nah, maybe we should go our separate ways?'

Martin glanced briefly at his son, then back to the water. James realised why, for a lot of men, fishing was a good way to bond easily, as opposed to say, having dinner at a restaurant. There was something to keep the hands busy, an objective, and no need for eye contact. For his father, this was helpful. In fact, since Jackson's diagnosis James had often wondered if his father had some minor signs of autism himself. He didn't know if he would be completely on the spectrum, but maybe from a personality point of view, it seemed to make sense. He hadn't been able to ask Stacey if there was any history of it in her family.

'Not really. There were times when that innate masculine fear of being trapped or controlled reared its ugly head, but I always knew I'd stay with her.' His fishing rod curved and he gripped it tighter, then wound the line up, a pale fish jerking and flapping on the end.

He took it off the hook and placed it with the others without a second thought, as though he could do it with his eyes closed. James had yet to feel the unmistakeable resistance of a fish attached to his line. Some people were just lucky.

'Don't worry,' Martin said, his mouth curving into a hint of a smile. 'Plenty more fish in the sea.' He chuckled.

Was he talking about fishing or Emma? There was only one 'fish' that he wanted.

'So it was Mum all the way, huh?'

'Yep.' He curved more bait onto the hook then cast the line into the sea. 'To be honest, son, I'd be lost without your mum.' James looked at his father's face from side on — the sun highlighting his ageing, tanned skin. Deep crevices showed where he had laughed, smiled, frowned, concentrated, and pondered life's journey. Lines that were starting to form on his own face. He wanted to have more laughter lines than frown lines, he wanted his face to resemble a life well lived, and a life well loved. He didn't know if that could be achieved without Emma.

'You still love her, don't you?' his dad asked.

James fiddled with the chipping paint near the handle of the fishing rod. 'Think so.'

They were silent for a moment, then Martin said, 'Things are a little different with you, though. You have Jackson to think of. He needs stability and an environment conducive to achieving his maximum potential.'

A twinge of resistance pinched at James' chest. Of course he did, but why did that and Emma need to be mutually exclusive?

'I know, Jackson will always come first. But I need to think what I want too.'

'Why don't you give Queensland a good shot? If Emma's meant to be in your life she'll adapt things for Jackson's best interests. And if she doesn't, then she might not be the one for you.'

James scratched his cheek and shifted his position on the pier. His dad had a way of making things uncomfortable sometimes. 'Actually, I'm considering other options for Jackson's best interests too,' James said. 'There are some good schools in the state here too, and there's also homeschooling.'

Martin almost dropped his fishing rod into the ocean. He turned to face his son, his frown lines deepening. 'Are you out of your mind?'

James leaned back. 'What? I'm just considering all options so I can make an informed decision. Apparently many kids on the spectrum do better with homeschooling, along with occasional inclusion in guided social activities. It's something I'm seriously considering.'

Martin shook his head. 'He needs specialist help. And think of yourself, you'll wear yourself out.'

'But I also like the idea of being around him for longer. I want to help him, teach him, and guide him. I want to be an active part of his life, not only in the evenings. I want to be around often, be there for him.'

A chill crisped the air between them.

Unlike me, he bet his father was thinking.

Martin tugged on the fishing rod a little. 'Damn, think I just missed one.' He adjusted the position of the rod.

'Dad, I—'

Martin held up his free hand. 'Look, I know I wasn't around much for you and Lizzie. I worked hard, wanted to make a good life for everyone.'

'I know you did, and I'm grateful. I wasn't saying that... that...' Oh, how could he turn this around without his father getting hurt? 'I just want to do what's right for my son, and me. For us. I'm realising that society's norms aren't necessarily norms after all. There's a lot of evidence that alternative forms of education can be just as good, if not better, for certain kids.'

Martin shrugged. 'I guess things have changed a bit from when you kids were young.'

They sat in silence, the strong briny scent that had greeted them on arriving undetectable now. There was calm here, and peace, but also an echo of emptiness. Although he knew his father loved him, he just wanted to feel for once that he was proud of him, and that he was good enough. To get some kind of inkling that no matter what decisions he made from now on, no matter how his life unfolded, that his dad would be okay with it. That he wouldn't wish it to be better or more successful than it was. He wanted acceptance. To feel loved, complete. The way he'd felt about Jackson when he was born...

Adrenaline fuelled James' body after hours of waiting for the big moment, and when that final push came and Stacey collapsed back in pain and exhaustion, all of a sudden his baby was out and in his arms. The tiny squashed being screamed at the top of his lungs as James held him with strong but shaky arms for the first time, and his heart overflowed with a love he'd never before experienced. He couldn't believe that this little baby boy was his. From his own flesh and blood, a part of him. For a brief moment he'd wanted to bring him to Stacey's side and let her share in the moment, see the magic they had created, but she had made him promise that he wouldn't do that. When he glanced at her on the hospital bed, she looked briefly at the child then turned her head to the side and covered her eyes with her forearm draped across her sweaty face. A midwife attended to her and James brought his attention back to the baby, then someone held up the scissors and asked if he wanted to cut the umbilical cord. He'd felt the firm cord give way under the snip, and with that, he knew, it was severing all ties to Stacey as well. She was now free of this child she didn't want, and he was free to raise the child the way he wanted.

When the nurses had pulled the curtain around Stacey and taken Jackson to the side to be weighed and measured, his arms buzzed with need to feel his son in them again. Just hearing his cries was bizarre, and he wondered what his voice would sound like as he grew up, how would it feel to hear him say 'Daddy'? At that moment, James had been filled with joy and wonder and excitement for what the future would bring. Nothing else mattered but this little human that would become his life, his purpose, his passion. He'd clamped his lips together in a smile as tears welled at his eyes. This was it. This was his son. He was now officially: a father.

James stole a glance at his dad again, who appeared to be lost in thought. Had he felt the same way about him when he was born? Was he overcome with love and joy like he'd been, or were his only thoughts ones of aspirations for the future, like what could this boy achieve? How will he make me proud? A bitter sadness crept through unchartered territory in his heart. It was only through becoming a father that he had started to question his relationship with his own.

James let his mind wander, recalling moments from his childhood...

His mum was always in the picture, always there, doing what the majority of mothers of that generation did — cook, clean, play, teach, discipline, and love. Plus she still worked part-time as a librarian. His mum did it all. His dad would come home late after work and tell them of his achievements, then he would ask them what they learned that day. He would often give them 'trivia of the day' too, some sort of random piece of useless fact that he'd read in a newspaper or memorised from years gone by. And he'd ask them to remember the previous days trivia to keep him and Lizzie on their toes. James always remembered though, because he secretly kept a diary with all the trivia, which he'd run off to write down when his dad had his shower. Before his father would get home, James would read the diary to recall the trivia so he'd be able to impress him with his memory once he got home. It gave him a thrill, knowing he would get a 'well done' pat on the back from Dad that night.

Martin Gallagher would also build intricate, complex Lego constructions with James until his bedtime, until Marie said, 'That's enough, bed and bath for you kids.' James could have gone on all night building Lego, there never seemed to be enough time to complete anything.

His father hadn't been around much, but when he was, he made it count. Maybe that was his way of showing his love — quality, not quantity. James' sadness floated away and was replaced with understanding. Martin had done what he knew how to do. Not everyone was cut out for long-duration parenting. Had his dad been around more, maybe it wouldn't have been as good for them. Maybe this was the best it could be, and the only way it could be, for his dad's personality.

As James realised that each parent was different and needed to approach parenting in their own unique way, he felt a light but firm touch on his shoulder. Martin Gallagher, eyes still gazing out at the ocean, had placed his hand on his son. James looked at the weathered fingers curving over his shoulder, then at the face of his father who had seen many more days on this earth than him.

'You're doing a great job, son.' Martin gave a firm pat with his hand, and a subtle nod of his head. 'You're a good father.'

A lump formed in James throat. He brought his hand up to his father's and gave it two light pats. 'I had a good teacher.'

CHAPTER SEVENTEEN

Emma decorated the wrapped gift with a ribbon, then placed it on the reception desk for Amelia to find the next morning. She smiled; glad she'd been able to get it finished by the end of work today. Amelia would love the drawing of the beach and headland with Tarrin towering above the holiday park, and it had turned out quite well, if she did say so herself.

She had thought of giving the drawing to James, but wasn't sure if that was getting a bit personal, and it could also be seen as a goodbye gift. She was still deciding whether it would be goodbye, see you later, or something else. But the more she thought about it, the more she thought it was probably best to continue on with her original plans and do what was right for her, first and foremost. They had each other's number; they could always get in touch if necessary, but everything seemed too sudden. At least with two days off starting in a few minutes, she'd have time to ponder everything and see James off when he left on Monday, get a sense of how they would leave things. And tomorrow when she'd be at Jen's party, he'd surely be focused on saying goodbye to his grandmother on what would have been her birthday, so it certainly wasn't the time to discuss other matters.

Emma switched off the desk lamp and locked the drawers, wiped down the countertop and eyed the other thoughtful gift on the desk. The one she'd been given by a guest who had checked out this morning; a six-year-old girl and her parents. The girl had made a little gift bag for Emma containing a few items she'd found and also bought: two seashells, a flower (which would of course wilt and die shortly, but it didn't matter), a miniature pack of playing cards, a whistle, and a cylinder of bubbles to blow. It wasn't every day that guests gave gifts as thanks for enjoying their stay, but apparently the little girl had thought of the idea herself. It had touched Emma's heart, but had also reminded her of the fact that she'd never be able to have a daughter of her own. After they'd left, she'd held back tears. They would often come and go unexpectedly, like changes in the weather. Just when she thought she was over it and had accepted her fate, something would happen and trigger the emotions again. She knew it would ease with time, like grief. She was grieving for something she never had, and never would.

Before closing up, Emma thought of Jackson and had an idea. She took the container of bubbles from the gift bag and brought it outside with her. She didn't have to walk to the cabin, Jackson and James were at the playground and Jackson was using leaves and twigs to make a shape around Owly as he lay helpless on the spongy ground. James' parents sat at a nearby picnic table with takeaway coffees in their hands.

'Hi,' she said to James, her voice catching a little in her throat at the memory of the night before, how they'd come close to letting go and letting their history take over where it had left off.

'Off duty?'

'Till Tuesday.' Emma breathed out with a whoosh and a

smile. She waved a hello to Marie and Martin. Both Martin and James had warm colour in their cheeks, their week in the sun starting to show.

'Thought I'd come by and see if Jackson was interested in bubbles?' She held up the cylinder.

James looked surprised. 'You know what? I don't think he's ever experienced them. Let's see what he thinks.' He moved closer to his son. 'Hey, buddy. Look at this.' He pointed to Emma and she pulled out the handle and blew through the circle, a glossy elongated bubble growing and releasing itself into the air. Jackson didn't notice, until she blew a few more and they floated around him. He gazed up at them, his eyes taking on a surprised and wondrous look, his mouth gaping.

James stuck his finger into one and it popped. Jackson flinched. James did it again and said, 'Pop!' then laughed. A wide grin stretched across Jackson's face, and he pushed his hands against the bubbles, laughing as they disappeared. He stood and left Owly in his virtual prison while he chased bubbles around him.

Emma eyed James and cocked her head towards the sand. He nodded. They could use them to try and entice him over to the sand.

As Jackson enjoyed the delight of the experience and Marie Gallagher took photos, James scooped up Owly as Emma blew bubbles further away from Jackson so he would follow them. She walked along the grass, Jackson following the bubble trail, leaping to catch them. She kicked off her shoes as she neared the edge where grass gave way to sand.

James already had bare feet, and so did Jackson, he had mentioned he was getting him used to being without them so his soles would desensitise to different textures. Emma stepped onto the sand and blew more bubbles, reaching up to pop them with her finger. Jackson glanced at the ground, aware he was veering into the unknown, and stayed put at the border, still reaching up on his toes to try to catch the bubbles. He made an urgent grunting sound as some were too far away to catch.

'James,' Emma said. She pointed to the owl and then to the sand. 'Maybe if he sees it on the sand?'

James put the toy close enough for Jackson to be near him but far enough away that he couldn't reach without moving forward. Emma blew bubbles in Owly's direction, and James made the toy jump up and pop them with his nose. They both laughed, encouraging Jackson to join in the fun. The boy was clearly mesmerised by these magical floating things, his fingers curled and wriggled in front of him, itching to pop them. Emma handed the bubbles to James and approached Jackson. She held out her hand in a non-threatening way, and waited. 'Let's go rescue Owly from the bubbles.'

James pretended that Owly was getting bumped on the head by the bubbles and kept collapsing, then James would rescue the toy and cuddle him. The next time he did it, he made the toy fall further away, and collapsed onto the sand himself, pretending he couldn't reach far enough to get Owly. 'Jackson, help me get Owly? I can't reach!'

Emma couldn't contain her grin at James' enthusiastic attempts.

The boy's face creased with concern.

'Quick, Owly needs us!' Emma had no idea if he could understand what she was saying, but she had confidence he probably could. For many with autism, comprehension wasn't the problem, expression was. They didn't know how to respond to the information bombarding their brain.

Emma tried to reach Owly too but stopped short. 'Oh no! We need Jackson's help!' She held her hand back to the boy and he grasped it, and with a gentle little tug she led him forwards, enough that he would feel the pull but not enough that it felt forced. He stepped one foot onto the sand and winced. 'Good work, Owly is going to be very happy when you get him.' Jackson put another foot on the sand, his toes curling and feet becoming rigid. 'That's it, almost there.' She tugged a little more, continuing to try and reach Owly with her other hand. James had given up trying to get the toy, his eyes were fixed on his son, his mouth open and his eyebrows raised. She noticed out the corner of her eye someone filming the moment on their phone.

Jackson took two more steps and squealed, but a different squeal, one of excitement, though he still looked a little terrified. Then in a flash, he dashed towards Owly, scooped him up into his arms and held him tight, then rushed back to the grass with another squeal like he was running away from a wave crashing onto the shore. He tumbled over on the grass in relief and laughter.

Emma's heart soared. Moments like these were what made life wonderful. She eyed James with a 'we did it' smile, and he blew bubbles towards her. She let one fall gently onto her hand, then popped it with a blow of air from her mouth. James blew more bubbles, and Emma glanced towards Jackson just in time to see the fluffy toy hurtling towards her like a meteor. It narrowly missed her head and landed on the sand. She pointed down to it then looked at Jackson. 'Oh, he's back! Owly loves the sand.'

Jackson inched forwards and stepped onto the sand, finding his footing, then rushed to Owly and picked him up again, returning just as fast to the grass and tumbling onto it.

'Again?' James asked, hands on hips, as Emma took over the bubble blowing.

Jackson threw the toy in the air then chased after it onto the sand, rescuing the owl then going back to roll on the grass. Repetition saves the day.

They stood there playing the game over and over, each time

watching Jackson's small feet scurrying across the sand, leaving footprints she bet James never thought he'd see. She finally looked up to see who was filming the scene unfolding — her mother. Barbara Brighton stood there with glossy eyes, hands poised on the phone as it captured the significant moment. Emma glanced towards James' dad who stood strong nearby with a small, but definite, unmoving smile. Marie had a hand on her heart, and James... well, she'd never seen him so happy. This gorgeous little boy was his life, and she wanted nothing more than for them to be happy and healthy. If it meant that she would need to leave them be, then she would do it.

In this moment, she got it.

With James, everything would revolve around the giggling, tumbling boy in front of them, and so it should. He needed his father, and would continue to do so. James had been given this gift, this responsibility, and she knew he would do anything for the son she would never have been able to give him.

She knew then that regardless of what may happen between them, now or in future, she would leave Australia for a while and experience new shores for herself, step into new cultures and landscapes, and have the experiences she wanted to have. It would be easier for James now, he no longer held the anger he'd carried for so long, and she'd been able to provide a small ray of help and hope for his son during their time in Tarrin's Bay. Helping his son walk on sand for the first time was in no way making up for hurting him, but as James looked at her with eyes of gratitude, she knew it mattered. *She* mattered. She never felt more alive than when she was helping someone, knowing she'd made a difference. And if they left now and never saw each other again, she would find comfort in the fact that things had ended on a positive note.

As Jackson sat on the edge of the grass and sprinkled sand over Owly's head like rain, Emma approached her mother.

'Sweetheart, that was so lovely to witness.' Barbara held up her phone. 'I got it all on video, so I'll forward it to you and you can...' she trailed off as James came over.

'You must be Mrs Brighton.' He held out his hand, and Emma realised that they had never officially met, as her parents had been travelling when Emma had first got together with James.

Her mother took his hand. 'Please, call me Barbara.' He smiled. 'I'll get Emma to send you the video I took.'

'That would be awesome, thank you.' He glanced at his son again, the smile still lighting up his face.

Marie and Martin came over and introduced themselves, and Emma and James exchanged awkward glances as they stood there surrounded by their respective parents, minus her dad. She hadn't expected them to meet in this way.

They chatted a few pleasantries, then Emma's mother touched her arm. 'I'd better head back to your father, I just wanted to come down and ask if next time you're out shopping, could you maybe pick up some DVDs from the library that your dad would like? He's much happier when he's watching movies, and I haven't figured out all that streaming nonsense yet.'

'Sure. I'll pick some up on my way to the city tomorrow,' she replied.

'You're not heading home, are you?' asked Marie.

'No, I'm still going to be helping out here for a while. I'm off to my friend's birthday party tomorrow in Sydney.'

'Oh, I see.' Marie's face slackened a little, and Emma remembered tomorrow would have been Nonna Bella's birthday too. 'I'll be back in the evening,' she added, mostly so James would know she'd be about so perhaps they could talk a bit, and she could let him know she still planned to go travelling. 'And I'll drop those DVDs around sometime, Mum. Tell Dad I'm onto it.'

Barbara thanked her and farewelled the group, and scurried back up the hill to her patient; the man she'd vowed to love and cherish till the day she died.

'I can't remember the last movie I watched,' said James. 'Except for animated ones.' He chuckled.

'Actually, I haven't watched one for a while either,' Emma added.

'You two should go,' suggested Marie. 'Tonight! It's Saturday, why not head out of town to the cinema and enjoy yourselves, we'll take care of Jackson.' She rallied her husband's support by sliding her arm around his back.

'I think it would be a splendid idea,' Martin said.

Huh? Both James' parents were now keen for their son to go out on a date with the woman who broke his heart? Her helping Jackson must have been more significant than she'd thought.

James exchanged an awkward glance with Emma, but his eyes held eagerness. 'Could be fun,' he said.

'It could,' she replied, clasping her hands behind her back and swinging side to side.

'Then it's settled.' Marie clapped her hands together. 'You kids go get organised, and don't you worry about a thing.'

No backing out then. It would have been so much easier to talk to James about her plans tomorrow night, rather than having to manoeuvre her way through what seemed to be a date, or a test, or whatever it was. But despite her new resolve, that part of her, that teenager, and that young woman who'd fallen in love with him, couldn't wait to settle into a seat at the cinema and share an armrest with the man standing right next to her.

CHAPTER EIGHTEEN

'This is the unhealthiest food I've eaten in five years!' Emma took a big bite of her humungous, processed pizza roll that she'd bought at the cinema for dinner in front of the big screen. 'Yum!' she mumbled with her mouth full.

'I know! Isn't it great?' James bit into his too, and found himself surprised by a burst of attraction to Emma in her moment of culinary enthusiasm. 'And the orange bubbles are bringing out my inner child.' He gestured to the jumbo-sized cup that housed his fizzy beverage.

'You'll probably end up hyperactive with all that artificial colouring.'

'Hmm, watch out.' He winked, and the lights dimmed as the movie previews screened.

Emma took her napkin and laid it on her lap. 'Don't want to drip hot pizza toppings onto my white capris.'

'I guess I should do the same.' James placed a napkin on his lap, though it didn't cover all of it. 'Maybe I should have grabbed more.'

'Don't worry, I have tissues if we need extra cleaning materials.'

'Always prepared, aren't you.'

'Of course.'

They ate and watched the previews, and had finished their meals by the time the movie started. Emma took a sip of her lemonade bubbles, or as he'd called them — *nude* bubbles — and settled back into the seat, crossing one leg over the other.

He noticed the way her thigh curved smoothly over her leg, the inner side of her knee facing him. His hand buzzed with the urge to touch her, to rest his hand on her leg like old times and enjoy the warmth beneath his skin. But he returned his focus to the screen.

At one point during the movie, Emma nudged him gently and said, 'Do you remember when...' and he had barely registered what she was saying, simply pleased she was slipping back into the memories of their past. The good memories. The ones they'd made together and would have made more of had she not left.

'Want one?' Emma took a packet of Tic Tacs from her bag and held them up.

'Only one?' he asked.

'Okay, you can have two.' She tipped the packet onto his palm but overdid it and a pile of the tiny pellets tumbled out.

'Have you forgotten how to do maths?' he asked with a quiet chuckle.

'Shush, you.' Her fingers tickled his palm as she gathered up the Tic Tacs. All of them.

'Hey.' James wrapped her hand with his, pulling it close to his chest. 'Where's my share?'

A smile lifted one corner of her lips. She put the mints back into the packet, bar two, and placed them carefully onto his palm. 'One. Two. There you go.'

He popped them both in his mouth and bit into them. 'Thanks.'

She leaned closer. 'You're not supposed to bite them, then the pleasure of eating them will be over too quickly. You're supposed to suck on them and take your time.'

He couldn't take his eyes off her. The taste of the Tic Tacs faded away and he could only think of tasting her lips. 'Sometimes it's best to just jump right in and don't hold back.'

Man, what had gotten into him? Being back in a movie theatre after all this time had brought back his inner teenager. He wanted to drape his arm around her, pull her close, and kiss in the back row till the credits finished and the cleaner came in.

'And sometimes,' she jabbed his chest with her finger, 'it's best to savour the moment, slowly, and carefully.'

'Then can I have another one?' He held out his hand.

She narrowed her eyes, then softened them and popped a Tic-Tac right into his mouth. He slid it around with his tongue and forced himself not to bite into it. Slowly, she wanted to take things, at least according to her Tic-Tac analogy. He would have to cull his desire, let the night unfold at the speed she wanted, to have a chance of making it work.

She'd wanted to kiss him. Desperately. Right when she'd heard the crack of the Tic-Tac as he bit into it. She'd wanted the minty sweetness to swirl between their mouths as they kissed and snuggled in their seats. But she didn't let it happen. She didn't want to keep giving in to her desire and losing sight of what was best. Tonight would be a simple, friendly little outing, and it would finish with a kiss on the cheek — nothing more — a hug, and they'd go off to their respective beds for the night. Tomorrow she would tell him about her travel plans. Not tonight. Tonight was for fun, an escape from the decisions and dilemmas of real life.

And although she didn't want to lose her inhibitions by having a touch of alcohol, the brightly coloured cocktail had called to her when they'd arrived at the beachside bar back in Tarrin's Bay.

James had opted for a martini, and after downing their drinks and mingling with a few locals and holidaymakers, they walked outside and crossed the park onto the beach. Emma slid her arms into her cardigan.

The ocean hummed and whooshed as they walked along the sand, the beach completely deserted. The good thing about this beach, cradled by the beachside cabins and caravan park, was that it was quieter and smaller than the others in Tarrin's Bay. Most tourists flocked to the main beach at the entrance to town, which was patrolled regularly. But here, now, this beach was theirs and theirs alone.

'I can't remember the last time I walked on the beach at night.' James slid his hands into his pockets.

'It's so beautiful here.'

'Yeah.' James spoke with a downward inflection, like he was sad about something.

'Welston has nice beaches too,' she said, thinking he might be thinking that he'll be out of here in a couple of days.

'True, but not like this one. There's something about it. It's small and intimate, like it belongs to whoever happens to be walking on it at the time.'

Emma breathed in the cool night air and revelled in the expanse of her lungs. 'So I guess it's ours for now.'

'It is. We should christen it.' He stopped, found a twig and scraped it into the sand: *JJ & Em's beach*. 'Now it just needs some sort of tagline.'

She laughed. 'It won't last forever you know. We'd need a more permanent sign.'

He glanced at her, his eyes sparkling in the moonlight. 'The water may wash it away but I'll remember it. We'll know it's ours.'

Emma took out her phone and snapped a photo with the flash. 'Not that clear, but here's another way to remember it.'

'I've already stored it,' he tapped at his temple, 'in here.'

'Well, just in case you need a reminder.' She jiggled her phone and he smiled.

They continued walking, each step cushioned by the sand as it gave way slightly. It was like their relationship: present, in some form, but fragile. Always changing form. Push too hard and it will give way. Avoid it and someone else may eventually step in and allow it to crumble away.

'So, my family's moving to Queensland,' James blurted.

'Oh?'

'They want me to join them. Found a good school for Jackson from a contact there who may be able to fast track an enrolment.'

Emma swallowed a lump. 'Right. Well, that would be good then, I guess.'

'Could be.'

'You haven't decided yet?' she asked.

'Nope. It's all a bit sudden. I need to weigh up the options.'

'Decisions can be so hard,' she said, feeling the truth of that statement weighing down her words.

Although she had decided one way or another she would continue with her travel plans, part of her wanted to tell him not to go, and she hated herself for it. Jackson was the priority here, not her. And *she* was going away, he could do whatever he wanted and she had no say in it, no right to object.

'Anyway,' his voice lightened. 'No need to talk about it, it's Saturday night, and one should never make important decisions on a Saturday night, ain't that right?' He smiled and swung his arms back and forth.

Phew. She'd started to wonder whether she should talk about her own plans too, but the moment had gone. 'Good idea. And hey,' she nudged him, 'what happened to the orange bubbles bringing out your inner, hyperactive child?'

'Oh yeah. I must have become immune to the artificial colourings in my old age.'

She whacked him on the arm. 'If you're old, then that means I am too. So I'll have none of that talk, please.' She put on her teacher's voice.

He raised his hands. 'Fair enough.' Then he stopped and looked towards the playground. 'I've got an idea.'

He grasped her hand and led her up the sandy hill, over to the deserted playground that looked kind of eerie and sad without the usual laughing, boisterous children and sun-drenched bright plastic.

'Are you looking for your inner child?' she asked with a chuckle.

'Yes. And I've found him. Over here.' He walked over to the swings and sat on the slack rubber, and it moulded to fit him. 'It's a tight fit, but I think it'll cope.' He looked up to the bar the swing was suspended from, as if checking it wasn't about to collapse on top of him. 'Oh, and your inner child, she's there.' He pointed to the swing next to him with a cheeky grin.

'Is that so?' Emma stepped to the swing. 'Maybe it won't cope with the weight of both of us at the same time.'

James reached over and jiggled the metal chains of her swing. 'Ah, I think it'll survive. C'mon.'

Emma glanced around, checking no one was watching the park manager about to have a late night swing on the children's playground. 'Okay then, just a quickie.' She caught his eye and laughed. 'I mean, a quick swing.'

'I know. What did you think I thought you meant?' He feigned seriousness then broke into a smile. 'Alrighty, let's see who can get the highest.' He swung his legs forwards, gathering momentum, and Emma did the same, though her delicate swings were no match for his powerful ones.

Emma's hair rushed backwards and forwards as she swung, the unfamiliar sensation bringing memories of childhood to her mind and a smile to her face. Cool air whipped around her, and as each swing took her upwards she felt light and free, weightless, for a moment.

'Fun, eh?' James said.

'I'd forgotten how much fun this is!' She giggled like a child.

James adjusted his swings so that eventually they matched hers, and they each rose forwards at the same time, watching each other. 'You reckon you can jump off from up here? Like the older kids do?'

The ground covering was springy, but Emma scrunched up her nose. 'Hmm, not sure. Don't want to twist my ankle or anything.'

'Then I'll go first, and if I survive, I'll try to catch you when you jump off. Yeah?'

'Okay. Yeah,' she said hesitantly.

James swung for a count of three, then as he swung forwards and went high in the air, he let go of the chains and leapt forwards, landing in a crouching position. 'Woohoo, I've still got it, baby.' He grinned and gave himself a clap.

'I'd clap too, but...' she shrugged as she gripped the chains.

'Your turn.' He curled his fingers towards his body, urging her to jump.

'Okay, here goes. One, two...' she swung forwards, 'three!' She let go and jumped off, crashing into James and falling forwards onto him as he tumbled backwards onto the ground.

'Whoa! You've got some power behind that swing, Em.'

Warmth radiated from his body and seeped into her as she lay on top of him. Had they not been in a public playground she may have been tempted to stay in said position a little longer. She scrambled up and laughed. 'I hope I didn't give you any bruises.'

James pushed himself up. 'A little bruise never hurt anyone.'

She scratched her arm, unsure what to do next.

James twisted sideways and looked down at the beach. 'See that rock?' He pointed and she nodded. 'Race you there on the count of three. Ready?'

She shook her head and giggled at his inner child's persistence, then readied her arms in running position.

'One, go!' He dashed forwards.

'Hey! You didn't get to three!' She ran after him.

He slowed a little till she caught up, then picked up speed again.

Emma found it hard to run as she laughed, and as they neared the rock he slowed again, allowing her to catch up. She reached the rock and sat on it just before him. 'Oh God, I'm so unfit!' She panted.

He sat on the rock next to her. 'Let's call it a tie.'

'Oh no, I won, thank you very much.' She crossed her arms.

'Okay, okay, you won.' He casually hung his arm around her shoulders and gave it a congratulatory squeeze. She turned her head and her laughter subsided. He moved his arm and lowered his head. It reminded her of the night she left him; all she could remember was the confusion and despair in his voice, and then his head hanging low and heartbroken.

After a moment of silence, she spoke up. 'I can't say it enough, James, but I really am sorry for leaving like that. I feel if I say it enough it might make it all okay. Make up for it, somehow.'

He looked her in the eye. 'It *is* all okay.'

'I mean, for me. You've been amazing how you've forgiven

me, understood where I was coming from. I'm still just finding it a little hard to not feel guilty around you.'

'Em, really, it's okay. I want to put all that behind us.' He kept his gaze on hers.

Damn, his dark eyes were so hypnotic, it was like there was a pendulum swinging in front of her, and a voice, instead of saying, 'You are getting sleepy', saying, 'You are falling more and more in love with this man'. Anticipation sparkled in his eyes, a strength of will gave firmness to his jaw, and he seemed to be waiting for some kind of response or sign to give him permission to kiss her.

The intensity of his gaze became too strong to maintain and Emma tore herself away from his focus. She turned her wrist. 'Oh, it's getting late.'

He brushed his fingers against her hand. 'But maybe it's not too late. For us.' She shivered at his touch, at his suggestion. 'What do you think?'

Emma looked away, and stood.

'Emma?'

'It's just...' She crossed her arms over her stomach and cupped her elbows with her hands. 'I just don't feel... I'm enough, for you.'

James stood and came close to her. 'Hey, don't say that.' He grasped her arms and uncrossed them from her body. 'You are *more* than enough.' His eyes bore deep into hers and a sharp breath hitched in her throat.

'I don't deserve you. I lied, I broke your heart. I just thought that one day, you'd find someone else. Someone you could start fresh with, without all this baggage.' She stepped back, but James closed the gap between them again.

He placed his hand on the side of her face and warmth spread across her skin, down her neck, and nestled into her heart. 'Don't you get it? There was never meant to be anyone else.' He took a deep breath and his exhalation tickled her skin as his face came closer. 'There was only meant to be you.'

James didn't wait for her response, she had barely even decided what her response would be, when his lips came crashing down on hers like a rush of waves tumbling onto the shore. He kissed her with rampant need, from every angle and position, devouring her lips as though they were essential to his survival. Like on the swings, her body felt weightless again. Free, yet contained; a juxtaposition of surrender and power as she both melted at his passion and came alive with her own.

She gripped the back of his neck with one hand, holding him close to her. Her other hand tucked under his shirt and met with hot skin as she trailed her hand up his back. Five years without feeling him close to her, without feeling like this. She'd forgotten how deliciously addictive he was.

As he took a breath and went to kiss her again, she gulped. 'Wait.'

'What is it?' he panted.

'This is amazing, you're amazing, but it's going to make it too difficult.' It took all her willpower to hold strong and not give in again.

'What do you mean, Em?'

'When I go.' She stepped back a little. 'I'm going overseas, James. As soon as things are settled here. I don't know how long for and I don't know what I'll do when I return, but I'm going. I need to.'

James pulled back too, his hands still holding onto her waist. So much for leaving big discussions till tomorrow, but she was worried that if she hadn't stopped, they would have ended up in her cottage and then there'd be no stopping.

'And maybe you *should* go to Queensland. You need to do what's best for Jackson and not think about me.' She caressed his cheek gently then stepped away. 'Sorry to lead you on.'

James tipped his head back and ran a hand through his hair. 'Geez, Em.' He planted his hands on his hips and pushed put a deep breath. 'First of all, there's no reason why you can't go overseas. I'll still be here when you get back. I'll wait for you.' His eyes confirmed the truth in his words and Emma bit her lip. 'Secondly, who says Queensland is what's best for Jackson? He could do just as well here, or even home-schooled. Of course my son comes first, but that doesn't mean I can't take into account what I want too.' He stepped closer. 'And I want *you*.'

'James,' she breathed as his face came close again. 'I'm scared.'

He grasped her arms. 'Don't be.'

She shook her head. 'I can't do it. Not now. What if my cancer comes back, like it did for Maggie?'

'Wait, who's Maggie?'

'A woman at the yoga class. Hers came back and now she's gone. What if that happens to me? I can't put you through that, and definitely not Jackson. He needs stability.'

James dropped his hands and his jaw stiffened. 'You're in remission. There's every chance it will stay that way. And anyway, no one's life is guaranteed. I could die tomorrow, but we can't live in fear of what might happen.'

'James, don't say that.' She turned away and pushed the idea from her mind.

'You can't plan for every contingency, you just have to go with what feels right and deal with whatever comes up.'

'I lived with uncertainty for too long, I need some certainty for a while, James.'

He turned away and kicked a twig on the sand. When he turned back his demeanour had changed. She'd pushed him away. 'I think what you're really scared of is the responsibility. It's not just me now, it's me and Jackson. He's not going to grow up and be independent like other kids. My life, our life, it's a serious commitment. That's what you're worried about, isn't it?'

'What? James, no.' She was the one stepping forward now. 'Jackson's a beautiful child, he's a gift. I'm not worried about that.'

As she spoke, a tightness gripped her from the inside. Was he right? Were the travel and cancer issues a mask for the real issue: that she didn't feel cut out to be Jackson's mother? A wave of nausea rolled through her. *Oh God.* She held her stomach. The reminder was constant. The emptiness within screamed, 'Can't you take a hint?' She hated that although she was great with kids, somehow deep inside she was convinced she wasn't meant to be a mother.

'But teaching children is a lot different to parenting one,' James said. 'It's ongoing, you can't just leave the hard stuff to the parents when you're done for the day. You have to deal with the challenges head on, there's no easy way around it.'

Ouch. It felt like he was the one saying she couldn't do it, that she wasn't good enough for this kind of responsibility. She crossed her arms.

'I've hit a nerve, haven't I. That's it. You still have feelings for me but you don't want the responsibility I come with.' He crossed his arms to match.

She stayed silent.

'I knew it.' He raised his hands and let them fall to his side.

'James, it's just, I just... I need to have some freedom for a while. I need to get away and see the world, do something for myself. It doesn't mean I'm afraid of responsibility, I think it might simply be a timing thing.'

James shook his head. His phone beeped and he looked at the screen. 'Jackson's having a night terror. I have to go.'

'A night terror, is he okay?' She approached him but James

held up his hand in front of her like a force field, holding her back.

'It's my responsibility, not yours. I need to go. You don't have to worry about a thing and you never will.' He turned around and walked.

'James, I'm sorry. Please, can we talk later?'

He spun around. 'You know what? Maybe I *will* go to Queensland after all.' And he turned back again and walked up the hill towards his cabin, back to the life he'd built for himself and himself alone.

CHAPTER NINETEEN

'It's so good to see you!' Jen wrapped her arms around Emma as she arrived at the party.

Emma held on tight and didn't want to let go. 'You too, you too.'

'Hey, I know I'm irresistible, but why the extra affection?' She winked as Emma reluctantly released her friend.

'I've missed you,' she said.

Jen leaned in close, as other guests mingled around them. 'Everything okay in James Land?' she whispered.

Emma flicked her hand. 'Oh, nothing I can't handle. So, here's your present. Happy birthday!'

Jen took the small box and envelope. 'Thanks! But let's talk later on, yeah?'

'Yeah.' She nodded.

'For those who don't know, this is my fabulous friend and ex-roomie, Emma!' Jen waved a flourished hand in front of her to present her to the crowd. Emma greeted a few people she already knew, and others introduced themselves.

This is what she needed, a fresh crowd and a bit of anonymity. Travel would give her that too. A place where no one knew her, and she could start with a clean slate without pity. New Emma. Healthy Emma. No One Knows My Past Emma.

A flute of champagne found its way into her hand and she sipped it eagerly. Better to get it in early before the drive back to Tarrin's Bay in the afternoon. Jen placed the present on the gift table but Emma placed a hand on her arm. 'Open it now.'

Jen's eyes narrowed with curious anticipation. 'Hmm, okay. Why not?'

While others chatted and ate and laughed, Jen slipped her finger under the pink and purple paisley design paper and withdrew a small silver box. 'Oooh, what is it?' Jen opened the box and lifted out the necklace with multicoloured glass beaded pendant Emma had bought from the Tarrin's Bay markets recently. 'Oh wow, it's gorgeous! Thanks, hun.' She kissed Emma's cheek and slipped the necklace around her neck, securing it at the back.

'I thought of you when I saw it. And look.' She turned the pendant over and showed Jen the engraving: *Thanks a million.*

Jen's eyes shone. It was a saying she always said, and now it was Emma's turn to say it. 'I couldn't have gotten through the last few years without you,' Emma said. Gratitude softened her heart and moistened her eyes.

Jen hugged her again. 'It's been an absolute honour.' This time Jen didn't let go right away.

'I guess I'm irresistible too, huh?' Emma laughed.

Jen pulled back and smiled. 'Of course. And I bet I'm not the *only* one who thinks so.' She tilted her head in a way that said, 'I expect a full detailed synopsis of the current situation later please'.

Emma wasn't too sure James would think that way now after her hot-cold performance from last night. She was glad to get away today, but regretted the way things had turned out between them. She didn't blame him if he did move to Queensland and forget all about her for the sake of avoiding riding in an emotional rollercoaster.

'Oops, I forgot that it's polite to open the card first.' Jen picked up the envelope and opened it. It was a handmade card with a drawing of two deck chairs overlooking the ocean. Inside it said: *Saving you a spot. Happy Birthday.* 'Wow, that's beautiful. Your handiwork, I take it?'

Emma nodded with a modest shrug.

Jen shook her head and smiled. 'You really should put all your drawings together into a book or something. I could flip through them for hours.'

Emma smiled. 'Someone else told me the same thing.'

'Oh? A *certain* someone?'

'Yes. But we won't get into that now. I'm starved, I think I'm going to grab one of those curry puffs.' Emma walked over to the smorgasbord of party food and popped one in her mouth before she blurted out everything on her mind. This wasn't the time to talk about her dramas, it was time for Jen to enjoy her special day.

And enjoy she did, because by the time everyone had eaten more food than was necessary and emptied multiple champagne bottles, Jen's boyfriend Sean gave a speech that would have any woman wishing she was the one he was talking about.

Jen's hand was glued to her chest, over her heart, at his words. Guests 'awwed' and cast smiling glances towards the lucky woman. And when Jen looked like she was about to walk up and give him a hearty thank you kiss, he came over to her and dropped to one knee.

'Oh my God.' Jen froze, her mouth gaping.

Emma's hand flew to her mouth. She had no idea he was planning this, she'd always thought he was a go with the flow kind of guy who never planned ahead.

'Will you marry me?' he asked, his eyes looking lovingly up at her, while Jen's eyes became glossy.

'After that speech, how can I not?' She got onto her knees as well. 'Yes. Yes!' She laughed and cried and kissed him, wrapped her arms around him, and eventually they ended up collapsing onto the floor in an ecstatic, tangled heap.

'C'mon you two, there'll be time for that later!' someone called out, along with a few wolf-whistles.

They helped each other up, grins wide. 'You might be wondering why I don't have a ring for Jen,' Sean said to the crowd. 'I'm taking her out this week to choose one. I knew my Jen would like something unique and I want her to be a part of the choice.' He looked back at his fiancée and smiled.

'He knows me too well!' Jen said.

Emma's heart overflowed with happiness for her friend, and for a brief moment a thought flashed through her mind...

James would know which ring to get me.

He knew her too well also. She imagined it would be a simple, solitaire engagement ring, white gold. Nothing fancy, just a pure representation of love and commitment.

Emma drank the last of her champagne in one giant scull. Why was she even thinking such things? She was just caught up in the moment and being silly. She tried to forget about James and went over to congratulate the happy couple.

'Did you know?' Jen asked Emma.

'Nope. Had us all fooled!'

'I'm good at keeping secrets,' Sean replied. 'So you know, if you have anything you want to tell me, Emma, I'm good for it.' He nudged her and winked. 'Though I can't promise anything after I have another drink.' He accepted a flute, along with Jen, for a congratulatory toast.

Oh no, there'd be no more secret telling. Emma had had enough of them. Now that she'd finally told James what had happened to her all those years ago, despite the current conflict between them both, she couldn't believe how much better she felt. From now on, there'd be no more secrets. She'd already told him she was scared, that she still had fear of the cancer returning, and that she wanted to go overseas. Everything was out in the messy open and no amount of tidying could put things back where they came from. Whatever happened now she would just have to deal with, and she knew she could. She'd beaten the Big C; she could handle whatever life threw at her next.

Empowered by the moment, Emma weaved through the crowd and went outside on the patio, breathing in the delicious afternoon air and filling herself with strength about her new life plans. A child bumped into her legs as he scurried past, being chased by another child, and she simply smiled as she watched them play.

'Huh,' she said out loud, surprised by her detachment. She didn't feel that pang of longing or jealousy, that 'oh how cute, I wish I had one' thought. She didn't feel anything, except a slight ache in her leg from the collision.

She could have a good life without a child in it. She knew she could certainly adopt, foster even, but right now, for the first time, she felt that even if it never happened, she'd be okay. Her life would still be fulfilling. A smile eased onto her lips and she took another deep breath, acknowledging the moment of realisation.

'Sneaking out for a smoke?'

Emma turned to see Jen standing next to her. She laughed. 'As if.'

'Look, I have a temporary engagement ring.' Jen held up her left hand.

'Classy. And versatile.' Emma smiled and nodded at the line drawn on with a pen, complete with a large diamond shape.

'I know, right? I can add an extra diamond whenever I want, or change the colour. It's really quite practical.' She giggled. 'Anyway, I want to hear about what's going on with you. Quick, while Sean is telling everyone the list of daggy songs he's going to choose for our wedding dance floor party.'

'Can't wait for the big day, when do you think it will be?'

'Early next year, I think.'

'Well, even if I'm overseas before that, I'll make a trip back just for you. I'm not missing your special day.'

'Good, because you're my bridesmaid.' Jen grinned.

'I am?'

'Whether you like it or not.' She draped her arm around Emma.

'Then it's a date.' They shook hands. 'Just don't choose a frilly, puffy-sleeved, lemon-coloured dress for me or anything.'

'I wouldn't dream of it,' Jen said. 'I'll make it peach-coloured instead.' She winked. 'Now, hang on. So you *have* decided to continue with your travel plans?' she asked.

'Yep. And Mum and Dad know now, about what I was planning. But I'll still wait till things are sorted with the cabins.'

'I'm glad. You need this. Have you told James?'

Emma nodded, and glanced at the wind chimes that jingled in the breeze as they hung from the patio roof, as though signalling a change in the direction of their conversation.

'And?'

'It's okay, we can talk when your birthday is over. You should be talking to your guests.' Emma turned to the patio door but Jen stopped her.

'*You* are my guest, and right now I want to talk to you. Besides, doesn't James leave tomorrow?'

Emma nodded.

'Then this is a conversational emergency! Spill it all. Now.'

She sat at an outdoor table setting for two and Emma took the other seat.

Emma sighed. 'Okay, where to start... Um, things were going well until last night,' she said. 'I've probably stuffed things up for good.'

'Oh no, what happened?' Jen leaned forward on the table.

'I told him I'm going overseas and that I don't know how long I'll be or what I'll do when I return, so in other words: I can't commit to anything and haven't made up my mind.' Emma lowered her head.

'And had *he* made up his mind?'

Emma nodded tentatively. 'He thinks it's worth another shot.'

Jen sighed. 'Oh dear. It took you so long to come to terms with leaving him and now he's back, willing and able to be in your life and you're virtually pushing him away?'

'Hey, I'm not pushing him, just telling him what my plans are. Anyway, he thinks I'm scared of the responsibility of Jackson.'

'Are you?'

Emma twisted her lips to the side. 'I started to wonder if I was on some deep level, that maybe, because of the hysterectomy, I wasn't supposed to be a mother. Part of me still feels like that, but when I think about Jackson, I'm not scared. I'm so fond of him, and I find myself thinking of ways I can help. The idea of him being in my life too doesn't trigger the apprehension I thought it might.'

Jen rested her elbows on the table and clasped her hands together. 'First of all, the cancer, the hysterectomy, it happened because it happened. It doesn't mean anything; it's not some cosmic sign that you're not cut out to be a mum, that's a load of absolute crap. Forget that now, you hear me?'

Emma shrugged.

'Secondly, despite the challenges of having Jackson in your life, I actually think you'd be in your element. James is just trying to protect himself by suggesting you're scared. He wants to give you a reason to back out now instead of once you're *in* the relationship. He doesn't want to be abandoned again.'

'Maybe I'm worried I *will* abandon him again. Either by choice or... the alternative.' Emma swallowed a lump in her throat.

'Hey, don't even think about that. You're well, and you're staying well, don't give any space in your mind for anything other than that.' Jen grasped Emma's hand and squeezed it.

'I know. I'm trying. And I'm feeling positive.' She smiled.

'Good girl. Anyway, so what led to having this talk, did he bring up the subject?'

Emma scratched her head and dropped her gaze from Jen's. 'Um, it sort of started with a kiss.'

'You've kissed again?'

Emma bit a tiny smile forming on her lips. 'Big time.'

'Hang on, shouldn't that have led to something else instead of what you just described?'

Emma's mind rewound back to the scene on the beach, and instead of stopping the kiss, she saw herself walking hand in hand with James back to her cottage. 'Exactly, which is why I stopped it.'

'Oh, Em.' Jen shook her head. 'Why the hesitation and indecision? Are you worried you will meet someone overseas and prefer them over James, and therefore have to let him down again?'

Emma thought about the possibility. A romance in France, an affair in Tuscany... it all sounded so movie-like, wonderful, and amazing, but not... real.

Emma breathed deeply. 'The thing is, I don't think I want to meet anyone else.'

'Emma. Did you tell him that?' She raised her eyebrows.

'No.' She breathed out with a whoosh. 'I only just realised it.'

'Oh Geez! Hun, you obviously still love him. You need to tell him.' Jen patted Emma's hand.

'But still, what if I say that and then get back from travelling and I've changed and we no longer suit each other or something?'

'What if, what if, what if... here's a what if: what if you come back and feel the same or even more in love with him and you've missed your chance? Ever think about that?'

Emma straightened up and adjusted her top as the strap dug into her shoulder. *That would be worse. Much worse.*

'Sometimes you've just got to make a decision and stick with it, trust it. Make it work.' Jen leaned closer. 'What does your heart tell you? Right now?'

'I think it—'

'No, not I think, I *feel*.'

'Okay, I *feel* like... that...' She buried her face in her hands as she leant her elbows on the mosaic table. 'That I can't imagine living my life without him. That I love him more than I've loved anyone. That I just want all the fears to go away so I can dive right in and be with him, make it up to him, love him.' Emma's hands moved about as she spoke, as though her feelings were overflowing and her words weren't enough to express them.

Jen stood and leaned her hands on the table, as though gearing up for an interrogation. 'Love like that doesn't come easily. If you're lucky enough to feel that and he feels the same, then oh my God — you need to get your arse back to Tarrin's Bay and tell him right this instant.' She slammed her fist on the table. 'Ow.' She rubbed her hand.

'You okay?'

'Of course I'm okay, but you won't be if you don't do as you're told.'

'I can't go now; it's your party. And anyway, he's spreading his grandma's ashes, so it's not the right time.'

Jen held out her hand. 'Then come inside, enjoy the party, and when it's all over, you will drive back and tell him that even though you're going overseas for a while, you're coming back to him, and you're one hundred percent committed to having a relationship with him. And Jackson. Got it?'

Emma took Jen's hand and stood. Was it really that simple? Could she make a promise like that when life seemed so uncertain right now? Emma looked into Jen's eyes, then down at the makeshift engagement ring on her finger — a promise, a sign of commitment. Jen and Sean didn't know what was around the corner either, no one really did, like James had said. But still, people made promises and made things work. They rode through life and navigated the speed bumps together. Was she prepared to finally turn that corner, say goodbye to the fears that had held her hostage in the past, and tell James she was ready and determined to start over with him, no matter what?

A warm, bubbly sensation rose up inside and solidified into crystal clear perfection.

There'd be no more dancing around the what ifs and the buts, it was time to grab the opportunity with both hands and tell him she was back for good, and that once she returned from her trip, she would never hide anything from him again, never run off, and never decide his future on his behalf.

Was she ready to do what her heart was screaming for her to do?

Yes. One hundred percent yes.

CHAPTER TWENTY

With each step up to the lookout, the sun sank lower, descending gradually behind the vast coastal landscape. Warm, earthy pink hues washed across the sky, as though it was blushing, knowing all eyes were witness to its beauty. James had one hand shading his eyes from the early evening glare of dusk, and the other holding Jackson's as his little feet walked three to his one, clutching Owly to his side.

His parents walked on ahead, his dad holding on tight to the wooden urn, his last chance to hold his beloved mother.

'Do you need a hand?' James asked André as his brother-in-law got out of the car he'd parked as high up as was allowed, so that Lizzie didn't have to walk uphill.

'Could you carry this?' André handed him a fold up chair, then helped his wife out of the car.

They all walked the few extra steps to the flat surface of the lookout that was cradled by a safety fence, and beside Tarrin, the earth man. James looked further up, towards the old lighthouse that perched higher on the headland. He liked to think that its light would be a reminder of Nonna Bella's light that she shone on the world, and he smiled, knowing that this was where she had accepted a marriage proposal.

James lowered his gaze and scanned the rough, rocky face of Tarrin, reminded of the weathered skin of his father as he'd sat at the pier fishing with him. How time flies. Life was ever changing, and yet people adapted as best they could.

Nonna Bella had lived a good ninety years. That was more than fifty years away for James if he lived that long. It was hard to imagine Jackson as a man in his fifties, but some day, he would be, and it was up to James now to ensure his son had the best upbringing he could offer. He hoped that there'd be some degree of independence in Jackson's future, for when he was no longer around for his son. A scary thought. Because, despite the adaptability and duration of human life, it was fleeting in the scheme of things.

James eyed the urn and a twinge of sadness rolled through him. He shouldn't be sad, his grandmother had lived a happy, long life, but he missed her. His life wasn't the same without her in it, and her absence was also a reminder of the cycle of life. Nothing lasted forever, except memories.

He unfolded the chair and Lizzie sat, her hands clasping her belly, her hair flapping in the breeze. She looked sad, like him, and the pallor of her skin was tainted with the grey shadow of exhaustion. André stood behind her with his hands on her shoulders.

'Bella would have loved this,' Marie said, looking out at the view, the ever-present ocean, the headlands and rocky cliffs curving around the beaches. The burgeoning sunset gave everything a magical glow, and like life, it would pass by and give way to something new.

With Lizzie settled and Jackson happily cooing to Owly, James approached his father. By simply standing beside him, he was expressing his support. He knew if he touched him, his dad may not be able to get through it without breaking down. Even though Martin often kept his emotions to himself, James knew his dad was finding this day a struggle.

Martin cleared his throat. 'I know we said everything at the funeral, but I'd like to say a few words to mark the occasion and say... say our final goodbyes.' He looked at the urn then out at the ocean, as though drawing strength from its beauty. 'My mother was an amazing woman. She and Dad gave us a good life, a good legacy, a heritage to be proud of.' Scattered clouds moved slowly behind him as the colours in the sky shifted and merged. 'It was here that her journey as a wife and mother began, and it is here that we now lay her to rest.' He rubbed the urn with his hand. 'Though I can never remember my mother resting. I'm sure she'll continue to scurry about keeping busy, keeping everyone in line, and making sure everyone is okay.' He offered a crooked smile. 'Mum,' he said, his voice softening, 'thank you. Thank you for...' his voice cracked and he lowered his head, rubbing his temples with one hand. Marie placed an arm around his back, rubbing it, whispering, 'It's okay, it's okay.'

'Thank you for everything,' he continued, his voice thick with both grief and gratitude. 'For my life, for our lives.' Martin glanced around at the small gathering. 'We'll never forget you.'

James' heart lurched as he watched his dad wipe a tear from his eye, something he rarely did. And he realised that once, his father had been a little boy like Jackson too, a boy who needed love and support and guidance to navigate through life. Everyone needed someone, no one could do it alone.

'Would you each like to say something you'll always remember about Bella before I...' He glanced at the urn.

'Of course. I'll start,' said James' mother. 'It sounds small, but I'll always remember the way she rubbed cream on her hands, as though it was an extremely important thing to do. She always carried that lavender hand cream around with her and

used it often. She had lovely hands, much better than mine!'
Marie chuckled, holding up a hand and rotating it. Martin took
hold of it and kissed it.

'Although I didn't know her as long as all of you, I'll
remember her positivity,' said André. 'She didn't seem to let the
little things get her down.'

Everyone nodded, and Lizzie patted André's hand as it
rested on her shoulder.

'And I'll,' Lizzie said, her voice shaky and bottom lip
trembling. 'I'll never forget her... her...' She sniffed, and André
leaned down and kissed her cheek. 'Her hugs.' She sobbed, then
took a breath and added, 'They were like magic. One hug and
the world was alright again, problems disappeared. I can't
believe I'll never,' she sobbed again, hanging her head, 'that I'll
never get to have one again.'

André crouched down beside his wife and wrapped his
arms tight around her, rubbing her arm and whispering
reassurances into her ear. James stepped to his sister and ran his
hand across the back of her head, the silkiness of her hair
cooling his hand. Jackson looked at Lizzie, then collected
pebbles and put them in a pile near his auntie's feet.

'There are so many great things to remember about Nonna,'
said James, 'but I've got to say it: she knew how to feed a hungry
herd of people.' He smiled. 'There was nothing quite like her
cooking. And just like the hugs,' he patted Lizzie's shoulder, 'I'm
sad that I'll never get to taste her food again.' He clamped his
lips together. 'But I'll always have the memories. And Mum,
your food is pretty fantastic too.' He glanced towards his mum,
who smiled a thank you. 'One more thing,' James said. 'She was
also a perfect parental role model. She raised a caring, dedicated
father,' he glanced at his dad, 'who married a caring, dedicated
mother. And each of you have helped me become the father I
am myself, and the father I hope to be.' He pressed his fingers to

his lips, kissed them, then held up his hand to the sky. '*Grazie,* Nonna Bella.'

'*Grazie,* Nonna Bella.' Everyone did the same. Five kisses made their way into the air, as though preparing it for what was to come.

James' father took the lid off the urn and handed it to Marie. With his hand over the opening, he lifted the urn over the railing and took a deep breath. Then, in time with his slow exhalation, Nonna Bella's ashes slowly released in a soft haze.

The delicate dust wafted through the air, riding on the wind that once caressed her face as she stood in this very spot, and once floated into her lungs as she breathed with life. A lightness enveloped James, like he too was floating. He watched the breeze carry his grandmother's spirit through the sky. She wasn't falling, she was soaring, circling around, up, and down, finally free, and forever a part of this magical place she loved.

Jackson gripped the bars of the safety fence, his eyes wide, Owly behind him at his feet. James touched a hand to the boy's head as he peered through the fence and down into the ocean. James returned his focus to the sky, the ocean, the vast beauty of the view, breathing in deeply and imprinting the moment in his mind, and his heart.

'Bell-la.'

James turned to the soft voice that came from his left. He froze, his eyes glued to Jackson.

'Bell-la.'

There was no mistaking it. His four-and-a-half-year-old, non-verbal, autistic son had spoken. And not just any word, the name of the grandmother whose ashes floated into the sunset this very moment.

James' mother gasped, and Lizzie stopped crying.

Everything went still.

'Jackson?' James whispered, a new, fresh, surreal sensation

growing inside him, his heart thumping, his head spinning. 'Bella,' he echoed. 'Bye, bye, Bella.'

'Bell-la.'

James' heart expanded with joy, and a smile mirroring the euphoria grew on his face. He dropped to his knees beside his son and flung his arms around the boy. Jackson stood there, unmoving, peering out into the horizon. 'You said Bella! You said her name! My beautiful, amazing, special boy.' Tears welled instantly, spilling out onto his cheeks and streaming onto Jackson's blue top. 'Oh, my boy. My boy,' he spoke as he cried, one hand gripping his son's back and the other caressing his mop of wavy hair in a lovingly fierce tangle. His chest throbbed and he stayed on his knees, embracing his son like he had just come to life. James didn't know if Jackson would ever speak like that again, but it didn't matter. He didn't care if he never said another word again for the rest of his life. He would never forget the pure, utter beauty of what he'd just heard. And now, he knew without a doubt that his son, his unique gift of a son, was there in that body; a living, breathing reminder that not everything needed to be heard or seen to be present. Jackson probably knew more than he let on, and was perhaps tuned into things others didn't even notice, and, for some unknown reason, had chosen this moment to show his father that everything would be okay.

As James held on tight to his son, Jackson remained still, letting his father enjoy this moment. A hand touched his back, and without looking he knew it was his own father. Three generations of men, united together in a moment of purity and simplicity beyond anything he'd experienced. And in that moment, as every emotion, every fear, every bit of grief that he'd bottled up poured out, he found himself smiling. It was only a simple word, a name, from the mouth of a child. But its significance was profound. And there was only one word to describe it: a miracle.

As the light dimmed, James wiped at his eyes with a tissue his mother had handed him. He picked up Owly and gave it to Jackson, who until then had continued to be hypnotised by the view. Everyone's eyes were red, everyone's except Jackson's. 'C'mon, Jax, time to go have some special dinner.' He patted his back. James turned around to find his mother with arms outstretched, and he let her scoop him up into a motherly hug. Martin couldn't take his eyes off Jackson, and although he'd just farewelled his mother, his face appeared brighter than before.

Lizzie blew her nose and shoved the tissue into the pocket of her cardigan, then nodded to André that it was time to help her get back to the car. He hooked his arm under hers and she rose, then Lizzie gasped as water gushed between her legs. 'Oh no. Oh no, André,' her voice shook, then her head dropped backwards and she wilted onto the chair.

'Lizzie?' André had caught her before she fell, and James rushed to his sister's side. 'Lizzie?' He patted her cheeks, but her mouth hung open and her eyes had rolled back.

'What's happening? Lizzie, sweetheart!' Marie dropped to her knees in front of her daughter, her hands on Lizzie's thighs. 'She's unconscious! Call an ambulance, quick!'

Adrenaline surged through James' blood and he punched in an emergency call on his phone.

His dad put down the urn and slid an arm under Lizzie's legs. 'Let's get her to the car.' André lifted his wife under the shoulders, Martin her legs, and Marie helping support her back.

'Here, Mum, you give the details, I've got her.' James handed the phone to his mum as the operator answered, then helped carry his sister to the backseat of the car where they laid her down. Martin took off his jacket and folded it under her head.

'Lizzie, wake up!' André touched and kissed her face repeatedly.

James put two fingers against her neck. He held his breath till he felt the light throbbing, weak but definite. He'd seen people on TV shows rub the chest on top of the sternum, so he made a fist and rubbed at it with his knuckles. 'C'mon, Lizzie, c'mon.'

Her eyes flickered and opened.

'Oh, thank God, Lizzie?' he asked.

She opened her mouth but no words came out. Her eyes appeared drowsy but aware. André kept kissing and fussing over her.

'Are you in any pain, sweetheart? They want to know.' Marie asked, one ear against the phone.

'Head,' Lizzie managed. 'Head hurts. And everything's blurry, can't focus.'

'She has a sore head and blurred vision,' Marie said. 'No, she didn't bump it, her waters just broke and she fainted... Yes, high blood pressure. The doctor had been talking to her about pre-eclampsia.' James listened to the one-sided conversation. 'André, make sure she's only semi-reclined. Is there something else to raise her body up a bit?'

Martin grabbed a towel from the boot and handed it to André. André manoeuvred onto the backseat into a kneeling position, placed the folded towel on his lap, then adjusted Lizzie to lie back onto him.

'Don't worry, sweetheart, ambulance isn't too far away,' Marie said, reassuring not only Lizzie but everyone else.

'André,' Lizzie whispered, her chin trembling. 'It's too early, it's too soon.' She tried to sob but didn't appear to have the energy.

'It's okay, the doctors will know what to do. You just take it easy, *ma cherie*.'

She grasped his hand. 'I don't feel good.' Her hand shook, as did her voice. James took off her shoes and tried to make her more comfortable. Martin found another towel and James put it between her legs just in case. He'd seen Jackson's birth and knew how much blood was involved.

'Honey,' Lizzie spoke again, looking directly into her husband's eyes. 'Make sure they save the baby. If you have to choose...' she sucked in a sharp breath, 'please — the baby.'

André's face paled and James' stomach churned. 'No, no, *ma cherie*, you're going to be okay, okay?'

'Promise me,' she urged. 'We tried for *so* long to have this baby. Promise me, baby first.' The eerie tone of his sister's voice pinched his chest.

No. No, Lizzie.

Lizzie didn't look away from her husband. She gripped his hand. André caressed her face and nodded as a tear dropped off his cheek. 'I promise.'

With his words, Lizzie's eyes rolled backwards again and André sobbed into her hair and pleaded for her to wake up.

CHAPTER TWENTY-ONE

Emma parked her car behind the cottage and locked the door with a beep. As soon as she was inside she planned to text James, both to offer her condolences on his grandmother and say that she hoped all went okay, and also to ask if they could talk before he left in the morning. But when she made her way around the side of the cottage towards the front door, she glanced up to the right. She'd picked up some DVD's for her dad before arriving at Jen's party and could probably drop them off now. She walked along the path as it gradually inclined, and glanced out at the beautiful warm pink of the sky. Maybe she should go up to the lookout, snap a photo, then use it as inspiration for a drawing.

She changed direction and headed up the hill towards Tarrin. As she neared, she stopped for a moment. *Oh, of course, James and his family must be spreading the ashes.* She thought they'd be finished by now as Jackson would surely need dinner soon, but she could see his mother and father, and someone's car, and... James was kneeling on the ground, leaning into the car. Jackson was beside Marie as she held onto his hand, but where were Lizzie and André?

When she came closer and saw the looks of despair on James' parents' faces, she knew something was wrong. They weren't just emotional from the events of the day, something had happened.

A siren blared in the distance and grew louder, and Emma turned as an ambulance bumped along the gravel road into the holiday park and headed towards her.

Oh no.

She ran up the hill towards James and arrived just before the ambulance. 'What's happened?'

James' face was red and lined with worry. 'Lizzie's water broke and she keeps passing out.'

'Oh God, is there anything I can do?'

He shook his head, then moved out of the way when an ambulance officer approached and took his place, the other one approaching the other side of the car where André was. Marie hung up the phone and filled them in on the situation. It didn't sound good. Emma's heart pounded and ached.

As the ambos worked quickly, Emma looked at Jackson, seemingly oblivious to the trauma unfolding. He seemed quite placid and zoned out, one hand clutching Owly and the other in his grandma's hand.

'Love, we should head down to our car so we can follow the ambulance to the hospital,' said Martin to Marie, clutching a wooden urn.

'I'll drive André in his car,' said James. 'Oh, dammit, I can't.' He ran his hand through his hair. 'Jackson.'

'Just bring him, he can come with us and we'll grab his booster seat when we get to the car park,' Martin said.

James shook his head. 'He's okay now but it'll be a nightmare at the hospital, he won't cope there.'

'Do you want me to come and I'll wait in the car with Jackson?' suggested Emma.

James looked her way. 'But we could be a while. And he needs dinner, he'll get tired too, and then he'll... oh God, this can't be happening.' He looked at his son, at Lizzie, and down towards the cabins.

'Then I'll look after him. Here.' Emma touched his arm. 'He'll be okay, don't you worry.'

'Emma, you are a lifesaver,' said Marie. 'C'mon, Martin, let's go so we can get there as soon as possible.' She let go of Jackson's hand and gave him a gentle nudge in Emma's direction, 'There you go, Emma will take care of you, darling.'

'Hey there, Jackson.' Emma crouched to his level. 'Hello Owly. Are you going to have some dinner too?' She patted the toy's head and smiled, though her expression was totally forced.

'Ooo,' Jackson cooed.

'But his dinner, he needs...' James said.

'No gluten, no dairy, I remember.'

'And he'll need a bath or he won't calm down before bed,' James said, as the ambulance officers loaded Lizzie into the vehicle and Martin and Marie scurried down the hill. 'Oh, you'll need keys.' He patted his pockets.

'It's okay, I have keys to all the cabins,' Emma replied. 'You keep yours so you can get back inside in case it's late.'

He nodded. 'And at bedtime, his favourite book is on the bedside table. Sometimes I have to read it twice. And leave the hallway light on, and—'

'James.' Emma stepped close to him and took a firm hold of both of his hands. She looked him in the eye with calm, capable confidence. 'I've got this.'

Emma distracted Jackson from the fact that all his family were leaving by playing a game with Owly as she walked with him down the hill. She tossed Owly into the air, he landed on the ground a little way ahead, then she counted to three and encouraged Jackson to run towards him and try to be the first one to rescue him. Gradually they made their way down the hill, and Emma noticed her mother hurrying towards her.

'What happened?' she asked. 'I saw the ambulance.'

Emma explained the dire situation and how she was looking after Jackson for the night.

'Do you want to bring him to our place so I can help, would he be okay with that?'

'Thanks Mum, but I think he's probably better off in familiar surroundings.'

'Okay, but call if you have any trouble.'

'I will.'

'I'll let you get him settled then. Gosh, I hope that poor lass will be okay.' She touched her hand to her forehead.

Dread gnawed at Emma's stomach. 'I hope so too, I really hope so.'

Emma ducked into the reception office to pick up the keys to James' cabin. She remembered Amelia's text message she'd received this morning, thanking Emma for the drawing.

> I love it! You are very talented, Emma. I'll cherish it forever. xx

And speak of the devil, as she walked along the pathway towards the cabin, she noticed Amelia sitting on a park bench facing the ocean, having what looked like a deep conversation with someone. Someone who looked slightly more stylish than when he was wearing his tradie getup. Bob. Was there anything going on between them? If so, it must have just been kickstarted because he (and she) had not said anything on Friday. Emma managed a brief smile. The two would get along well, she didn't know why she hadn't suggested they get to know each other earlier.

As sunset darkened, she entered James' cabin with Jackson and turned on the lights. Jackson withdrew his Sound Machine from his pocket and pressed the bouncy spring sound, then dashed to the end of the hallway, banged his palm on the wall, then ran to the other end and banged his palm near the door, then repeated his little routine a few times. It gave her a few moments to get her bearings and think what she needed to do.

Dinner, bath, reading, bedtime. Right, she could do this. No worries.

And as for her talk with James, she would probably have to come visit him in Welston sometime. Right now Lizzie was the priority, and her realisation at Jen's party and the subsequent urgent desire to tell him would have to wait. Still, there was no guarantee he'd believe her declaration or be willing to risk his heart on her again, but she knew she couldn't miss her chance to make things right with him once and for all.

As for tonight, she had to make things right for Jackson.

Emma opened the fridge. A couple of uncooked lamb cutlets sat in a plastic container. She presumed James had defrosted them overnight for Jackson's dinner, so she took them out.

Now, what to have with them?

There was another container of some rice dish, but she wasn't sure if it was free of the things he couldn't eat. On the counter there was fruit, and a paper bag with potatoes. Potatoes, they would surely be acceptable to Jackson?

Emma turned on the grill to heat it up for the cutlets, then peeled a potato and cut it into thin chips. She poured some olive oil into a frypan and when it was hot, slid the chips into the pan. They sizzled, and Jackson stopped his running back and forth and came over to the pan.

'Ooh, careful sweetie. Hot!'

He pressed his Sound Machine and a laughter sound blurted out. Emma laughed to match and the boy gave a small smile then ran back to the wall and banged on it. It would probably have little four-year-old hand marks dented into the plaster by the time they left tomorrow, but it didn't matter.

As the chips cooked she put the cutlets in the grill, then heated up the rice dish in the fridge for herself. Hopefully James wouldn't mind.

When the food was ready she put it on a plate. 'Here you go, Jackson!' She patted the table next to his meal. Jackson didn't respond at first so Emma sat and ate a mouthful of hers. 'Mmm, yum!'

Jackson rubbed his nose and came over, propping his hands on the table's edge. He looked at his plate, then at Emma's.

'That's for Jackson. Yum, yum!' She patted the chair and he climbed up and picked up a cutlet and bit into it.

Phew. Emma would have hated it if he wouldn't eat anything she cooked. She ate quickly, wanting to make sure she was completely ready to handle any sudden change in behaviour, as sometimes occurred with children on the spectrum.

Emma's phone beeped and she took it from her pocket. A text from James:

Lizzie is in theatre, we don't know much, just have to wait. Is Jackson ok?

Emma took a deep breath. Not long ago the woman was saying goodbye to her grandmother and now she was having surgery. She closed her eyes and made a wish that Lizzie, and the baby, would be alright. Then she texted James back:

Jackson is great, eating dinner now. Don't worry about a thing, I will stay as long as needed. Sending positive thoughts to Lizzie and all of you. Em.

Although it seemed strange to be sending a message like that and signing off with 'Em' after their argument last night, it also felt good, even though a disaster was unfolding. Because it at least shone a light on what was really important. And it only reinforced her decision to try her best to convince him she was ready to make a commitment. Now, more than ever, she wanted to be there for him.

Another text came in:

Thanks Emma. Let me know if there are any problems.

She replied:

There won't be. You be with your family and I'll see you whenever you get back.

Jackson finished his meal and jumped off the chair, making his way to the DVD player. He put a disc in and Emma smiled at his independence. As The Wiggles danced and sang, Jackson moved about and flapped his hands. When a song ended and they clapped, Jackson pressed his Sound Machine. Correction, he jabbed at it. He made a high-pitched squeal as he continued to jab it with his finger.

Uh-oh. Emma walked over to him and looked at the machine. She pressed a button but no sound came out. Jackson screamed and Emma scrunched her face instinctively. The boy had a set of lungs on him.

'It's okay, Jackson, let me look at it.' She managed to pry it from his grasp. It probably needed new batteries. Hopefully it wasn't a problem with the actual device. She frowned. The red plastic box needed a screwdriver to open the battery compartment, and she knew for sure that the cabins didn't have any, unless James was in the habit of bringing them with him.

Emma opened the cutlery drawer to see if there was anything she could substitute, while Jackson's face turned red and he cried. The knives were too big for the tiny screw, and so were her fingernails.

Damn it. She realised also that owing to the small size of the machine it probably had those little round batteries instead of AAA batteries. Wonderful. So getting the compartment open was only half the battle. She knew there weren't any of those batteries here, and she had no idea if there were any in the cottage. She'd have to look, as Jackson would probably be lost without his Sound Machine and she didn't like her chances of getting him to go to sleep when he was this wound up.

She grabbed her bag, picked up Owly and gave it to Jackson (who threw the toy on the ground and tried to reach for the Sound Machine), then picked up the owl and put it in her bag. 'C'mon, Jackson, let's get the Sound Machine fixed.' She held out her hand, but he wouldn't grab it. She took out her keys and jiggled them like she was about to leave, hoping he'd follow her. 'Time to go! Let's get new batteries and fix the sounds, hey?'

He rushed to her side, still in tears, arms reaching for the device. Emma handed it to him and he jabbed at it. She turned it over and pointed to the compartment. 'See? Needs new batteries to make it work. We can get some from my place.' She held out her hand, again to no avail, so in one quick swoop she put her hands under his arms and scooped him up. Her back spasmed a little but she grunted and put up with it. She needed to get out the door and find new batteries ASAP. It was only when she was out of the cabin and had locked the door when she realised maybe she should have called her mum and asked her to bring some over, but either way Jackson would still cry. And besides, barely an hour into babysitting duties and she's calling her mum for help? No, she wanted to take charge and handle it her own way.

With Jackson on her hip she walked as fast as she could along the pathway until she reached her cottage. Jackson squirmed a little, his body tense and stiff, but she managed to keep hold of him until they were inside the house. He immediately ran around looking at every corner and crevice, every room, every cupboard, still wailing, while Emma rummaged through drawers and boxes. She found a screwdriver and opened the compartment. Yep, just as she'd thought. Two tiny round batteries were required. She looked around but it was no use. Time to go to her parents place.

'Time to go again, Jackson. Up the hill, so we can find batteries, okay?' She pointed to the machine and showed him how she'd opened the compartment so he (hopefully) knew she was trying to fix it. His forehead furrowed and lips scrunched up as he noticed the machine looked different, as though it had been operated on and was displaying its internal organs. She scooped him up again, tightened her core to avoid a back spasm, then locked up and made her way up the hill. Jackson's cries had settled somewhat but he still repeated a high-pitched moan. Her mother opened the door before she got there.

'I thought I heard something going on, what's happened to Jackson?' Barbara asked.

'His Sound Machine is out of batteries, please tell me you have those little round ones here?' Emma said.

Please, please.

'Oh dear, come on in. Hey there little fella.' Barbara moved aside for them to enter. 'I'll have to have a look, hang on.'

Emma went inside and put Jackson down. He ran to the back of the room and huddled in the corner, turning his face to the wall and fiddling with the cord on the vertical blinds. Then he let out a scream.

'What's the matter, mate?' her dad asked, as he sat watching a movie.

'Dad, maybe press pause on that in case it's too loud for him.'

He did as she said, and the movie sounds were replaced by clattering and clashing of items in drawers as Barbara searched.

'Do you know where the batteries are, Don?' Barbara asked in a loud voice.

'Aren't they on top of the fridge?' he replied. 'Not that I can reach them, but I think I put some up there a while back. Shame the machine can't run on the kid's lung power.'

'Dad, this is no time for jokes,' Emma said.

'Just trying to make light of the situation.'

She wasn't in the mood for his 'sense of humour'. Emma went to Jackson and placed a calming hand on his back. 'It's okay, it's okay.' She took Owly from her bag and hugged it to her chest. 'Look, Owly needs a hug. Can you give Owly a hug too?'

Jackson looked at the toy and snatched it from her, pulling it close.

'That's better.'

'Found some!' Barbara exclaimed.

Hallelujah.

She came over and handed them to Emma, and she popped them in and secured the screws. Showtime. Emma hoped like hell it would work. She pressed the applause button that had a small symbol of a hand on it, and exhaled in relief as the sound of clapping filled the room.

'Hey, I need one of those,' said her father. 'I can press it when I need your attention, Barb.' He chuckled.

'Does it have a "not now I'm busy" button, Em?' her mother asked.

Emma smiled. She looked at Jackson and gave him the machine. He had dropped Owly and now his eyes were fixed on the red device. He pressed the laughter button, then squealed, this time in a happy way.

'All fixed! Yay!' Emma clapped and picked up Owly.

Jackson then went through what seemed like every sound on the machine, testing if they worked. Applause, laughing, bouncy spring, cash register ka-ching, game show sounds, drum roll, wolf-whistle, big idea ping. Emma watched him and noticed he avoided a few buttons; one had a picture of a face with something coming out of the mouth. A burp, just lovely. No wonder he didn't want to press that one. And a screaming face, and a broken wine glass. But all the others he kept pressing, laughing and squealing as a cacophony of random sounds filled the room, and both Emma and Barbara ended up in fits of laughter.

'Okay, now I will definitely have to get one for myself if it keeps my two favourite ladies so happy,' said Don.

'I'll ask James where he got it,' Emma said, then remembered they had still not yet resolved their situation, and of course, where he purchased Jackson's Sound Machine would be the last thing on his mind right now.

She wondered how Lizzie was and if her baby had been delivered yet. An emergency caesarean wouldn't take as long as other surgeries. But as for Lizzie, she had no idea what sort of treatment was needed for her.

'Any word yet?' Barbara asked, as though reading her mind.

Emma shook her head. 'Only that she's in theatre.'

'Let me know when you hear.'

'I will.'

'Can I put my movie back on now?' Don asked.

'Don, I think Jackson is the priority right now,' said his wife.

'It's okay, I'll take him back now and get him ready for bed. Thanks for the batteries, you saved the day, Mum.' Emma hugged her mother.

'I was the one who knew they were on top of the fridge,' said Don.

Emma rolled her eyes, but went to her dad and gave him a hug and a kiss. 'Thanks, Dad. You saved the day too.'

'Just call me SuperDad.' He pointed his good fist in the air like he was flying, and Emma realised what a good sign it was that her dad's sense of humour was strong. He may be a bit too honest and direct sometimes, but if he had a smile on his face, the other stuff didn't matter. He seemed to be coming to terms with his situation more, and for that she was glad.

'C'mon Jackson, time to put Owly to bed?' She put her hands together and against the side of her face, thinking it was probably a good way to show him that it was bedtime.

Instead of going towards her, he ran to every room in the house and pressed the bouncy spring sound in each one. Emma decided to wait. Eventually he came to the front door and grunted and pointed.

Thankfully, she didn't have to carry him back, he held her hand as they walked, Jackson's eyes wide and looking around as though he had never walked at night before.

When they got inside she turned on the bath taps, and when she came out Jackson had put Owly in his bed, patting him. Her heart softened and an emotion she wasn't prepared for bubbled up. It was indescribable, but she knew that if she never saw this boy again, it would leave a huge hole in her heart. And the same went for the boy's father.

She checked her phone to make sure she hadn't missed any calls or texts during the screaming episode, but there was nothing. She hoped everything was okay.

As the bath filled with water she wondered...

How deep should a four-year-old's bath be?

It probably wasn't that important, but it struck her how many little things parents had to think about each day. Somehow they learned how much water to put in the bath, and what types of batteries to leave in the house for electronic toy emergencies. James knew all these things, and no doubt many more. He did everything for his child, he became the father he always wanted to be, and more. Emma wondered if he knew how amazing he was. He, too, was a SuperDad.

When she turned the taps off and was about to get Jackson, he beat her to it and came into the bathroom. He must have recognised the sound abating and knew it was time. He took off his shoes and to Emma's surprise, jumped in the sand tray. Sand sprayed outwards onto the floor and he laughed. He stepped out and approached the bath and peered in, and seemingly satisfied with how it looked, pulled his top over his head and took off all his clothes. Emma chuckled. The kid could practically babysit himself.

She hoped the temperature was okay as he climbed in, but he seemed fine with it. She plonked a few bath toys in and he played with them in his own little way, making random sounds as though having his own conversation with them. Emma sat on the bathroom mat and found herself humming a tune of *Twinkle Twinkle Little Star*.

As he played she typed a message to Jen on her phone, filling her in on what had happened, otherwise she'd probably call tomorrow and ask how James had reacted to her declaration. She checked a few other messages then put the phone in her pocket. Worried that Jackson would end up looking like a prune if she left him in there too long she held up a towel.

'Time to get dry,' she said, rubbing her arms with the towel to demonstrate. She wondered if James had flash cards that he used, but she didn't want to leave Jackson alone to look for them. He was probably old enough to stay in the bath himself, but she wasn't sure what his level of independence was in this case.

Jackson stood abruptly and climbed out, water dripping from his wavy hair all over his face and onto the bath mat. She enveloped him in the towel and rubbed his skin as dry as possible. Then she realised she didn't have any pyjamas ready for him.

She pulled the plug from the bath, then, keeping the towel around his shoulders, ushered him to his bedroom. 'Now, where are Jackson's pyjamas?'

Jackson hopped on the bed and jumped up and down, his towel flapping like a cape and poor Owly being flung up and down without any choice in the matter.

She opened the drawer of the wardrobe and found a few items folded up, including cotton pyjamas with spaceships on them. She picked them up and also some underwear.

Oh, hang on. Is he toilet trained at night?

She didn't want to text James to ask. In another drawer there were a few pairs of disposable pull-up pants, so maybe he wore them at night. Or maybe they were for long car trips or emergencies.

Emma held up one pair of the pants and one pair of undies towards Jackson. 'Which one, Jackson?' He ignored her question so she went closer and repeated herself, holding both up against him.

He grabbed the pull-ups and stepped into them.

Once he was dressed, Jackson raced into the bathroom again and shut the door. Emma waited near the door. The toilet flushed and she smiled. This boy may have his challenges but James was doing a phenomenal job teaching him how to look after himself. Emma waited a little then peered into the bathroom to find the boy brushing his teeth. Once he'd arranged everything back in its correct position and adjusted the handtowel after using it, he raced into the bedroom and Emma followed. Jackson grabbed Owly then hopped under the covers as Emma held them up for him.

'Time for your bedtime story, hey?' She picked up the book on the bedside table; it was about a monkey's trip to space. But as soon as she opened it and started reading, Jackson pushed the pages closed and grunted. She tried to open it and read again but he did the same, then threw off the blankets and dashed out of the room and into his father's.

Jackson looked around the room, under the bed, and in the wardrobe, his body stiffening and hands flapping.

'Oh, Jackson, Daddy's not here right now. He had to help Auntie Lizzie. I'll read to you tonight and then Dad can read tomorrow.'

He hopped on his dad's bed and stamped his feet, making urgent sounds. Emma approached and gestured to Owly. 'Shall we put Owly to bed?'

He twisted his body away from her and huffed.

Okay, maybe not.

Emma hoped his unhappiness at his father not being here wouldn't escalate into the domain of Flat Battery In Sound Machine status. Instead of pushing him further she tried to remain calm, and sat on James' bed. As Jackson stomped around, Emma read from the book and when he tried to close it she moved it away from his grasp and continued reading. When she got to the bit that mentioned a loud clap, surprisingly, Jackson made a loud clap sound with his hands. Emma glanced his way and smiled, then clapped as well. She kept reading and when the monkey gasped, Jackson did too.

Okay, now we're getting somewhere. Comfort in familiarity and repetition.

As she neared the end of the book, Jackson sat next to her and listened, and she was overcome with a sense of accomplishment. Not only that, she felt privileged to have this experience; caring for Jackson for the night, however unprepared she'd been. The emptiness inside her didn't feel so dark and lonely anymore.

The book ended and she closed it, and now, in contrast to his earlier actions, he forced it back open.

'Again?' she asked. She started all over again.

On the third reading, Jackson lay down on the queen-sized bed as he listened. Emma didn't want to encourage him back to his own bed in case it upset him again. Whatever worked in the moment, she'd keep doing.

On the fourth reading (so much for only needing to read it twice!), she glanced down at Jackson. His eyes were closed and his chest rose slowly and rhythmically. Success.

She read till the end of the book anyway, just in case, then quietly closed the book and put it on the bedside table where James had a few other books. She picked them up out of curiosity and her heart ached for James, to tell him how she really felt and to tell him he didn't have to do this alone.

Raising the Autistic Child

Single Parenting the Special Needs Child

Dietary Approaches to Autism

The man's head must be overflowing with information, and probably had been since Jackson was born. She flipped through the diet book and found it fascinating, and after about fifteen minutes decided to try and carry Jackson into his own bed.

She gently eased her arms underneath him, careful to keep Owly on his chest. Jackson didn't rouse, he was probably exhausted after the stress of the day and being dragged to two new houses in the space of half an hour. She activated her core like she'd learned in yoga class to avoid hurting her back, and walked as slowly as possible to Jackson's room, then placed him under the covers.

Success again.

She tucked Owly into the crook of his arm and adjusted the blankets, switched off the lamp, then she couldn't help herself. She gave the boy a light kiss on his forehead.

She crept out of the room, hoping he wouldn't wake suddenly and freak out.

With the hallway light on and Jackson's door open a crack, Emma went to the bathroom to tidy up after Jackson's bath and wondered if she should have a shower. She could be done in a few minutes. *Nah,* she thought. If he woke and came in, he'd probably get the shock of his life seeing a naked woman in the shower. Emma freshened up instead with a face cloth and some soap, then took off her shirt, leaving her bra and spaghetti-strap singlet on with her linen trousers. She went out to the living room and switched on the outdoor light in readiness for James, then made sure the door was locked and everything else turned off.

She went back to James' bedroom and kicked off her shoes, sat on the bed. It felt strange to be in here, even though it wasn't his house. It was still James' domain, and she could sense his presence and familiar scent.

There was a charging dock on the bedside table so she placed her phone into it and put a playlist of relaxing, cruisy songs on a loop, though at a low volume. She needed to charge it anyway and keep it on in case James needed to reach her.

Checking the time, Emma thought she might as well relax while she had the chance in case Jackson woke or there was news from James, so she leaned back into the pillows and opened the book, *Raising the Autistic Child.*

As she devoured the information, a fair bit of which she knew from her teaching training and experience in special needs, she thought about James' opportunity to go to Queensland and be closer to his family support network.

If she was ready and willing to be with him when she got back from her travels and he was ready and willing to have her, would she move to Queensland? Or would James want to stay here, especially if he knew she'd be sticking around?

She pondered different scenarios like a *Choose Your Own Adventure* book as they played out in her mind. Yes, there was still uncertainty in her future, but in each scenario one thing was the same: She knew now that she was prepared to do anything and go anywhere to be with James. And as soon as it was appropriate, she would tell him.

CHAPTER TWENTY-TWO

I f it weren't for Jackson, James would have stayed all night at the hospital. But he needed to get back and make sure his son was okay, then get some sleep so he could head back to the hospital with at least some restored energy. Although he hated asking for help, he hoped Emma might be willing to help out with Jackson again, considering it was her day off on Monday. But he'd have to check out of the cabins, they all would, before the next load of guests arrived. James would need to pack everyone's stuff and do it on their behalf as soon as he woke. He thought about all the practicalities, as his mind was trained to do, while he drove back to Tarrin's Bay, the roads mostly deserted this late at night. Thinking of the practicalities also helped him handle the emotional upheaval, buffered it somewhat.

When he parked at the holiday park's car park, he stopped for a moment and rested his head on the steering wheel. Images of Lizzie's seizure gripped him with pain. Her body tensing and convulsing as they wheeled her from the emergency ward into the operating theatre, needing to deliver the baby as soon as possible. Then came the frustration at not knowing how she was doing, if she was okay, and having to wait outside for news from the doctors. And then, the unbearable anticipation of watching one of them walk towards them later on.

James lifted his head and took a deep breath. There was nothing more he could do, he needed to get inside and deal with things tomorrow.

He walked around the grounds to cabin number one, his keys at the ready. He'd thought of texting Emma to let her know and to tell her he was on his way back, but wasn't sure if she had maybe dozed off on the couch or if her phone sound would wake Jackson.

The outdoor light was on, and it gave him slight relief, a reminder that she had been there for him tonight and that his son was probably perfectly fine.

He unlocked the door quietly and walked inside, switching off the outdoor light and locking the door. The living room was empty. He went straight to Jackson's room and peered through the slightly open door. Light from the hallway speared through and landed on Jackson as he lay sleeping in bed, Owly tucked up by his side, his space pyjamas on. More relief relaxed his shoulders.

She'd done it. She'd looked after him successfully and he was safely nestled in his bed. James didn't know what he would have done if Emma hadn't been there tonight. Despite their argument and her indecisiveness, she had a heart of gold. Right now, all that other stuff didn't matter. Life was messy, emotions were volatile, love was unpredictable and uncertain. Tonight showed him what was most important, what really mattered. He wanted to take all the mess and chaos and pain from their past and scrunch it up like a piece of paper into a crumpled ball, then toss it into the ocean to wither away and lose itself in the vast expanse of sea.

He wanted to kiss Jackson and hold him tight, feel his son

breathing and warm in his embrace, but restrained himself. He didn't want to risk waking him, he could do that in the morning. He closed the door until it was almost shut, then tiptoed to his bedroom, the melody of a love song emanating through the wide open door. The lamp was on. He half expected Emma to be sitting up reading, waiting for him, but when he walked into the room he stopped. She was lying on her back, fast asleep, a book splayed open on her chest. A brief smile tugged at his lips, despite the trauma from the night still hanging over him like a shadow.

He closed the door behind him, kicked off his shoes, and approached the bed. His heart warmed when he noticed the book she'd been reading: *Raising the Autistic Child.*

Had she simply been passing time or was she really interested in learning more about the topic? He carefully picked up the book and placed it on the bedside table, surprised that Jackson's favourite bedtime story was also there. He wondered if his son had been reluctant to go to sleep in his own bed without him there. Maybe she had read to him in here so he felt like he was still around. Whatever she'd done tonight, it had worked.

James placed his phone on the table also, leaving it on, and undid his belt. He considered waking Emma but she looked so beautiful he didn't want to disturb her, so he simply slid under the sheets beside her and revelled in the feeling of finally taking the weight off his body.

He switched off the bedside lamp.

Emma stirred beside him, a deep breath filling her lungs. She rolled sideways towards him and her forehead bumped his.

'Huh?' she mumbled, then shot up. 'James!'

'Shh, it's okay.' He patted her arm.

'What happened? Is Lizzie okay? And the baby?' The dim moonlight curved around her face, highlighting her soft features and her concern.

'She's alive. She got worse when she arrived at hospital but they said the condition usually resolves after delivery, so they'll have a better idea tomorrow how she's faring. But they're confident she'll recover fully.'

'Oh, James!' Emma covered her heart with her hand, then placed it on his hand. 'I'm so relieved, I've been worried all night.' She exhaled loudly. 'And the baby?'

James recalled the tiny human he'd seen briefly after they stabilised her. 'A girl. Don't know her name yet, André is waiting for Lizzie to wake up. She's premmie of course, so is in the NICU. Doctors and nurses have filled us in on the potential complications, but also told us that many born this early still do as well as they possibly can. She'll be in there for quite a while, I'm guessing.'

Emma shook her head. 'Wow, all this in one night. How are your family holding up? How are *you* holding up? Especially after today being... an important occasion.'

'André was a wreck, understandably. He was dreading having to make an impossible choice, as Lizzie had...' the words caught in his throat and he covered his mouth. 'Lizzie said,' he closed his eyes, 'to save the baby instead of her if it came down to that.' Unbearable pain of an alternate reality swept him away, taking him to a place he didn't want to go. He rubbed at his temples with his thumb and fingers, pushing what *could* have been back down into the abyss of where it belonged.

A soft hand warmed his cheek. Emma stroked his skin with her thumb, backwards and forwards, easing his turmoil.

'They're all staying there the night. I wanted to get back to Jackson. And you. And we need to check out tomorrow, I'll have to sort all that out and pack things up and—'

'Hey, it's okay. I'll help. And you can put any of your family's things in my cottage if you can't fit everything in the one car. And I'll take care of Jackson again all day if you need me to. He's an amazing little boy.'

Emma's helpful nature sprung to action, and James wanted to wrap her in his arms and shower her with love. 'Emma, thank you.' He brought his own hand to her face, then ran it down her neck and shoulder, encouraging her to lie back down by his side. 'I don't know what I would have done without you tonight.'

Or ever.

She rested her hand under her cheek as she lay on her side. 'I just did what needed to be done. I wished I could have done more.'

'You did more than enough. You're an angel.'

He looked deep into her eyes. The pain and trauma he'd seen before was gone. There was now only peace, acceptance, and love. 'Don't go. Stay here tonight, with me?' he spoke softly, running his hand slowly up and down her bare arm in time with the slow, sexy rhythm of the music.

Her gaze moved to the door. 'Will that be weird for Jackson?'

'He rarely comes into my room anymore. And in the morning he's been getting himself up and making his own breakfast.' James smiled. 'Anyway, after tonight, I'm sure he thinks you're part of the family.'

Emma smiled. 'Okay. I'll stay.'

When his fingers reached the end of her arm, he took hold of her hand and threaded his fingers with hers.

'James. About last night,' she said. 'I'm sorry. I've had time to think. I don't want to muck you around anymore, I just want...' she breathed, 'I just want...' She released her hand from his and brought it to his chest, running it up and over his shoulder then around his back, pulling him closer to her. 'I—'

James put a finger to her lips. 'Shh. Let's talk about it tomorrow.' He kissed her forehead. 'Right now, I just want to be with you. In this moment. No past, no future, just now.' He put his hand around her back too, rubbing it up and down.

'I want that too,' she whispered.

James moved closer to her, his lips parting in readiness for hers. He kissed her with a raw, pure need, but not with the same passionate intensity of last night. This time it was different. There was no rush, no suddenness, only a simple, beautiful, natural progression from one moment in time to the next. Her mouth danced with his, soft and warm and magical, and heat crawled throughout his body and heightened his senses.

Her hands moved under his top, pulling and lifting. He raised his arms and let her take the shirt off his back. She ran her hand down his spine, then back up again, her fingers reaching the back of his neck and tangling themselves in his hair.

He deepened his kiss, lifted his body, rolling her onto her back. His hands cradling her face, he moved his lips to her neck, trailing kisses down the firm, corded muscles to her collarbone. He slipped a finger under her singlet strap and moved it aside, kissing the spot where it had been, then traced the neckline of her singlet with his lips, exploring her curves as her chest rose high with a breath. James wriggled himself lower, lifting the hem of her top and circling her belly button with his tongue. Her skin felt like home to him; a sanctuary, a haven, and he longed to rediscover every inch of her.

When he kissed a little lower, Emma flinched. He realised why. He paused a moment, grasped her hand that had been tangling in his hair, and brought it to his lips. He kissed each finger one by one, then uncurled them and pressed his lips against her palm. He wanted to reassure her, to remind her, that this was not just physical. He'd never felt so connected to anyone on *all* levels, and he wanted her to feel adored, cherished, and worshipped.

James lowered the waist of her pants slightly. With only a

dim wash of moonlight in the room, he felt across her abdomen with his hand and became aware of the change in texture on her skin. He traced the scar with one finger, from beginning to end, and a small sigh escaped Emma's mouth. This was what had taken her from him all those years ago, what had made her feel she couldn't stay. But now, it made her even more beautiful, unique, and strong. Pride and love overtook him and he leaned closer and kissed the middle of her scar. Then he placed a gentle kiss on one end of it, sprinkling kisses one by one along the length of the permanent reminder of her infertility. With each kiss she whimpered, from sadness, or relief at finally exposing her vulnerability he wasn't sure. But she didn't ask him to stop. Still she caressed his hair, his neck, and allowed him to shower affection on an area she probably never thought would receive anything but pain. He reached the end of the scar and gave it one last kiss in the middle, allowing his lips to linger a moment longer.

'James,' she whispered, and he gazed up at her. She curled a finger and he eased himself up to level his face with hers.

'It's been a long time for me,' she breathed into his ear. 'There's been no one else.'

James stroked her hair and tucked strands behind her ear. 'It's been a while for me too.'

'Was Jackson's mother the last one?' she asked.

He nodded, and it was only then that he realised just how much time had passed since he and Emma had been together. It seemed like a lifetime. And yet, being here with her now, her skin smelling sweet and hot, her touch filling him with longing he ached to fulfil, it seemed like they'd never parted.

'I barely remember that side of me,' Emma whispered. 'All I've been focused on is getting well.' He kissed her face gently as she spoke, then she grasped his face and looked him in the eye.

'Thank you for understanding me, for being here with me. I just hope it's worth the wait. I hope *I'm* worth the wait.'

'My beautiful Emma.' James looked into her deep brown eyes with a smile. 'You already are.'

CHAPTER TWENTY-THREE

E mma became faintly aware of the morning sun warming her face, but her eyes remained closed. She was also faintly aware of her memories from last night, floating in and out of her consciousness as she drifted between awake and asleep...

The moment James had kissed her scar had sent a healing wave through her body. The beauty of the moment took her breath away, and the moments after even more so. The way he'd taken his time rediscovering her, showing such tenderness and respect, had reinforced her feelings for him and reawakened her desire for him. For the first time in a long while, or even ever, her body had felt beautiful, scars and all. Never had she been so overcome with bliss and a sense of connectedness with another human being, it was like they had reached new levels of intimacy they'd never experienced before when they'd been together. Emma sighed, remembering the moment she'd felt truly one with him, their bodies entwined, like all these years he'd been a missing part of her and now they'd re-established their bond. Nothing could break that bond now, nothing at all.

A phone rang and Emma's mind switched from half asleep to awake and alert. She rolled over to the sound on the bedside table. James eased himself up to sit on the edge of the bed with his back to her, the phone to his ear.

'Hello, Mum?' he asked, and Emma smiled as she saw that James was still completely naked. Then she remembered what else had happened last night.

Lizzie.

'And what do the doctors say?' he asked.

Emma propped herself up on her elbows and realised she too was completely naked. She fossicked around for her clothing. She found her bra under the pillow and her undies on the side of the bed, and put them on.

James turned briefly as he listened to his mother on the phone and half-smiled as Emma tried to discreetly get dressed. 'When is the best time to come see her?'

Emma was worried Jackson might come into the room, so she crawled on the bed looking for her pants and singlet. She reached over the end of the bed to grab her pants from the floor, but from the incoordination of waking from sleep or her rush to get them, she lost balance and toppled off the end of the bed. She grabbed the pants and covered herself with them as James looked at her and held back a laugh.

As he spoke to his mum she fed her legs through the pants, then crawled back on the bed to find the singlet, which she yanked out from under James' pillow. James didn't seem in a hurry to get dressed, and Emma, to be honest, wasn't in a hurry for him to do so either.

She lay back on the bed, trying to ascertain what the situation was with Lizzie and the baby from the one-sided conversation. It didn't sound like there were any major concerns. She reached out and ran a supportive hand down James' back, then ran it sideways to curve around his hip. He swapped the phone to his other ear and placed his right hand on hers, giving it a squeeze. Had this not been an important and serious conversation she might have been a bit more playful, but she kept her hand on his hip.

'Right, well I'll come by around midday. I'll get everything sorted out here first. See you then.' James ended the call and placed the phone on the bedside table. He twisted sideways to face her. 'Lizzie is much better, her blood pressure is almost at normal levels, and protein levels are improving. Baby has a long way to go yet but is responding well.'

'James, I'm so pleased. Your parents and André must be exhausted. Let me know if there's anything I can do.'

He lifted the sheets and slipped back under the covers with her. 'I know something you can do.' He teased her nose with his, then gently kissed her lips.

'You know what I mean,' she replied, teasing his nose back.

The sound of the toilet flushing turned their heads towards the door, and it was soon followed by the clattering of cutlery and what sounded like a bowl on the kitchen counter.

'Stay right there,' James said, planting a quick kiss on her forehead. He turned to the side and leaned over, then stepped into his trunks and stood, pulling them up over his shapely, tight muscles. He had kept himself in good condition over the last several years, no doubt about that. In fact, he seemed in even better shape now. James picked up his trousers and put them on, then fed his top over his head. 'Back in a sec,' he said with a smile.

Emma stayed on the bed as he went out to the kitchen. She heard him say, 'Good boy,' to Jackson and, 'I missed you.' Moments later The Wiggles blared from the TV, and James came back in the bedroom and closed the door.

'He got his own cereal, and he'll be occupied for the near future, so, we can spend a bit of time alone.' He climbed over the bed and laid his warm body next to her.

Oh, how she'd missed this. Missed him. How many years she'd let slip by without him, but never again.

'You know, he spoke yesterday. Jackson.'

'What? Oh my God, James, that's amazing. What did he say?'

'Bella. My Nonna's name, can you believe it? And right when we spread the ashes.' He shook his head. 'It was bizarre, surreal.'

Emma's mouth gaped. 'Holy cow.' She too shook her head. 'He didn't say any words last night, if you were wondering. But he was a good kid, it was a pleasure to look after him.' No need to tell him about the battery incident now, or the bedtime story near-disaster. She could fill him in on the details another time.

'I'm so grateful.' He brushed the hair from her face and nuzzled into her neck.

'James,' Emma said. 'I still plan to go overseas for a while, maybe a couple of months. But before then, after then, I want nothing more than to be with you. Properly, officially, no holding back.' She moved his face to meet her eyes. 'Whatever you choose to do for Jackson, I'll support you. I'll be there. I'll move to Queensland if I have to. If you want me, that is.'

He traced the curve of her face and brushed his thumb across her bottom lip. 'I've never wanted anything, or anyone, more.'

Emma smiled, revelling in his unblinking gaze that saw right into her heart and soul. It felt good to be seen, *really* seen, understood, and adored. She couldn't imagine that any other man could be more suited to her than James, and even if there was, she didn't want them anyway. She only wanted the wonderful creature right in front of her.

'I promise not to lie to you again. I'll tell you everything. No more secrets,' she said, and James nodded.

'No more secrets.'

'And as for Jackson,' she clamped her lips together, emotion welling up inside and tears threatening to spill. 'I'm so amazed that not only do I get to be with my ideal man, but to have a child in my life too? You've made my dreams come true, James.' She swallowed hard.

His eyes became red at the rims and he smiled with a sigh. 'You have no idea how amazing it is to hear that. To have someone regard Jackson as a gift and not a burden is just...' he shook his head. 'I'm just, so grateful.' He hugged her close.

'Will you be okay with me going away for a while, once the cabins are all sorted?'

'Of course. I want you to do what you've always wanted to do. Take the opportunity. Just don't fall for any sexy foreigners and I'll be right,' he said.

'Maybe I'll have to wear a fake engagement ring to ward them all off,' she suggested.

James chuckled. 'Why not a real one instead?'

Emma looked at him, her eyebrows raised.

'Don't worry, I'm not proposing, not yet anyway, but... watch this space,' he whispered, nuzzling into her neck again.

'Oh, is that right, JJ?'

'Indeed. I might surprise you when you least expect it, just you wait.'

Excitement bubbled up inside Emma at his promise, and she couldn't believe that in the space of one week so much had happened. If her dad hadn't had the stroke, if she hadn't come to run the cabins, if it hadn't been his grandmother's would-be birthday... they never would have reconnected. Emma smiled at the amazing way life seemed to orchestrate things to occur at exactly the right time, as though there was someone up there, slotting dates into a complex spreadsheet or calendar in order to manage a schedule that would bring about the best possible outcomes for all involved.

'So, are you going to get me some cereal too or do I have to get my own?' Emma asked.

'You're a big girl, I'm sure you can get your own,' he teased. 'I'm kidding. How about I cook a hot breakfast? Eggs, toast, bacon... I'm so hungry I could eat the proverbial horse.'

'I could eat *you*.' She giggled, nibbling at his lips.

'Hey,' he said, tickling her in the ribs.

Emma laughed, then gazed into his eyes as he rolled slowly on top of her, his weight bringing comfort and security. 'I love you, James.'

It was so good to say it again. To feel it again. To know that he felt the same.

'And I love you.' He kissed her cheek, and as she closed her eyes to enjoy the moment, he kissed both of her eyelids with a tender softness that sent tingles through her body. 'I never stopped,' he whispered.

She held onto the sides of his face, and with her eyes, told him that she too had never stopped, and that she *would* never stop. As his lips connected with hers in a delicious, passionate unity, a sound came from the living room. A very appropriate sound, which made Emma and James laugh against each other's lips.

On the Sound Machine, Jackson had pressed the applause button.

EPILOGUE

Spring...

James' heart beat faster as he waited at the airport, his anticipation buffered by the amusement of watching people both scurrying around in a rush and standing still in boredom, checking their watches. He was one of those waiting, but he was far from bored. His chin held high, he peered through the crowd so he could spot her as soon as she emerged through the gate.

Five years without the love of his life had been easy compared to the past two months, now that he and Emma were committed to each other. His body ached to be near her again, his lips buzzed with the desire to kiss her, and his heart longed to cement the future of their relationship.

He glanced around at the other people waiting and wondered what their story was. Were they meeting a loved one they hadn't seen for months, or perhaps years? Or maybe they were greeting a business colleague or an old friend. Airports were rife with untold stories.

When he glanced back, a hint of caramel brown hair caught

his attention as it bounced around her shoulders. As travellers filtered through and dispersed, she came into full view.

James smiled wide.

'Emma,' he called with a wave.

She spotted him and her eyes lit up. She waved back with a freshness in her smile, and an air of rejuvenation that filled him with joy to witness.

She picked up her pace and dashed towards him, he opened his arms out wide. Emma leapt into him and he lifted her off the ground in a twirl of an embrace.

'Oh, I missed you!' she said.

'I missed you too. So glad you're back.' He kissed her cheek then her lips, grasping the sides of her face with his hands.

'Does absence make the heart grow fonder?' she asked with a wink.

'It sure does, among other things!' He chuckled.

'How's Jackson? I can't wait to see him.'

'Good. He even had a haircut! You probably won't recognise him.'

'Really? How'd you manage that?'

'Well, let's just say you might not recognise Owly either,' James explained.

'Oh, Owly had a haircut too?' Her eyebrows rose.

James nodded. 'Not that she had much to begin with, but she's got quite the crew cut now. Very military-ish.'

Emma laughed and her head tipped back, happiness radiating from her. 'Love it. A pink army owl. Lucky I wasn't there or Jackson may have made me have a haircut too.'

James ran his fingers through her hair, tangled a little from the long flight. 'I've missed doing this.'

'And I've missed you *doing* this.' She smiled. 'What else have you missed?' she asked with a cheeky grin.

'I could tell you, but one thing might lead to another and we might get arrested for indecent exposure.'

Her cheeks flushed. 'Well, we can't have that. At least, not right now. But I'm looking forward to tonight, I'll probably be wide awake come bedtime.'

'Lucky me.' He kissed her again, then took her hand. 'So, let's get your bags.' They walked along with the flow of the crowd. 'And your art book, is it all ready to send to the formatters?'

'Yep, finished writing the notes and poems to go along with my drawings. Never thought I'd be writing and drawing in Parisian cafés, it was totally clichéd but wonderful.'

'I bet. And did you think up a title?'

Emma had sent emails updating James on her progress with her book, which she'd worked on in between shopping, tours, eating, and admiring Parisian architecture and Tuscan vineyards.

'*Healing Art — a journey of cancer recovery through creative expression,*' she said proudly.

James squeezed her hand. 'I love it. And I spoke to Olivia at Mrs May's Bookstore, she said they'd be happy to buy a few copies to sell in the store.'

'Oh you did? That's great! Thanks, gorgeous.' She smooched his cheek and he smooched hers back. 'And the cabins are running smoothly?'

'Of course. You trained me well before you left, remember? Amelia's reliable as ever, and our newbie Christine's history in hotel management has sure come in handy. She's dynamite for business.'

'I'm so glad.' Emma jiggled a little as she walked. 'I'm so looking forward to getting back there and making the place our own.'

'I know. Still can hardly believe I bought it. Your parents faces when we told them, I'll never forget!'

'Me neither. They're so glad we're carrying on the business, though I didn't want to when I first arrived, but now, well, things are different.'

James pondered how significantly things had changed in the past six months since he reunited with Emma. 'Things are the way they're supposed to be.'

Emma nodded and smiled. 'Absolutely.'

They made their way towards the baggage claim.

'Can you believe, another year and a bit and we'll be starting our new roles?' Emma asked.

James shook his head at how time was flying. His boy was growing up and he felt one hundred percent certain he'd made the right choice in deciding to home-school him, along with Emma's help. With Christine as park manager, their role in running the cabins was more to oversee things generally, freeing up more time. 'I know. I'm looking forward to it. And by then, my VIP program will have run its course. I'm glad I added the option to train a handful of up-and-comers to be my clones.' He chuckled. His program had been well received by his clients, and now he was further leveraging his expertise by licensing a few of them to become law business coaches with his unique system. It had provided enough income to add to his net worth in order to secure the holiday park, not to mention buying Emma's parents' house to live in as their own, while the pair moved further up the road to a one-level, wheelchair-friendly property. But in another year, it would be time to focus solely on running the park and schooling Jackson. It was time to live his dream with his newly formed family unit. Speaking of which...

James took a deep breath as they arrived at the baggage terminal, his heart rate rising a notch.

'You okay?' Emma asked.

'What? Yes. I'm fine.' He slipped his hands into his pockets and rocked back and forth on his feet.

'You look like you've had several cups of coffee,' she said.

He grinned, and as he removed his hands from his pockets, he pulled something out along with one of them. James cleared his throat and lowered himself to one knee.

'Shoelace undone?' Emma asked.

He laughed. She really had no idea. He'd said she wouldn't know when it was coming and he'd been right.

'My shoelaces are perfectly fine,' he replied, looking up at her and holding up the velvet box, opening it with a muffled pop.

Gasps and whispers sounded around him, and he noticed someone with a phone camera, but most of his focus was on her face, taking in the moment as best as he could so he could remember it for years to come. Her mouth hung open and her hand flew to her chest, her eyes brightening in realisation.

'Emma Brighton, my favourite woman in the world,' he said, 'well, apart from my mum, my sister, Nonna, and... well, the chick in the grocery store is pretty cute too.' He winked, then prepared for the cheesy poem he'd promised he'd write for her when she returned home. 'Complete will be my life, when you become my wife.' He grinned. So it had only been a two-line poem, but she hadn't specified length, so he figured that was enough to get the message across. 'My beautiful Emma,' he continued. 'Will you marry me?' He gazed up at her as she gazed down at him, her eyes becoming shiny and her hand shaking.

'First of all,' she said, 'your poetry needs work.' She giggled. 'And secondly...' she moved closer, holding out her left hand towards the white gold solitaire ring he'd bought on a whim, thinking it would be perfect for her. 'Your ring-buying skills are spot on.' She smiled. 'So here's my poem: I can't imagine a better life, than one where I'm your wife.'

Intense love rose up inside as he took the ring from its box. 'I take it that's a yes?' he asked.

'It's a definite yes,' she replied, her voice shaky.

Onlookers cheered and applauded, and James slid the ring on her finger, securing the future he'd always wanted, with the woman who, though she'd once broken his heart, had healed it back together to create a new and improved version 2.0.

———

Summer...

'You ready?' Jen asked, as Emma neared the pathway at Tarrin's Bay Beachside Cabins.

Emma took a preparatory breath. 'I'll be asking you the same thing in two months time.'

'I know,' Jen smiled. 'Isn't it exciting?' She rubbed Emma's arm.

They exchanged happy smiles and with an eagerness in her eye, Jen turned around and began her walk down the aisle, AKA — the concrete pathway alongside the cabins — the chiffon sash of her baby blue bridesmaid dress trailing behind her.

Emma waited behind the tree as Jen had her moment, and when she was halfway along, she walked up to meet her mother and father at the back of the arrangement of chairs with blue and white chiffon ribbons around each one.

'All set?' her mother asked, and she nodded.

Barbara gave her an excited smile and turned to walk along the grass to take her seat in the front row.

'So,' she said, glancing down at her dad. 'I guess this is it.' She patted his shoulder and he grasped her hand.

'Wheels and I are ready when you are.'

'Wheels?'

'Yeah, I had started calling my constant companion

Marilyn, but your mother got jealous. So, Wheels it is now.' He smiled.

Emma did too, and glanced over at the playground behind and to the right of the congregation, where Amelia and Bob were keeping Jackson amused. He had grown quite fond of the two in the last few months, and they'd become Jackson-Approved Babysitters, Registered Carers of Owly, and Qualified Operators of the Sound Machine. With James' parents now living in Queensland, it had been great to find two other people who Jackson could cope with when Emma and James needed time alone. She smiled as he played with Owly on the equipment, realising that in a few moments, she would officially be his mother, and her dreams of becoming a parent would be fully realised. It had taken a while, but she'd come to know that her fulfilment didn't need to come from pregnancy and childbirth, but from being part of a child's life and helping them reach their full potential with love, commitment, and dedication. With Jackson, and James, she'd been gifted with more than she thought she'd ever receive.

'Well, c'mon Wheels, do your thing.' Emma gestured to the controls on the automated wheelchair, and her dad was about to press one when she put her hand in front of it. 'Wait.' She moved in front of the chair. 'If you can't technically walk me down the aisle, Dad, then I'm going to roll with you.' She sat on his lap and adjusted her simple, elegant wedding dress so it wouldn't catch in the wheels. 'Am I too heavy?' she asked.

'No. Half my body can barely feel it anyway. Let's get this show on the road.' He instructed Wheels to start moving forward and gripped the steering handle.

Emma giggled as they began their journey towards the front. Guests chuckled and snapped photos, including Marie Gallagher who stood at the front next to Martin and Lizzie and her nine-month-old daughter, Hope.

Emma smiled at the crowd, a light breeze wafting around her face as it moved from the ocean towards her, as though embracing her with the promise of a fresh new life. The occasional fluffy white clouds in a perfect blue sky complemented the blue and white theme, and seagulls swooped overhead in what looked like a synchronised dance of bliss. The salty scent of the ocean felt like home as she got closer to the front, and her heart rate rose as she caught the gaze of the singer and guitarist who was filling the great outdoors of the holiday park with his soulful, earthy voice. He winked at her and she smiled wide. She never thought that international superstar and Tarrin's Bay born and bred, Drew Williams, would be singing at her wedding. Thanks to her yoga teacher, Chrissie, who'd been able to set up the surprise gift for her. His romantic, cruisy melody filled her with joy, and anticipation of what was to come.

She basked in the perfection of the moment as she saw James standing next to his best man, André. Her fiancé wore a blue-grey suit with white shirt open at the top, showing a hint of his tanned chest. His thick, dark hair was expertly styled in sexy waves, and his face beamed. He didn't take his eyes off her. She locked eyes with her soon-to-be husband, while admiration, appreciation, and electrifyingly magnificent love filled her heart to the brim and overflowed.

'I love you,' he mouthed as she got closer, and Emma mouthed it back.

Birds chirped and the breeze danced around her in celebration, and she realised how lucky she was to have been given a second chance in not only life, but love, and to be rolling down the aisle towards her one true love, her soulmate, her miracle.

THE END

ALSO BY JULIET MADISON

ACKNOWLEDGEMENTS

Thanks always to my editor Belinda Holmes for working with me on these books to polish them until they're squeaky clean, and also have fun along the way. And thanks again to Bloodhound Books for helping to get these stories out to the world!

This writing journey would not be the same without the support and friendship of other writers, in particular Diane Curran, Alli Sinclair, and Rachael Johns who have helped with either critiques, feedback, ideas, or general moral support and encouragement. You make my writing days extra fun!

I'd also like to give a shout-out to the members of my Readers Group on Facebook who share in my progress of writing my books and offer their enthusiasm, feedback, and loyalty. Thanks to the readers, reviewers, and bloggers who take time to write about books and help spread the word to support authors.

A special mention to those who work in the field of autism awareness and care, something close to my heart and an important part of this story: thanks for your dedication and passion for helping those on the spectrum and seeing them as the gifts that they are.

Thanks always to my family and friends, especially Mum for always reading my work in the draft stage. And to my sons, Jayden and Zaki, for showing me that miracles can and do occur.

ABOUT THE AUTHOR

Juliet Madison is a bestselling and award-nominated author of books with humour, heart, and serendipity. Writing both fiction and self-help, she is also an artist and colouring book illustrator, and an intuitive life coach who loves creating online courses for writers and those wanting to live an empowered life.

With her background as a naturopath and a dancer, Juliet is passionate about living a healthy and positive life. She likes to combine her love of words, art, and self-empowerment to create books that entertain and inspire readers to find the magic in everyday life.

Juliet lives on the picturesque south coast of NSW, Australia, where she spends as much time as possible dreaming up new stories, following her passions, being with her family, and as little time as possible doing housework.

You can find out more about Juliet, her books, and her courses at http://www.julietmadison.com and connect with her on social media at Facebook http://www.facebook.com/julietmadisonauthor and Instagram http://www.instagram.com/julietmadisonauthorartist

A NOTE FROM THE PUBLISHER

Thank you for reading this book. If you enjoyed it please do consider leaving a review on Amazon to help others find it too.

We hate typos. All of our books have been rigorously edited and proofread, but sometimes mistakes do slip through. If you have spotted a typo, please do let us know and we can get it amended within hours.

info@bloodhoundbooks.com

Printed in Great Britain
by Amazon